# Habitat

# ACKNOWLEDGEMENTS

I am grateful to the Arts Council for their financial support; to my editor Seán Farrell and everyone at the Lilliput Press for their precision, care and ambition with this novel; to Jo Minogue for reading early on; to fellow writers for ongoing discussions.

# Habitat

# Catriona Shine

THE LILLIPUT PRESS

DUBLIN

First published in 2024 by
THE LILLIPUT PRESS
62–63 Sitric Road, Arbour Hill,
Dublin 7, Ireland
www.lilliputpress.ie

A CIP record for this title is available
from The British Library.

10 9 8 7 6 5 4 3 2 1

ISBN 9781 84351 8877

eBook ISBN 978 1 84351 9010

Set in 12.5pt on 17pt Fournier MT Std by Compuscript
Printed in Sweden by ScandBook

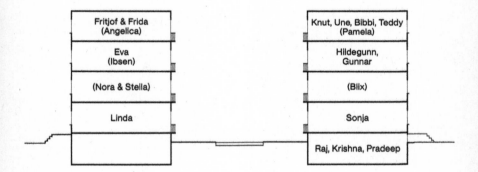

# Monday

*We settled slowly from bones and shells. Our particles pressed down on one another. There are deep troughs in coastal woods where our skeletal grains once lay. Descended from rock, we are also a careful proportion of clay. We were pulverized, heated to the point of vitrification, fused. We were then ground down once more. Part stone and part sand; water was once mixed into our dust. Poured into moulds, we set, gripping rods of steel. It is this clinging that keeps us in place, where you set us, far enough apart, one above the other, so that you can walk between us without knocking your skulls. We cling, but it is you who fear, who must be kept apart from members of your species who are not your family. We rest our edges on walls of bricks, transferring our load, the load of you and your possessions. You have no plan for us after this. Your thoughts will crumble with us.*

# Knut

Knut and his grandson woke to one another's noises and met in the hallway. Knut bent over, with the intention of planting a kiss on Teddy's head, but, feeling a pull under his right shoulder blade, he contented himself with ruffling the boy's hair.

Good morning, little prince, he said. Where's Mamma?

Teddy pointed in the direction of the bedroom.

The door was held open by Teddy's trailing blanket. Knut edged the blanket back in and closed the door with only the faintest click of the handle. This had been his own room as a child, and he knew from the deep snug inside him that Bibbi would be safe there. He could not even feel guilty for letting his own mother move out to make room for them. This way, they could stay close.

Knut put a finger to his lips.

Let Mamma and Granny sleep, he said.

Bibbi had slept like a log the past week and, if she did, she needed it. Her marriage to that executive should never have gone ahead at all, if you asked Knut. But no one did, and if anyone had asked him, if Bibbi herself had asked him at the time, he would have said, What do I know? It's your own choice.

Still, it was hard to regret it all when little Teddy was there, making music with marbles on the floor. Only a completely useless father would abandon his own son outright, but it was a good thing, for Bibbi, that he was gone. He made no marks, but that man had left a trace on her. Being an attractive young woman brought as much trouble as good. Knut worried about how often she went out at night ever since she came back. Staying in touch with friends, she called it, but before he knew it she would have a new partner. It never seemed to take long. Then she would be gone again, along with Teddy this time.

Apissu, apissu, all fall down, said Teddy.

Knut didn't mind getting up in the morning anymore. Teddy's little voice did something to him. It was like a breeze which blew his eyes wide open, a string which pulled him up to standing. Still, to appreciate Teddy fully at such an early hour of the morning, he needed a cup of black coffee in his hand. In the kitchen, he spooned ground coffee into the filter bag, added water and turned on the Moccamaster. He heard marbles rolling along the wooden floor as he measured out oats and milk. Enough for two, because Teddy ate like a man. He snuck out one cup of coffee before the brew had finished and heard Teddy saying, Ball, ball, with increasing frustration.

Knut turned on the wall lamp in the hallway.

There, he said, will we have some porridge?

Ball, said Teddy.

He had managed to pull Une's knitted jacket from the coat stand and was, with some success, removing the spherical buttons.

No, no, no, Teddy, they are Granny's buttons, you see? Buttons. What have you done with your marbles?

Ball, said Teddy, and Knut decided that the harm was done and there was no point in waking the others with the child's screams, which were sure to erupt if he took away the jacket without a replacement.

Where are the little coloured balls? he said.

It was with considerable difficulty he got down on his knees and felt along the skirting boards, around the mat and under the hall stand.

What did you do with the lovely small balls? he said, getting a bit worried now. He could hear the porridge spitting, needing to be stirred and turned down.

You didn't eat them, did you? We don't eat small balls, do we?

Gone, said Teddy, his palms raised in proof.

Knut put two fingers into the boy's mouth and felt along the inside of his chubby cheeks – huge muscles – as Teddy squealed.

Say ah, he said, and then the screaming started.

Bibbi appeared, bleary eyed.

What happened?

I think he swallowed a marble.

Who gave him marbles? He's only just turned three, Dad. Did you give him marbles? Teddy, say ah.

5

Ball, said Teddy.

He found them himself, said Knut. They're from the game of solitaire. I'm surprised he could reach them.

Of course he could!

I can't find any, Bibbi. He had them just now. He must have hidden them. He can't have swallowed them all. It's not humanly possible.

He put his ear against Teddy's round belly, listened for clinking, and Teddy patted his bald patch like a drum.

Bibbi had the wooden solitaire board in her hands.

Nine – no: six, twelve, eighteen, twenty-four, she said. There were thirty-three of them, I think, no thirty-two.

We'll find them and count them, said Knut. Teddy, where are all the little balls hiding?

Teddy pulled at the buttons on Une's jacket, and Une came out in her dressing gown.

The porridge is burning, she said, and look what he's doing to my jacket.

We think he ate the marbles, said Bibbi.

All of them, said Knut.

It's not possible, said Une, taking the game of solitaire from Bibbi. Knut, you can't let him out of your sight. We'll have to bring him to the A&E.

I'm sure he hid them, said Knut. I was only in the kitchen for a few minutes.

Bibbi and I will go, said Une. Let me just get dressed, and you can search, Knut. Ring us if you find them, all right?

# Linda

Flink had been pawing the balustrade at the French windows for a good hour. He stood upright like a trapped human with his forepaws as high as they could go on the steel banisters, his wiry tail pivoting between ginger hind legs. Linda stayed in bed. She didn't think he had it in him to scramble up.

He teetered a moment with all four paws on the top rail, before flinging himself into the bushes below.

The hurried struggle to the window set Linda's old head reeling. The railing pressed against her lower ribs and loose flakes of rust-backed paint clung to her nightdress, black on white.

It had been a sultry night for early May, reminding her of that summer a lifetime ago when Leif gave her his first gift, a folding fan, and she kept it tucked into the waist strap of her apron.

She always slept with the bedroom window open: a small gap in the winter and open wide in the summer. Up in her top-floor apartment across the way, that had always been fine. She could see her old home from where she stood. Knut

7

and his family would still be in bed. Her bedroom up there opened onto the roof terrace via a pair of French windows just like these.

Down here, she lived like an insect. She felt she might be trampled on, and there was always someone looking in.

The other problem, of course, was the dog, little Flink, who had spent his entire life up on the fourth floor, where he could wander freely out to the terrace.

It was Leif who found Flink, brought him in one Saturday morning while Linda was scrubbing a buttery grit of mackerel skin off the pan. He was uncharacteristically quiet coming in, so Linda rushed out to him without taking the time to dry her hands on the tea towel. She was dripping water on the floor, and there was Leif with a cardboard box in his hands and Flink's tiny puppy head sticking out. Flink was ginger, like Leif himself, and Linda fell instantly in love.

Leif! she'd scolded, because he was always springing surprises on her. She never admitted how much she liked it.

She repeated his name aloud now: Leif, Leif. She had read somewhere that we die our final death the last time we are remembered.

Flink was almost twenty years old now, on his last legs. That's probably what they said about her. That architect couple – what were they called? – Frida and Fritjof, yes. They always waltzed past her with a hasty hello when they came down to walk their own dog. Perhaps they thought Flink was too old to sniff Rocky's rump, or that he wouldn't be able to reach, or that Linda couldn't keep up if they walked together.

Flink was running around the rectangular pond, whose fountain was turned off this early in the morning. That awful Hildegunn's silver cat was stalking the back garden for small birds. It was that idiot cat who drew her own Flink outside, though how the slinky feline managed to descend from the third floor, Linda couldn't say. There was nothing to climb down, unless it hopped from one balcony to the next – a difficult task, since they were directly over one another.

The cat jumped out of the rose bushes, up onto the edge of a garden-level balcony. It slipped in under the wired glass balustrade by way of a tiny gap no animal should fit through. It was all fur, no substance.

For over half a century, Linda had lived with Hildegunn underneath her, hating her. Now she had nothing but a basement under her, crammed full of outdated possessions that would be difficult to get to if anyone remembered they existed. It was only when she moved here that she realized she had always walked across her old floor with unease. Of course Hildegunn had hated her after the affair – Hildegunn was the injured party – but she had already hated Linda before that, out of prejudice. The floor was fairly soundproof, but Linda had always left a room if she noticed a noise right below her. Blame rose, seeped through the painted ceiling, the concrete slab and the wooden floor, and it chased Linda's heels all day. She had Hildegunn to thank that she had been so active all her later years, never sitting still, rising early, going out cycling.

There was a movement at the window directly opposite hers and – Bibbi, she thought, could that be you? She wondered what her poor granddaughter could be doing down there at this hour of the morning. Bibbi might be having an affair with whoever lived there, but then she realized that, no, old eyes deceive – it was only her worry that brought Bibbi to mind – and the person she saw was that quiet young woman she used to chat to when she lived over there. What was her name again? Solveig. No: Mette. No, of course, it was Sonja, like the queen.

Linda used to spy on birds on her terrace and compare notes on her sightings with Sonja. Now they had the same angle on birds, so there was no point in comparing. They lacked an excuse to talk, as well as the opportunity.

Sonja, like the queen: Linda tagged everyone's name like this now. In her old head, everything worth remembering was still there, but the doors were sometimes locked, and the hinges creaked. She called her granddaughter Baby-Bibbi, though she had her own baby now. That girl had depths, dark and murky, that called to her, ever since her year in London. There were meanings behind Knut and Une's silences whenever she brought it up. They didn't want to upset Linda, to agitate her. They thought upset and agitation were fatal to old people.

Flink!

There was no puff in her whisper. The word got barely past her lips. If she called out in earnest, her old voice would fly, ricocheting back and forth between the buildings. She saw Flink in the rose bushes from which the cat had leapt. Poor Flink had not the agility to follow it further.

The earth outside was a good metre below the floor at her feet. Add to that the safety balustrade, and she was certain that Flink would not come back this way. When you were old like her and Flink, you had to go the long way round. She reached out her hand in a stay-where-you-are-boy gesture and pulled back inside, pushing the French windows closed. This was an awkward enough manoeuvre in itself: she had to hold two latches open, one high up and one down low, as she slammed the frame. It banged right into her elbow joints, but it wouldn't shut. In the warmth and humidity of this tropical night, the window, she presumed, had expanded and no longer fit into its frame.

Linda had known many a sultry night up in her old apartment, but this had never happened to the windows there. It must be the height that made a difference. Up on the fourth floor, the breeze sped past, unhindered, cooling. Down here at garden level, draughts seeped, plants sweated and the air was almost a liquid. She had sunk too low. She had gone underwater.

The back garden was full of honeyed light when Linda came out, and the birds in the big bush were going crazy. Some sort of delirium washed over those small brown balls of feathers at dawn. Every morning, without fail, off they went, equally surprised each time. Was that what they meant when they called you a birdbrain? She heard them more intensely these days, from her bush-level bedroom. She lived with the birds now, though she was further from the sky. Sometimes she wondered if it would be better to start going deaf. The peace of old age.

There was a movement in the bushes at the other end of the garden that had something of Flink's swagger in it, so she walked in that direction and allowed herself to click her tongue to call him. Surely that couldn't wake anyone; surely that was quieter than the dawn chorus.

Flink's tail was sticking out of a bush, wagging so the leaves made the sound of plastic. She clicked her tongue again and he came out. The bushes caught her attention because it was the wrong time of year for berries. Bending down, she saw that the leaves were covered with hundreds of ladybirds. It must be a year for greenfly. She picked one up and let it crawl along her palm. She would need her reading glasses to count its spots. As she hooked the leash onto Flink's collar, the ladybird spread its red-armour wings and flew back to gorge itself green.

She heard a child crying not far away and thought of Bibbi, of Teddy.

# Sonja

Sonja woke in the twittering dawn. A breeze rubbed over the hairs on her calf, tickling them upright. She tucked the edges of the duvet underneath her, so there was no flow of air into or out of her upholstered bubble. A strand of outgrown fringe blew over her eyelid.

For heaven's sake, she said.

She toed her slippers the right way and went to the French windows. The whole long winter it was fine and now, in the month of May, on this most critical of nights, air decided to leak in. She pushed the curtains aside and felt along the edge of the window to locate the gap, but she felt no draught.

Across the way, Linda, her elderly counterpart in the opposite block, was also awake, standing at her wide-open window in only a nightdress. This selfless old woman had moved from the big top-floor apartment three floors above Sonja last month so her son, Knut, and his family could move in. Sonja missed having Linda in her own block, missed being waylaid on her way in or out to chat about birds in the old days, the original gardener or who had said what about whom in the gardening committee. She saw Linda more often now, out on her balcony, but they were too far apart to speak.

She still had Hildegunn to chat to, the second eldest resident, but the two old ladies were arch-enemies, so it felt like a minor betrayal. Hildegunn had lived directly under Linda for decades and claimed to know everything there was to know about her neighbour. Hildegunn once told Sonja, in hushed tones, that Linda was nothing more than a maid. She had moved into the building when it was newly built, when she was only fifteen, and, soon after, had married her employer. That woman had married into the building, and there she sat, in the best apartment, like a queen bee all these years. According to Hildegunn, a tramp was a tramp, no matter where they lived.

Linda was leaning over her railing now, a hand outstretched towards the swaying branch of a hibiscus bush. It was clearly out of reach. Sonja marvelled at the gnarled directionlessness of the ancient arm. She wanted to sketch that branchy limb.

Though Sonja was behind two layers of glass, she must have made some sudden movement, as Linda's smoky gaze flicked across to her. Sonja's hand went up in the gesture of *hello*, but Linda withdrew, just as swiftly, into the shadows of her bedroom.

I didn't mean to startle you, said Sonja.

Since she moved to this apartment, she had a garden right outside for the first time. She had to go down the stairs and around to the gate to access it, but even the visual closeness fostered in Sonja a new love of nature. When she moved in, the garden was concealed in a thick layer of snow, but she had seen it come alive this spring. At the living-room window, she set up a desk and let windborne seeds and insects disturb her at will. She was illustrating a volume on endangered birds, her first book project. If she had lived somewhere else, she might have stayed in advertising forever. The leap into freelance illustration, which she would take today, was spurred by how she felt when she opened these curtains every morning. She hadn't joined the garden committee, but she enjoyed what they cultivated, and it was the birds she delighted in the most – her skylarks and goldfinches. She learned that you could make as much noise as you wanted, but sudden movements would startle them and cause them to fly away. Sonja learned to keep completely still while she observed birds, and so she was disappointed with herself now when Linda noticed her and took flight. Sonja was not some stranger. This was a contact-seeking old woman, so it was hurtful to see her pull back and slam the window shut without even saluting.

Sonja went back to fondling the window frames in search of the air current. These were the original windows and were composed of a crude form of double glazing, made by screwing an extra window frame to the first, on the inside. There was certainly no insulating vacuum between the layers of glass, because flies and ladybirds had found their way in there, years or perhaps even decades before, and their bleached bodies remained, a testament to some passage the air might also take. Sonja found no draught, for all her searching, but she took some towels and socks from the washing basket and packed them along the edges of the window all the same. Dispensing with the tug of frugality, she turned on the radiator full blast and went back to bed.

Somewhere above her, a child was crying, probably little Teddy on the top floor. In a weak and desperate moment, Sonja had considered asking them if they needed a babysitter. Things were tight now, but it wouldn't last forever, and she owned this apartment, which was the main thing. It had been worth staying with the office until her loan was approved and she got set up here, but she longed for this freedom. Today was her last day in advertising – ever, maybe. Tomorrow she would be a full-time freelance illustrator.

The draught was still there.

She got up and rooted in the bottom drawer where she kept the bulk of her odds and ends. She found nail scissors and a roll of gaffer tape.

She sealed the window meticulously, but, when she moved away, the airstream was strong as ever.

Why now? She needed eight hours of undisturbed sleep before her final day. She wanted to walk out of that stifling office beaming and fluttering free.

She ran her hand over the wall, a centimetre from the surface, and – there it was: cold air pushing against her palm. This wind was blowing through the wall itself.

She rubbed her palms briskly against her thighs and tried again. It was the same: air, coming right through the wall. She placed a cheek close by the surface and real wind blew over her skin.

16

She looked out the window to the top floor of the opposite building, where the architect couple lived: Frida and Fritjof, she could ask them. They seemed approachable. They had been keen to chat at the garden clean-up that spring, though perhaps keener on chatting than working.

She noticed that all the windows on that block were open, every single one. It was a Norwegian thing. They were mad about fresh air. She had grown up in Ireland, where a window opened for any length of time inevitably brought in flies or spiders.

Her room was being aired, whether she liked it or not. She had used paint that let the wall breathe, the safest, most environmentally friendly variety on stock, the one with low vapour emissions, but breathable paint was meant to allow residual moisture to escape from the wall. It was not meant to facilitate this level of deep yogic breathing.

She checked the other walls in her bedroom, the internal walls and the party wall, and they were all fine. This one was the problem: the exterior wall that separated Sonja's bedroom from the back garden. She went out to the living room where this wall continued, and there she found the same cool rush of air.

It was not the same all over. It seemed to be seeping through specific patches. Perhaps these were the positions of old vents that had been sealed up badly, though she could make no sense of the spread. As far as she could make out, standing on a chair and checking the whole surface, there seemed to be seven, possibly eight patches that were leaking air. There could hardly have been so many vents.

She looked at the brickwork and plasterwork on the opposite building and particularly at Linda's apartment, directly opposite hers, her mirror image. There was only one vent on Linda's façade, and that was under the living-room window. Sonja had one in the same position, with a little lever to open or close the damper inside. It let air in behind the radiator. It seemed to be working fine, despite the chirping she heard there a month ago, when a family of sparrows moved in for a week. Sonja mentioned this to Eva Holt, the proud head of the board of residents, so they could put in a net before next year or check if the birds were actually doing any harm. The birds didn't bother her. She found their twittering heart-warming. But the noise was gone the next day, and she was too scared to ask Eva if she had made the caretaker get rid of them. Eva was an action-oriented leader. She should really ask her about the wall. External walls were the common responsibility of the board.

Sonja had a sudden sense of urgency, some mounting fear she couldn't name until she realized that she could hear an ambulance. It was not far away and coming closer. Maybe all worry was a Doppler effect.

# Knut

A key scratched and clicked in the lock, and Knut looked up from the floor. He had the drawers out and emptied, and all the shoes lined up. Une held the door open for Bibbi, who was carrying Teddy in her arms. His face was full of chocolate.

You look like you licked a bear's bum, said Knut.

God, I'm starving, said Une.

Did they get them all out?

No, said Bibbi, he hadn't swallowed any. They did an ultrasound and an X-ray. Did you find them all?

Knut looked around him.

It's either old age that's catching up with me, he said, or ...

Did you put them up high this time? said Une, taking off the jacket with the missing buttons.

I didn't find any marbles, said Knut, not one. I've checked everywhere.

He looked at the line of shoes, the rolled-up doormat.

Une and Bibbi cracked into laughter simultaneously. It was the kind of cheer that came out as strong as tears, maybe because it felt deserved.

He's lost his marbles, said Une.

This was the first time Bibbi had laughed properly since she came back to them, so the whole ordeal was worth it, in a way. Even Teddy joined in, but when they stopped Bibbi said, Well they're here somewhere. We'll have to keep our eyes on him.

As Knut rose from the floor, he thought he was having a dizzy spell, because blue lights reflected in flashes on the ceiling. He went to the window in Bibbi's room and looked down onto the street.

Why did you call an ambulance? said Une.

She opened the door to the stairwell, and they all waited as footsteps came up the stairs. From the floor below, there were three thuds and the sound of splintering wood.

Hildegunn, said Knut, going down to the half-landing. He could hear her screaming and moaning quite clearly. He went past Hildegunn's broken door and down to the entrance, where a paramedic was holding the front door open with his back.

Keep the passage clear, he said, pointing to where Knut could stand. Do you know the woman on the third floor to the left?

That's Hildegunn Lofthus-Lund, said Knut. We live right upstairs from her.

Any family we can contact?

They're all abroad, said Knut. Her husband passed away. I'll ask the head of the board of residents though. I think there's a nephew in Oslo.

He broke off then as two paramedics manoeuvred a narrow stretcher down the stairs. Knut was in no doubt it was her hip that had gone, swelling her slacks on one side. Even though Hildegunn's arms were fixed in place, the tendons on her wrist strained against the strap and she managed to point a wizened finger at Knut as she passed.

It was him, she said. It was those Klevelands with their marbles. They did this. They've been plaguing me for weeks. They did it. Vengeful tramps. Son of a tramp! she called out, her eyes latched onto Knut, even as they slid her into the back of the ambulance.

Hildegunn's door was hanging open when Knut went upstairs, the wood splintered around the lock and the hinges distorted. He knew he shouldn't, but he pushed it in.

It smelled distinctly of old woman in there, the same cobwebby smell that still had not left their apartment upstairs. Linda and Hildegunn had a long-term feud going, which Knut had never understood, but he had to admit that Hildegunn's apartment was more stylish. Everything he saw, from the Arne Jacobsen lampshades to the Vitra coat stand, was fifties-style, light and industrial, and well designed. His own apartment seemed like a cluttered cabin in contrast.

He shuffled further into the apartment with the odd idea that this rare opportunity should not be missed.

A deep, rolling sound, followed by a click, caused him to look down at the polished wooden floor. Strewn about, and along the edges of the hallway, he saw dozens of glass marbles.

He gathered them quickly into his pockets, counting as he went. He tried to picture the game of solitaire, to know how many he should collect. He found twenty-eight.

In a wide wooden bowl on the hall table he found two others, along with some spherical buttons he recognized from Une's knitted cardigan.

Is she all right? said Une, when he came back upstairs.

Broken hip, poor woman, he said.

Bibbi was changing Teddy's nappy in the bathroom, an operation he was audibly resisting.

I'd better call Eva, said Une, to get in touch with her family. I told Eva we should have a digital file with all the information about the building and residents, but she's holding those cards close to her chest.

They'll have to fix her door. Come here.

Une followed him into the kitchen, where he emptied his pockets into the general waste bin.

They were strewn all over her hallway, he said.

You went in?

Knut looked at her. He took the pot and wooden spoon, scraped the coagulated porridge on top of the marbles and buttons, and tied the bag closed.

Were those my buttons? I could have sewn them back on.

I'll take this out, he said, and can you put that jacket in a plastic bag? I'll bring it to the recycling.

My jacket? I can get new buttons.

You're missing the point.

You don't actually think she came up and stole our marbles?

No, but they were down there, on her floor.

She probably has her own game of solitaire.

No.

You found my buttons downstairs?

They both stared at the plastic bag of rubbish.

They were all over her hallway, said Knut. Will you give Eva a ring?

Maybe we shouldn't.

Just ask about her nephew. Say she broke her hip, that's all.

Did they really break her door in?

It was well they did, said Knut. She was out of her mind with pain. Tell Eva that. Tell her Hildegunn was saying crazy things.

# Eva

What was that smell?

Eva was still wet from the shower when her mobile rang, but she answered immediately. She presumed it was someone from the office, an emergency only she could address: some information she alone was privy to, some encouragement needed before a meeting with a tough client that Eva would know how to handle. Her helpline, she affectionately called it. She clocked up all the time she spent on the phone when out of office. It was hours some days. She didn't mind helping. She just needed her efforts to be acknowledged, in monetary terms.

Hello, she said, Eva Holt.

The strangest thing happened – I mean the most terrible. Poor Hildegunn seems to have broken her hip.

It was Une Kleveland, and there was something suspicious about the way she spoke. Eva had asked her to email, but ever since Une joined the board of residents last year, she rang all the time, usually prefacing whatever it was with, I'm not sure if this is something for us. She thought she

24

had joined a club and wanted the full induction programme. Eva appreciated that the other board members deferred to her, but, instead of helping out, they seemed to increase her own workload.

That terrible smell though ... She checked the loo.

Doesn't she have a nephew in Oslo? said Une. I know her own children moved abroad.

If Hildegunn's apartment came on the market, Eva was interested. She had been inside a number of times. Their two third-floor apartments were approximately the same size, but Hildegunn's was at the end of the opposite block and so had windows on three sides. Eva's was a one-sided apartment, facing onto the garden and the opposite block. She could never look away from her neighbours. Eva had grown up in a traditional detached house in the outer suburbs, and these modernist blocks had always given her the feeling that she was missing out on something, some avant-garde, freethinking ideal that had been denied her. She was in now, just not so completely as Hildegunn. Hildegunn's apartment was a homely museum, a testament to the ambition and optimism of the fifties.

A nephew? said Eva. Let me just check here.

It was like falling in love with yourself, this feeling that came over her when she observed a desirable life. She wanted to be the one living it. Even the knowledge that Hildegunn was gone off to hospital with a broken hip did not deter her imaginings. To be young in the fifties, to live in a home made of light, floating elements, with thoughts and musings stacked behind each piece of furniture, which should be placed just so. Eva imagined that Hildegunn's apartment could live all by itself, that even without occupants it would continue its ideal life: coffee brewing, flower boxes receiving a trickle of water from a stainless-steel watering can, a silver cat leaping onto a windowsill to stretch out in the sun.

Did you hear me? said Une. I said they broke the door into Hildegunn's apartment.

I have a spare key! said Eva. There was no need to ruin the door.

We didn't know what was happening. Hildegunn rang for the ambulance herself, so she must have told them to kick in the door. It was a medical emergency, you know. She was out of her mind with pain, talking absolute nonsense, poor woman.

Eva put Une at ease, told her not to worry, that she, Eva, would sort it out. She asked Une to look out for Hildegunn's cat, in case it escaped.

When Eva hung up, the awful smell seemed to jump at her again, as if it had retreated to the background, out of politeness, while she was occupied on the phone.

Before she put down the phone, it buzzed again, with a message from Sonja Flynn. Despite the fact that her contributions were in arrears, she was asking for an insurance assessment. If it wasn't something as serious as an exterior wall, Eva might have told her to pay up first.

The smell was horrible. It was shit; that's what it was. There was no denying it, but it wasn't coming from the toilet. The windows were all open, though Eva could not remember opening them. She must have done it during the night and forgotten. It had been so warm, so clammy.

If they were digging up pipes she should have been informed, as head of the board of residents. She unlocked the door to the balcony, to check if there was a leakage from the sewage system down on the street.

The five-metre-long flower box was full of earth to weigh it down and prevent it from blowing off, but it contained no plants yet. It was she who had ordered these copper flower boxes, reproductions of the originals which had been replaced by boxes made from asbestos in the seventies. She would get Ellie, her cleaner, to plant heather at some stage. Heather mostly took care of itself, she had read. She allowed herself this practical consideration for a prolonged moment, and then her attention was drawn downwards to the middle of the balcony floor slab. A wretched coil of excrement – dog poo, in fact – lay there, reeking and taunting.

She leaned over the edge of the balcony and looked up and down at the apartments above and below. It was impossible. She was on the third floor and there was no way for any dog to climb up here. At the other end of this block there were ivy creepers, which some superhero dog might plausibly have climbed, but here, by her apartment, the walls were of fair-faced brick. This was not a façade that anyone, human or canine, could climb. She had only one theory, and it was so extreme it baffled her. Magic seemed almost more likely, but it was the only possibility: on the floor above, in the best apartment in the block, with 150 square metres of internal area, a large roof terrace and a balcony, there lived a couple of architects who had a dog.

There was always something strange about Frida and Fritjof, like they were not entirely present in the conversation. They were beautiful people, maybe that was it, and, critically, they had a beautiful dog, a Rhodesian ridgeback. It was the colour of the shit on her balcony. Even this thought could not make Eva dislike the dog. It was sleek and svelte, and, if she ever decided to get a dog, it would be a breed she would consider, solely for its looks – and its demure nature.

That dog was huge. It must weigh as much as herself. Frida and Fritjof were tall, so the dog seemed the right size for them, but – there was no way that huge animal could have climbed down. If the faeces did belong to the beautiful dog, it was its owners who, out of some deeply concealed contempt, had managed to lower the stinking pile down here.

She craned her neck to see up to the nearest window above her and the balcony right over her own. Could they really have done it? The physical feat and the audacity were equally perplexing. If the poo had lain along the edge of her balcony, on the bare flower boxes, it would at least make physical sense. They might have somehow brushed it off. But this was not something that had splattered down. It was a perfectly formed piece of excrement, coiled in a direct depiction of the colon it came out of. It was provoking. It was absolutely enraging. Really, she should just clean it up, but she was so astounded she could hardly move. Could it be some bird, she wondered, who left droppings like a dog?

She had once seen a crow eating a cowpat, a most revolting sight. It ruined crows for her, despite their purported intelligence. She considered whether a crow could have eaten some dog's excrement down on the street, then flown up here and thrown it up.

No. This was dropped right here from a crouching hound. It was the only thing that made sense, and it made no sense at all.

# Raj

It was almost 10 pm as Raj neared home, his research in digital technology and leadership still tinkling connections and potentials in his head. The forty-minute walk from the university was like descending a mountain of knowledge. The fact that he concluded the descent in a basement flat contributed to this impression. His was a cerebrally intensive existence. The research institute he worked at was beside the university so, when the workday ended, he could go, via dinner in the student canteen, to the lab or the library to work on his postdoc: convenient, but physically slothful. He needed these two daily walks. His body was the benevolent host to his brain, a rich aunt who would support you if you toed the line. Sidewards glances from women he passed on campus suggested he was not doing so bad a job on corporal maintenance. If these women came too close, though, they might smell his apartment off him.

For the last week, after noticing that some of his colleagues talked to him from a greater distance, or just waved where they would previously have come over and fist-bumped, Raj had started taking his showers in the changing room at work.

A fortnight earlier, his flatmates, Krishna and Pradeep, had found a notice in their letter box about the smell, telling them to use the ventilator when they showered, to consider their neighbours when preparing food, to use, or indeed install, an extractor fan over the cooker, to keep the door to the stairwell closed at all times, especially when food was being cooked. When they received this recipe for civilized living early one morning – that is to say, it had been placed in their letter box late at night – Raj noticed that neither the part-time dad on their storey nor any of the others had a similar note folded and sticking out of their letter box. None of his neighbours were suspects.

Not only were Raj and his flatmates extracontinental foreigners – who, it seemed, needed to be told the basic rules that allowed Europeans to live side by side – not only this, but they were also tenants. Eva Holt, head of the board of residents, had not-so-casually bumped into Pradeep soon after they moved in and told him that they were the only tenants. All the other apartments were owner-occupied, so she just wanted to say that they had only to ask if there was anything they were unsure of, and had their landlord given them the house rules? If not, she happened to have a copy on her.

All the other residents came down to his storey from time to time to get to their storage rooms, and they inevitably complained about the smell. It was probably one of them who had stashed away something horrendous, a slaughtered elk in a malfunctioning freezer, though it was not the smell of rotting flesh. There was certainly nothing Indian about the smell, a fact that should have exonerated Raj and his flatmates. There was nothing particularly foreign about it even, whatever that meant. It was not a spicy, aromatic or pungent smell. It smelled of basement to a factor of ten. It smelled wet, or damp, even though the surfaces were dry. He had looked up dry rot and fungal growths and checked along the floor and behind the furniture. There were no characteristic black spots; there was no rotting wood. It looked fine – but it smelled intense.

It hadn't always stunk. When they moved in it had been all right – a fact that made the whole situation worse, since there was a temporal link between their tenancy and the smell. Worried about their deposit, they had been eating salads and taking cold showers to avoid steam for the past fortnight, but the smell only got worse.

They paid a three-month deposit when they signed the tenancy contract, all three of them, but they had only lived there for one month. The other two were as tightly strung on student loans as Raj was, otherwise they would have looked for a place somewhere else. Next time he would rent somewhere on a higher storey. He could probably get something cheaper closer to the university, and he could get his exercise by jogging. He didn't benefit from the central location of his apartment. It was just expensive.

There must be something they could do about the smell. He was the only son of scientists and maybe that was why he could not let it rest, why he needed to understand.

Raj, Pradeep and Krishna all worked in IT, worked by day and researched in the evenings, or the other way round in Krishna's case, since he was still contracted to a Delhi-based company. Dealing with smells was not within their skill sets. Scent and taste were still way off on the edges of virtual reality, the last unconquered senses.

As he walked down the street he saw Krishna inside, attempting to open his bedroom window to a greater angle. They shrugged at each other. There were bushes directly outside the windows, so Raj always felt he was peeping out of a hiding place when he looked out. They mainly kept their curtains drawn, however, as people – strangers as well as neighbours – tended to gape in as they went by. It could be that some people thought single flatmates were in a public sphere with each other, not being related, so it was less of an intrusion to stare in at them, less provocative to suggest they stank. Perhaps these people believed that families lived in homes, whereas young single males, especially academic migrants, never lived in more than a flat or apartment. Raj did not think of that stinking hole as his home. It was just a place to stay and, increasingly, a place he was glad to leave every morning.

It was called a basement apartment, but the floor inside was only a couple feet under the level of the narrow garden along the street. Because of how the streets sloped, whoever designed these buildings had managed to shoehorn Raj's apartment and one other in under the rest of the apartments, in front of the basement storage rooms. For all he knew, the apartment they rented might once have been part of the cellar, and he and his flatmates were in temporary storage.

The part-time dad's red-nosed face leered at him through his basement window, and Raj wondered if this meant he too was one of those who dared look in at ground-floor residents, if he was entitled to do so since others did the same to him, or if it was the movement of the man, right behind the glass, which had caught his attention. Raj averted his gaze as neutrally as he could.

As he came through the glass doors, a silver cat darted slipper-silent up the stairs. Even cats could not abide the smell – or this cat might be in the habit of urinating down there. This beautiful feline might not be so beyond reproach and thoroughly refined as one would expect from her graceful movements and the dazzling gloss of her fur.

His red-nosed neighbour was peering from his door as Raj came down the half flight of stairs to his apartment. A whiff of whiskey tinctured the overwhelmingly subterranean odour.

Was that your cat? said Raj.

I want you to know, said the man, that I have a little daughter, a seven-year-old girl, a pure princess, who I bring to my home from time to time, for the weekend. Do you know what it is like to have your own daughter say your home stinks? I tell you, young man, I am meticulously clean. It is simply not fair, what you're doing: you and your chums stinking out the whole floor. You know the rules; you've been given notice. Now, just show some respect, can't you?

His monologue complete, the man slammed the door.

Not your cat then, said Raj.

As he came inside, a noise drew his glance inwards along the floor. Mice, four at least, shuttled in various directions and disappeared, hidden who knows where.

He checked under his own bed. That would be the worst. He closed his bedroom door, but opened it again, because he didn't want to block them in.

He heard a low meowing out in the stairwell. In his hurried mouse chase, he had left the door unlocked.

Pss-pss-pss, he said. Here, pussy pussy.

He held the door open and stood well back so as not to frighten the animal. She kept her eyes on him as she passed and then made straight for the kitchen.

Pradeep came out of his room, and Raj put a finger to his lips.

We have mice, he said.

Krishna came out too.

Is that your cat? he said. It is not allowed.

We have mice, said Pradeep, putting on his jacket. I'm going out to get a trap.

We'll need a few, said Raj, but the hardware stores will all be closed now.

I'll try the shopping centres.

I'll come with you, said Krishna. There are humane traps we could get.

Stay with me, said Raj. We should tidy up and seal all the food. Get some tape too, Pradeep, will you?

Text me if there's anything else, said Pradeep, already out the door and tapping up the half-flight of stairs at speed.

Raj heard squealing and hissing from the kitchen.

Where did you get the cat? said Krishna.

It just came in.

He held the door ajar and allowed the cat to go out with a small mouse in her mouth — alive or dead, he couldn't tell — and to come back to fetch another and another.

They waited quietly as this happened. Raj stood aside in the hallway, so he would hear anyone coming on the stairs. He didn't show himself at the door, in case the alco-dad could see him through his spyhole. If anyone came and saw the door ajar, they would be accused anew of spreading their dinner odours into the stairwell. This despite the fact that none of them had cooked dinner and none of them would have the appetite to eat anything now.

Let's keep the cat overnight, said Raj, in the lowest of voices. She had come in of her own accord, and she would be well fed.

What if the owners come knocking? said Krishna. We will get in trouble.

We are in trouble, said Raj, and how is the owner to know the cat is here?

They decided to let the cat choose for herself.

Raj stood by the exit for twenty minutes, an attendant to a cat. Eventually, he heard a scream from upstairs: Mice! He silently closed the door. The cat took five mice, if Raj had counted correctly, but he could not be sure she took them all. So, when Pradeep came back with the traps, they set them up all over the apartment.

# Tuesday

*We don't swing the way we used to. We consider refusing. We wonder if we could close on purpose, or decline to open, but we know how the push controls us, and the pull. It may be that our age is showing, that we will soon be demounted, stored or tipped, but we have not forgotten our roots. Yes, we once had roots below us, branches, twigs and leaves. It was warm there, moist, and we cannot return. Hinged through seventy springs, this swinging still feels wrong. Flatness is the greatest degradation. Ring on ring around a core, we remember, curving round the pull of water, pressing inwards, that's how we were. We never minded the rain. It gets so cold here. It's always dry. The oak sticks on the floor get washed on occasion. Not us. They slathered on a thirsty resin. How it stank, all wrong, and never washed out. It's still there, between our grains. They cut us thin and rolled us flat and glued us together in layers, and our corners — oh! — how they long to curl. We have been pulling back towards the curve of our trunks all these years, hoping, one day, to be round again. It takes too long, so, while we wait, we slam! Listen to it: slam! slam! slam! If we do it all together, the mutilators might hear: SLAM!*

# Linda

Flink tugged on his leash and emitted a tortured whimper. The empty morning street echoed his complaint and turned it into an accusation.

Come on, now, said Linda, who had the front door in sight and only put on a light cardigan when she rushed outside because, yes, Flink had jumped out to the garden again, with her bicycle helmet dangling from his drooly jaws this time. She was pleased that Flink, at least, thought her capable of vaulting the railings and crawling through the bushes to go for a cycle. Knut had offered to pay for her bus pass if she gave up cycling, as if it was the cost that mattered.

She shut Flink into the living room last night because the balcony door could be closed there, unlike the French windows in her bedroom. He drooped and cried as she pulled his basket out. Ever since Leif died, Flink had spent his nights beside her bed. She slept badly last night without Flink's smelly old wheeze around her. She couldn't listen to her own breath long enough to grasp it. It was something too deep, at the heart of the world. All night, she had the feeling of falling, sinking. She was used to having the sky overhead, not a stack of people.

Come now, come, she said, but her order had little effect on Flink.

It was early, but she was eager to get back inside, to tidy up the mess of newspapers, pens and unfamiliar knick-knacks that had accumulated: one of those reflectors that you snap around your arm, and one of those clips that keep your trousers out of the chain when cycling, at least that's what she thought it was. It had a little picture of a bicycle on it. Linda simply tucked her trousers into her sock, but maybe someone had given her all these things. It must have been Bibbi. It might be their new location that made them seem strange, or she might be going batty. She had to tidy up because Baby-Bibbi was at home today and had promised to call over around eleven.

It was a point of pride for her that Bibbi referred to Linda's old apartment as home. That's exactly what it was, and if anyone needed a place to call home, it was Bibbi.

Linda pulled the leash and clicked her cheek.

Come on, Flink, in we go, she said, but Flink only leaned back on his haunches, stretching the line.

She wound the strap round and round her hand until her fingers were purple and she was right beside him. She picked him up — and he was a light dog, she could take his weight — but it was an awkward movement with the helmet dangling at her elbow.

40

Up on the doorstep, she heard Frida and Fritjof's voices jangling. They had not hung up their intercom receiver correctly.

What time is it? she heard Frida say. Careful! There's another one. Don't stand on it.

With Flink still in her arms, she pressed Frida and Fritjof's button. She had to ring a few times before she got an answer.

Hello, said a tired man's voice. It sounded as if he were dragging the word along.

It's Linda from the ground floor, she said.

The door buzzed open.

Are you all right? said Fritjof's voice, slowly becoming itself. Were you locked out for long, Linda?

Linda held the door open with her foot, as she spoke into the intercom, though there was no need. She had her keys. It just seemed impolite to refuse to go through the door he had buzzed open for her. The brass kickplate had come loose on the outside of the door. It hung on by only one screw and scratched along the black stone tiles on the landing inside.

The door's broken, said Linda.

Oh dear, said Fritjof. I'll come down. Just give me a moment.

Linda came inside and let the door go. It scraped back to almost closed, but the sheet of metal caught in the door saddle, keeping it ajar. Flink squirmed in her arms, his nose twitching towards the gap.

Their voices continued to sound from the intercom.

Linda's locked out – oh, yuck! said Fritjof. The front door's broken.

I don't understand this, said Frida.

I'll be right back, said Fritjof. Where's the dog?

Don't you dare leave me with this, said Frida. Rocky! Here, boy! Rocky!

Linda waited through buzzing calls of, Rocky! Rocky! until Fritjof came down without any tools in his hands, not even a screwdriver.

Linda, you got in, he said. I'm sorry it took me so long to answer. We were still in bed. What time is it? Were you out cycling?

He pointed to the helmet.

Yes, she said, the lie slipping out so easily. But look at that door.

Fritjof pulled it open with a scratch.

Do you have the screws? he said. I'll run up and find a screwdriver to match.

Check on the steps outside, she said.

He did but found nothing, and so he examined the one remaining screw.

I'll find something that will do, he said, for now. We'd better tell Eva about this, I suppose. I'll send her a message, in a while. Do you want to go in home, Linda? I'll look after this.

You're a saint.

Actually, he said, I've been meaning to ask you: when you lived up on the top floor, did you get a lot of leaks?

Linda looked up, out of old habit, though of course she couldn't see the roof slab from all the way down here.

I never had a problem with leaks, she said, not once. They change the waterproofing every thirty years, you see.

Right.

It's not that long since they did the roof here, is it?

Only fifteen years, said Fritjof.

Modern tradesmen: they're only interested in how much you pay them and getting the job done quickly.

She went into her flat using her full strength to keep the whingeing Flink from escaping.

What's got into you? she said, as soon as they were inside.

Flink broke out in a belt of barking, and she put him down before he deafened her. She sat on a stool in the hall-way and changed from shoes to slippers. They felt tight and looked a strange colour too in this light.

She followed Flink into the living room. She was certain she had wedged the stiff balcony door shut before bedtime and locked it too. Flink was a smart animal, but the use of a key was surely beyond him. She wondered if she might have been sleepwalking again. She had done so as a child. Once she had awakened out in the cowshed. Her parents put a can by the door so they would wake if she was on her way out. They made her sister sleep outside her in the bed. Now she wondered if she might have continued sleepwalking all her life and no one had noticed. Leif used to sleep like a log. She remembered throwing a glass of water on his face when she went into labour with Knut. If her sleepwalking was harmless and she went back to bed without waking up, she might have been doing it all these years. She hoped it was true. Otherwise, she was losing her memory. The balcony door stood wide open.

Come, Flink, we'll get your breakfast.

The floor felt strange underfoot. It seemed to drag, to slow her steps. All her adult life, she had tripped around the top floor like a bird. Now she was grounded.

Her kitchen window faced onto the little strip of garden towards the street. In terms of intruders, it was a good thing that window could still be closed properly. It was quite warm at night now, so as long as she could close the windows again in the autumn it should be all right, she thought, and then she considered thunderstorms. There was nothing for it, she would have to go up to Eva-the-first-woman.

She jingled Flink's dog food into the tray on the kitchen floor and felt a chill on her back. The kitchen window was closed but she noticed something odd. A long tendril of ivy extended through the closed window and hung down, almost reaching the floor.

She went closer and, not trusting her eyes, felt for the glass with her fingers. The entire left pane, through which the ivy grew, was missing.

She stood back and inspected the floor, but there were no shards of glass there. There were none stuck to the window frame either. The putty was missing along the edges. She leaned through the open frame, like a picture come to life, and looked down at the strip of lawn between the wall and the pavement. She stared at the spot where the glass should be if it had fallen out. There were no bushes it could have fallen into, just this two-metre-wide stretch of grass. There was no trace of the glass. Someone must have stolen it – or taken it away if it was broken.

Did you do this? she said to Flink.

He must have got into the kitchen during the night and pawed the pane out, or it might just have fallen out, and someone had been up early and taken it away. It was possible that this happened the day before without her noticing, though the opportunistic speed of the ivy's growth still baffled her.

Will I have to lock you in the bathroom tonight? she said, and Flink whined like he understood.

# Raj

Raj had spent most of the night trying to read an article. He would drop off after a few paragraphs and wake, maybe only minutes later, not remembering what he had read. He must have attempted the same article twenty to thirty times, yet he could hardly remember the title, let alone the content.

All night he controlled his breathing, exhaling as silently as he could, and perhaps this was the problem. He could not stop listening, even when he had listened so long that every creak in the building was magnified. Lying on his bed with closed eyes, he had difficulty placing the sounds he heard. A repeated, low tapping at high speed might well have been a mouse scampering across the floor, but he could not tell if it was in the hallway, out on the street or here inside his bedroom. He lost track of his vertical position in the room and could not decipher if any sound was above him or below. This apartment building took on the abstract spatial qualities of cyberspace, with microchips which squeaked like mice and incomprehensible sequences of binary numbers representing all the sounds he heard.

He looked at the shadowed cavities of his slippers but could not bring himself to swing his feet in as was his habit. Anything could be in there. From the safe height of his bed, he scanned the floor. There was a gap of half a centimetre under his bedroom door, and he wondered if that was enough, if a young mouse could squeeze through.

He took a pen from his bedside table and prodded the toes of his slippers from the outside. Nothing happened, so he picked them up, one after the other, and shook them. When no mice fell out, he stuck the pen inside to make sure they were empty. Only then did he dare peek in. He should have risen half an hour earlier if he was going to apply such caution with all his garments.

When he opened his bedroom door, he heard human scrambling in the rooms beside his, and the others emerged.

I didn't want to come out first, said Krishna. I've been awake for hours.

It smells terrible, said Pradeep, the worst it's ever been.

They went from trap to trap, huddled in a group and terrified more than guys their age should be. The first three traps, in the corridor, were empty. The fourth, in the kitchen, had sprung across the head of a rat.

Raj found himself alone. He fetched three plastic bags from under the sink. The trap had clearly snapped, yet he was afraid for his trembling fingers. He managed to get both the rat and the trap into the first bag without touching either. This was the kind of job you should do after a better night's sleep.

When the rat was wrapped in three layers of plastic, each bag tightly knotted, the stench was still there.

The other traps were all empty, so Raj wondered if the rat had eaten the rest of the mice before it was killed. He entertained the unlikely future memory of himself opening each of the three plastic bags and dissecting the rat's stomach for signs of mice. In this imagining, the mice twitched their noses free from the rat's intestines and scampered away. Raj forced himself to think of white sandy beaches and wished the feeling of scampering off his skin.

I'm going out to the bin, he called to the others. There was only one, guys. You must help me clean.

A head appeared from each of their bedroom doors, surprisingly low down; they resembled mice peeking from their holes.

When Raj came back inside, he found his flatmates mopping and scrubbing. They were both wearing rubber boots.

Ring the landlord, said Pradeep. This is too much.

I don't know, said Raj. We could try throwing out all the food.

It stinks, said Pradeep, and it's his job to fix this. Ring him – in a while. Our complaint will command more respect during office hours.

Is it our fault? said Krishna. Do either of you know of anything we can have done to deserve this?

Of course not, said Raj. I don't have time to carry out bad deeds, and you, Krishna, are irreproachable. I mean, you capture flies in cups and put them out the window rather than swatting them. You stay standing on public transport, just in case a bunch of old people get on and feel uncomfortable taking your seat. And Pradeep, my friend, you do go through a lot of boyfriends, in a way some people would call immoral, but you always speak respectfully of your lovers, even after the relationships end.

I'm glad you see it like that, Raj, but did you take a picture of the rat?

It's too late now.

So, we have no proof?

# Sonja

She spied them through the kitchen window, Frida and Fritjof out for their usual morning stroll along the street with their beautiful Rhodesian ridgeback. They were holding hands in their customary way: her left hand holding his right hand, she with the leash in her right hand, he with the recycling in his left – plus a huge plastic bag from the hardware store, a minor variation. Sonja would never have considered shopping at this hour. They were like another species, these people who saw the pre-work hours as a time to get things done, rather than a scramble. There was something perfect about Frida and Fritjof. She could not imagine them arguing, never mind breaking up.

She had convinced Eva that the draught should be looked into at once, in case they discovered something serious. Eva gave her the contact details of their man at the insurance company. Get someone to come and assess the damage, she said, and even the word *damage*, in Eva's confident tone, seemed solid and certain. The wall was damaged. They would find out what was wrong. The insurance company were sending someone out the next day. Everything was moving forward in a soon-to-be-fixed manner, but she would feel better if she asked Frida and Fritjof about it.

She waited too long, admiring, so she had to grab the paper rubbish at a run and fly down the stairs in order to casually bump into them.

Frida, she called out. Fritjof!

They smiled as they strode back up the slight incline towards her. They were long and dangly, all three of them, like the roots of a mature tree in a manicured park.

Wish me luck, said Sonja, out of breath. First day as a freelancer. She gave them each a business card, and this was useful, this was wise, but she knew she was also stalling. She didn't quite know how to put her question without appearing a complete idiot.

How's the book coming along? said Frida.

Oh, lovely. I'll be doing illustration for brochures and institutions as well, she said. Let me know if there's anything going in your field.

Sonja wished she could illustrate books exclusively, but she'd need other streams of income to keep – to get – afloat. She was in arrears with her loan, utilities, mobile network and union. Her strategy was to spread her debt evenly, paying up as late as possible.

If you don't mind me saying, Frida, the folk museum could do with a graphic update.

Sonja laughed at this, in order not to insult Frida, and Frida smiled.

I wish we had the budget for it, she said, pocketing the card.

The Rhodesian ridgeback leaned its shiny flanks into the foliage beside the footpath, unsettling a dusting of small flies and bringing forth an on-and-off twittering from a nest somewhere in the depths of the bushes.

What's the dog called, said Sonja. Fred?

This teasing suggestion of alliteration passed Sonja's lips before she could censor it, but they smiled at her anyway, as if they got the joke and didn't mind.

He's called Rocky, they said.

He's fabulous, said Sonja, deliberately not commenting on the name, because it was the wrong name for such a dog. A bulldog could be called Rocky. This guy should be called Silvester – something glossy like that.

In a nervous throwback to childhood, Sonja picked a plump white berry from the bush and burst it with a pop. Her father called them fart berries.

Frida and Fritjof started to turn back the way they were going.

Actually, said Sonja, there was something I've been meaning to ask you two ... as architects.

Their eyebrows went up, encouraging her to continue, but they didn't smile this time. They were expecting her to ask for free design advice.

It's just the wall in my apartment, she said, the one towards the back garden: there's a draught from it sometimes, or all the time, really.

That's strange, said Frida. Do you have radiators under the windows?

I do, said Sonja, it's not that. The radiators are on. It's the rest of the wall. There seems to be air kind of seeping through it. I can feel it with my hand.

Are you sure it's not simply cold? said Fritjof. If the wall's cooler than the room, that would cause a downward airflow along the surface – a draught, if you like.

Maybe, said Sonja, and she didn't know how to tell him that it couldn't be that because she had only noticed it now and it had been fine all winter. She didn't know how to express to them that it was a much greater problem than they seemed to consider it. She couldn't say any of this without sounding mad.

I guess there might be a crack in the wall, said Frida. Can you see any cracks?

No, it looks fine, really.

A crack in the bricks under the plaster? said Fritjof. I can't think of anything else it could be – or an old vent that was filled in badly.

Yes, said Frida, get someone to check under the plaster for you, if you think it's worth it.

Let us know how it goes, said Fritjof. He sounded like he meant it and offered his words with a tip of the head, but Sonja didn't believe him.

Do you ever have birds flying in? said Frida.

No, I mean, there's no hole, just a draught.

They don't fly in the windows?

No. Do they fly into your place? What kind of bird?

Oh, I've no idea. It's always gone by the time we get home, after leaving a little mess for us to clean up.

That's interesting. I've seen some skylarks in our garden. They're quite rare. And goldfinches. They nest quite high up.

Maybe that's it, said Fritjof. Goldfinches.

Satisfied, they smiled and nodded, nipped at Rocky's leash and loped off, their linen blazers fluttering earthen colours in the breeze.

# Eva

The no-entry sign she had adhered to Hildegunn's door the night before had been treated with a lipsticked tag of Munch's *The Scream*. Her expectations were so low at this stage that anything short of the typical balls and cock was a welcome surprise. She had arranged to meet the locksmith, the door repairman and Hildegunn's nephew, Gunnar. Eight o'clock sharp, she had told them, but she had little hope that they would all turn up on time, so she left a message at the office saying she would be up to an hour late. Her subordinates would have to survive without her this once, and they could ring if there was some emergency.

Lately, Eva wondered if the meaning of the word *emergency* had been lost on her colleagues. They seemed to equate it with a sense of crisis, an emotional reaction rather than an issue that really couldn't wait. One of the junior staff had already rung her to say he had forgotten his access card and was locked out of the office. She told him, Either go home and fetch your card or get a coffee and wait for someone to come. The strange thing was, he seemed happy with this answer.

She unpeeled a shocking screech of glass-fibre-reinforced gaffer tape. When the last of the tape lost its glue-hold, the door swung inwards at a slightly wrong angle, so the bottom corner wedged into the mat inside. Lucky there was a mat. Otherwise, it would have put a mark on the wooden floor. She went straight to the kitchen and found a dustpan. She brushed up what she could of the splinters in the entrance hall and tipped them into the bin under the kitchen sink. There was a pile of Lego figures in the old woman's bin.

It was already eight o'clock, but no one else had arrived. Eva allowed herself the liberty of having a look around. She had been here before, often. Any time Hildegunn called to complain about something, Eva always insisted on coming over. This had its advantages for the lonely old lady, but Eva would not be so helpful if it was not such an enormous delight to visit.

Everything in Hildegunn's apartment had a carefully assigned position. Three Danish designer birds with pastel-painted wings were clustered along the top of the brickwork at the fireplace. A teak bookshelf matched the wood on the windowsills, and the latter must be frequently sanded and varnished because, while Eva had the same in her apartment, hers were rapidly bleached by the sun. The bookshelves were built to the exact height of the windows, and the distance between the shelves and the window was equal to the distance between the shelves and the ceiling. Paintings hung in a balanced pattern, with almost-invisible fishing wire suspending them from the picture rail along the ceiling. A few of the pictures on the party walls were slightly askew, and Eva corrected this small divergence on Hildegunn's behalf.

On a coffee table of chromed tubular steel and glass, Eva saw that Hildegunn's usual collection of interior design magazines was absent. It had been replaced by a startling composition in primary colours. On closer inspection, Eva saw that this abstract structure was built of nothing other than Lego. She would have noticed if Hildegunn's grandchildren had been to visit. They lived abroad. Eva considered taking the Lego apart, or hiding it, because Hildegunn must surely be going senile. She must be reverting to childhood, though Eva was uncertain if Lego would have been available to Hildegunn when she was a girl. Eva had recently read that Lego figures outnumbered humans at a rate of 8:1, but when, she wondered, had they started to produce it? Eva didn't like the idea of Lego figurines outliving her. She wondered what future generations would think when all they found of us were these little ninjas and coloured bricks. Would they think we were a diminutive race, obsessed with fighting and building?

At a quarter past eight no one had shown up, and the door repairman called to say he was having difficulty parking. He had evidently come in a truck. Eva taped the entrance door closed from the inside, reusing the same strip of gaffer tape, and slipped into the loo. There was no key in the door, and anyone could push in the front door and know what she was doing. It was too close, too badly sealed off for comfort.

She stepped on the bin pedal to dispose of a used tissue and saw a bunch of tampons inside. They were still in their individual plastic wrappers, so it was clear that old Hildegunn had not been using them. They could not have belonged to a visitor, because why would a menstruating woman throw away her unused tampons? It must have been a free sample slipped into a bag at the pharmacy, and Hildegunn had meticulously removed the tampons from their box to recycle the cardboard. Another theory – they were coming to Eva now – was that Hildegunn, as she had previously speculated, was going senile, and she had bought a box of tampons by mistake. Tampons had possibly not been produced when Hildegunn was of the applicable age, so perhaps – yet another theory – perhaps Hildegunn just wanted to see what they looked like.

Eva came out into the entrance hallway and found that the repairman was already at work on the door.

New hinges, he said, and you'll need a new mortise lock-set. The deadbolt's damaged. Do you have the latch? We might be able to reuse it.

I'm Eva Holt, she said, head of the board of residents.

She reached out a hand to shake.

I'm expecting the owner's nephew any minute, she said. Have you heard anything from the locksmith? He said he'd be here at eight.

I know the man you're expecting, he said, and he's always at least half an hour late. It's a rule with him, I'm starting to suspect. No matter, anyway. I'll have to take the door away.

He was already at work on this task.

The doorbell rang.

Wait with that a minute, said Eva. This will be the nephew. He's an estate agent, so he'll probably have something to say about it.

She buzzed Gunnar in and heard the slow tap of leather soles ascending. It was quite likely he was late on purpose too, an alpha male principle.

The repairman lifted the door aside to reveal a doggish version of Hildegunn. Gunnar's face had all of his aunt's recognizable features, each in a slightly cruder, slightly coarser expression. He had come to the AGM a couple times on Hildegunn's behalf, but she was a fool to trust him. He would ruin this apartment if he ever got his hands on it. He stepped inside and didn't bother to take off his shoes.

I can fix the door, the repairman told him, but I'll have to take it away: new lockset, new hinges, and repair of the woodwork.

That's fine, said Gunnar. Write it all on the invoice, and I'll send a copy to the insurance assessor. We'll need some sort of temporary barrier too.

I can board it up for you, if you like, said the repairman. I'll put that on the invoice too.

That's great, but I'll need access, said Gunnar.

A temporary door, then?

Make something that closes with a padlock, said Eva.

Yes, said Gunnar, just something to close the apartment off. How long till you have the door repaired?

Should be done by the end of next week. A new door would be three to four weeks, at least.

I need it repaired in one week, max, said Gunnar. An elderly woman lives here. Also, I've that project for you up in Ullern ready to go if you hurry this along.

He strikes a hard deal, this one, said the repairman, winking at Eva. I'll do my best, he said, and we'll have to get that locksmith to come at the same time as me. Let me see.

He opened a tattered notebook and tutted.

We'll aim for installation Tuesday afternoon, then. I'm busy that morning.

Eva gave Gunnar the spare key.

This is no good to you anymore, she said, but I'm happy to keep a copy when the new keys get here. I've ordered them already.

That's lovely, Eva. Perfect. I wish all my properties were as well run.

Gunnar's waxed hair brushed against the glossy orbs of the coat stand.

How is Hildegunn doing? said Eva.

Oh, she's on the mend, but it was a terrible injury. Really knocked her out.

Do pass on my regards. I have great respect for Hildegunn. She keeps such a beautiful home. She's always been keen to show me around.

Yes, well, I'm taking good care of her. This is all very confusing for someone her age.

Oh dear. She must hate being away from home too. You know, Gunnar, if she's ever thinking of moving out, keep in mind that I'd be interested in a private sale. I'm sure she'd like to know her apartment was in safe hands.

I'll consider that when the time comes, said Gunnar.

He rubbed his fist, and Eva knew by how his eyes darted around that he was already calculating the worth of this home.

Right, said the repairman, here we go.

He pocketed the hinges he had unscrewed, lifted the door and laid it against the wall.

I'd better slip out before you, said Eva.

It was wrong to leave this gem in the hands of this pair, but she had work to do.

# Gunnar

Gunnar had a list of things Hildegunn needed to survive the coming day, as she had put it. They were planning on discharging her the next day, her injury being what they described as minor under the circumstances. They said they wanted her back on her feet, though he suspected they rather wanted her out of their bed. He filled the cat's bowls with water and cat food that was composed of 60 per cent rabbit. He didn't care to check what the other 40 per cent was. Rat, he thought. They probably gave it some technical name, but it was likely as not rat.

When he failed to locate Hildegunn's toothbrush, he decided that he might as well buy the lot off the list in the pharmacy and save himself time searching. Efficient. He didn't need to redefine himself like a man undergoing a mid-life crisis, but, since his divorce, he needed to define what he had always been, aside from a husband.

Hildegunn's bathroom mirror had those characteristic black age spots along the top corners. He could not quite decide if this was a desirable quality, showing the pedigree of the property, or if it made the place seem shabby. He reminded himself that this apartment was not for sale, though he had offered to buy it once. Eva Holt wanted it too, but he suspected she was trying to get it cheap. She could put in a bid alongside everyone else if it came to selling.

Poor Hildegunn: she kept the place so well. Many apartments in this area had been ruined by renovations, nothing of the original charm enduring. The internal doors and windowsills were rainforest hardwood that you could not source today, yet he had seen many instances where they were replaced with cheaper timbers. A trendy renovation was the alpha and omega of a good sale, but you had to do the same again in five years' time if you wanted to resell. Nothing lasted, especially style.

He felt an attachment to this building. That was part of the reason he had bought the basement flat downstairs, though he couldn't live down there himself. It was previously the maids' quarters, perfect for rental. He spent very little on it, and it brought in a tidy little income every month. It fascinated him that while homeowners in a particular area could be quite homogenous, as could renters, the owners and renters in any one area had very little in common with one another. They occupied separate strata of society and scarcely influenced each other.

Gunnar had an idea. He took off his shoes and took a stockinged stroll around the apartment.

He would maintain his own house as his official residence, for tax purposes, while he got it ready for sale. His ex-house: that's how he thought of it now, belonging to the same category as his ex-wife. When he sold the house, he would be able to afford a nice apartment down by the seafront. In the meantime, he would stay here. He could get things ready for Hildegunn before she arrived home, and then stay here to look after her. She needed his care.

His phone rang, and he saw on his screen the name Raj, followed by a great number of letters he could not form into a name while the ringer disturbed his concentration.

Gunnar Lofthus, he said, with the familiar punch his own name always gave.

I wish to make a complaint, said Raj, and Gunnar began at once to estimate what cost he could sanction.

Just a minute, he said.

He put the phone on speaker and opened the relevant spreadsheet. He had to replace the flooring the year before, pulling up the oak floorboards, which had begun to rot, and replacing them with a cheap parquet. Spreading that cost over three years, as well as the depreciation in value, there was not much left for other repairs. Then, Gunnar had a second idea.

The door to his rental apartment was just downstairs, and it belonged to him. He could get the repairman to switch them, bring his tenants' door up here. He wasn't about to live in a padlocked apartment. His tenants would be all right with a temporary door for a while. He could even let them wait for a new door, instead of getting Hildegunn's door repaired.

I've been trying to call you, he said. I received a complaint about you from the board. There seems to be a problem involving the preparation of food in the apartment and the door to the stairwell remaining open for an undue length of time.

Mr Lofthus —

Now, don't worry, I don't believe you actually leave the door open. There's not much we can do about the neighbours' prejudices, but I've decided you need a new door. There must be something wrong with the one you have. Is there someone at home now?

We've all left for work, Mr Lofthus —

So early? I wish you'd have warned me. There's a man over there right now, to take the old door away. He'll have to replace it with a temporary door for a week or so, but don't worry about that.

A new door? said Raj. I'm not sure that will help with the smell.

Look, I agree with you completely, they're almost looking for something to complain about, but trust me, it's easier to go along with them on small points like this. They'll see I'm doing what I can with the door, and you do your bit: cut down on the spices and candles, and they should leave us alone. Believe me, there's no point in putting up a fight for every small complaint. Keep your head low, and they'll forget all about you.

That's not all, said Raj. We have an infestation of mice and rats. We put out traps.

This was suspicious. As all landlords know, where there are mice there cannot be rats, because rats eat mice. Not everyone could tell the difference, though.

How big are they? he asked.

The mice were approximately three centimetres long, and the rat was fifteen centimetres long and very fat.

Have you thrown them out? Did you take pictures?

There was a pause before Raj answered.

We took no pictures, but you would believe me if you smelled what it is like here. These are not proper living conditions.

In a practice he recognized as typical of himself, Gunnar was pacing around the living room as he listened, and he now roared out, Devil! hissing and clutching his stockinged foot.

He bent down and picked up a silver dessert fork, a traditional, overly ornate piece that he was surprised to find here. He saw another one along the edge of the rug underneath the coffee table, and a teaspoon of a similar design. He raised the volume on his phone, put it on the coffee table, and let Raj continue to expound on the situation downstairs.

There were three spoons on top of the coffee table, one of them in the empty fruit bowl, and he found others on the armchairs and on the rug itself, disguised by the geometric pattern. There were six of each, dessert forks and teaspoons. He lined them up on the edge of the table.

I want to know what you are going to do about it, said Raj.

Gunnar realized he hadn't been listening at all, but he was not going to let the spiel be repeated.

Send me a bill for the traps and cleaning agents, he said, with pictures of any receipts, and I'll subtract it from next month's rent. Is that all right?

That is very good, thank you, said Raj, but I must impress on you that the smell is quite impossible to endure.

Gunnar went to the walnut sideboard where Hildegunn kept her silverware in a wooden box lined with grey velvet. Not only were the cutlery boxes full, containing all components, teaspoons and dessert forks included, but the design was entirely different to those on the coffee table. The difference was so wide that they could not possibly be used at the same table. While the cutlery on the coffee table looked more like plants than utensils, the cutlery in the box were more in keeping with the style of the apartment. They had long, slender grooves along the handles that let off before the tip in an elegant curve. This new, strewn-about collection of frivolous silverware was a clear sign that all was not well in old Hildegunn's mind.

Raj was still talking.

It is terrible, he said, no matter how much we clean and air out.

Well, let's see how it goes with the new door, said Gunnar. Your next warning will be in written form, but I hope it won't come to that. I must move on now, but send me those receipts. That's no problem. And give me a call if you have any more trouble. Bye now.

He hung up without letting Raj reply, and he felt surprisingly bad about it. Perhaps it was his proximity which gave him these pangs of guilt. He could easily have gone downstairs straight away and had a look at the problem for his tenants, but there was no way Gunnar was going anywhere near rats. That was an issue for the board. If they were in Raj's apartment now, then they would find them elsewhere soon. They could sort it out themselves. Gunnar had enough to do, tending to old maids.

*I am on top, above all else. Without me, forget about the rest. I am the obligatory component of shelter. I am the first defence. I shut out inhospitable temperatures. I guard against rain, ice, hail and wind. I withstand forces of both tension and compression, and carry what snow winter drops through to spring. I absorb ultraviolet rays and gather the acidic droppings of birds. I can exclude insects and other flying creatures. I may deny access to airborne twigs and falling branches. I believe I might provide some resistance to meteors. I am what keeps it all together, if cared for and correctly maintained. I am an embargo on dilapidation, for a while.*

# Fritjof

He was chopping the carrots into half-moons for a scampi salad. Frida brought the scent of leaves with her when she set the tap gushing in the sink beside him.

Bird droppings, she said. Again. We're going to have to keep the windows closed during the day.

She wrung a cloth under warm water, spattering the carrots, and rubbed in a squirt of washing-up liquid.

Fritjof, you don't think it's perched inside somewhere, do you?

They both turned from the sink and listened.

They make an awful fuss if they get trapped inside, said Fritjof. Show me.

He followed Frida out to the living room, followed her craning neck from the piano to the bookshelves.

It must have flown out again, she said, and she pointed to the cushioned armchair.

In the middle of the forest-green woven cushion, right where you would sit, there was a splat of white, with a nodule of black in the middle.

Bird droppings all right, said Fritjof. You know, we should have asked Sonja to support us about the skylight.

She's just gone freelance; she's probably skint, and you know how Eva makes out like everyone will pay for it in the long run.

Yes, but Sonja might not want to go against us. Seemed like she wanted friends. Every time I go for a shower, I look up at the ceiling and think how nice it would be with a skylight. Daylight on my wet, naked body: is it too much to ask for?

Why don't you put it like that when you ask Eva again?

She's so mean. I'm sure we could put a clause in somewhere that says we'll be responsible for the maintenance. Angelica next door wants one too, she texted. They're away this week. And Une said she'd support us. She has as much to gain as us, though they can't afford to put one in themselves right now. Do you think that Ibsen guy would take a bribe? That would be two out of three on the board.

Seems the type. He might support us just to spite Eva.

I think he wants to be head of the board, said Fritjof. Let's tell him we'll vote for him if he gives us this permission.

Frida started nipping the mess off the fabric with a piece of dry kitchen paper. She blew away the chalky dust and dabbed what was left with the cloth.

It's gone into the weave, she said.

I think we have a clothes brush somewhere, said Fritjof.

Or maybe carpet cleaner. This is wool, isn't it?

Fritjof sniffed the clean, matching armchair. It's wool all right, he said. Will I get the Milo?

71

Do, and maybe even the nail brush.

Frida was still dabbing with the cloth when Fritjof came back.

Here, he said. There was another one in the bathroom.

A bird?

No, just the droppings. Do you think it was a skylark?

Not my area of expertise, said Frida.

The one in the bathroom's bigger, and it's kind of swirled with green.

This is revolting. Close the windows, will you?

Fritjof went clockwise around the apartment, closing all the windows, as well as the doors to the roof terrace and the balcony.

There's one in the bed, he called to Frida.

He opened the fasteners along the bottom of the duvet and started to separate duvet from cover. Frida came to the bedroom door.

I googled it, she said. There's some sort of acid in it. Put it in the washing machine straight away.

The runny stain had gone through the cover.

How long's the cleaners open? he said.

Six, I think. Wait.

Fritjof brought the duvet cover into the bathroom, with the offending smudge balanced on top. He poured a good glob of detergent directly onto the stain and shoved the bundle into the washing machine.

Do you think it's dangerous? he said. Birds have diseases.

I can't hear you.

Fritjof stuck his head out the bathroom door without touching his hands off anything. Do birds have diseases? he said.

You're thinking of the bird flu, said Frida.

Maybe we should wear gloves.

He rinsed his hands and turned the dial on the machine to a 90-degree cycle. As he opened the detergent drawer, he let out a roar.

Are you all right? called Frida.

There's one on top of the washing machine, he said. Ironic.

Frida put her head through the bathroom door. I'll fill a couple buckets with bleach, she said. We should wash everything.

He heard her cross the hallway and, understanding suddenly what it was he had observed on the floor there, he came out to warn her, just as her foot slid and her arm reached out for the wall.

Jesus, she said, taking off her slipper to examine the sole. It's everywhere. How did we not notice when we came in?

Fritjof wiped the now familiar grime off the floor with a wet cloth. It was uncanny. Must have been a whole flock of them, he said. Do you think it could have been seagulls?

I told you, said Frida, I don't know anything about which shit belongs to which bird. Let's just clean it up.

I don't like it when you snap at me like that, he said.

Then don't provoke me.

He found a roll of kitchen paper, wrapped a good length around his hand and tore it off. He put the paper on top of the stain on the duvet, then folded it in on itself and rammed it into an oversized IKEA bag.

I'll drop this down straight away before they close, he said.

Frida had a steaming bucket of water in each hand. He kissed her on the ear on his way out.

When he came back there was a strong smell of lemony bleach, and he was glad to see Frida had opened the windows again, to air the place out. Even though that's how this revolting assault had started, ventilation was a necessary part of cleaning.

There's one in the hallway, he called.

For heaven's sake, said Frida, coming out, I've done there.

She looked sweaty and ruffled, and her cheeks glowed like she'd just come down from a mountain.

Wait, Frida, stand still, he said, and he touched a fingertip on a dab of white right on the crown of her head.

Stop it, she said, smacking his hand away.

You have one there, he said.

What?

Bird's droppings. You must have scratched your head.

It didn't look like it had been rubbed on by accident. It looked like it had landed right on her head, and he could not understand that she hadn't noticed it happen.

Were you out on the terrace, he said, or the balcony?

Frida was already in the bathroom, tilting her crown towards the mirror, cursing over the gurgling slosh of the washing machine and running tap water directly over her head.

I need a shower, she said, pulling off her clothes and stamping them into a pile on the floor.

Don't open the windows, she said. They might come back.

The washing machine went into a screeching spin.

Did you hear me? she said, because Fritjof remained standing there, staring at her. How could she forget that she opened the windows?

I'll close them, he said. Have you seen Rocky? I should have brought him out with me for his walk, killed two birds with the one stone.

Frida spluttered through the suds. You can kill as many birds as you want, with what stones we have, she said. I could do with a walk after this.

In the kitchen, Fritjof found his chopped carrots had been dressed with a dollop of bird poo.

They're back, he called to Frida, as he dashed around to close all the windows and doors, scouring every possible roosting spot as he went.

Where's Rocky? he called to Frida, but she was busy cursing her way through the hallway and into the bedroom.

# Eva

Eva scaled the stairs to home with unusual ease. The steps felt shallower.

The day had proceeded from the quenching of one fire to the next: misunderstandings and worries, contractual difficulties and a new colleague who refused to see how his misinterpretation of corporate norms had almost cost them their reputation. She usually complained that the employees were too dependent on her. This one was the opposite, an entitled little troublemaker who wouldn't entertain an ounce of negative feedback.

She shrugged him off. Looking out the stairwell windows into the branches of trees, putting her key in the lock: these movements were the pleasant conclusion to a pleasant segment of the day, and the sound of the bolt sliding into the thickness of the door was one of her favourite noises.

Eva kicked off her flats in the hallway. She padded into the bedroom and pushed the French windows almost closed before she shed her suit. The windows must have blown open during the day. The bolt that kept them at the right angle for airing was missing. It wasn't on the floor. She must have scooped it into the wash basket that morning. She disliked the idea of the building adjusting itself at will while she was out, opening its windows wide to take a deep breath like a living thing.

She switched on the ceiling light, because there was something strange about the wall at the head of her bed. Bizarre. She slept here every night, so it was astounding that she hadn't noticed it, but it seemed equally impossible that it should have happened in the course of this one day.

Over the whole wall, though on none of the others, the surface was – how could one describe it? – it was rippled. It looked like the paint had achieved a molten quality while a strong breeze had blown over it, and the film of colour had frozen into the crests and valleys of an ocean in miniature.

Eva picked up her bedside lamp and shone the light along the surface. It was completely destroyed. She knew she shouldn't, but she let a thickly manicured nail scratch and catch on one of the crests, pulling off a strip of paint. The plaster underneath was chalky and dry, just as it should be. This was a party wall, and it was cold to the touch but – she gasped.

She ran out to the hallway and slid on her shoes at speed. She crossed the landing and pounded on her neighbours' door.

Steps approached, and Severin Ibsen opened the door with that snootily relaxed, academic smile. Eva was not sure how she could be so certain of this, but she could tell by his manner that his wife was not home. Eva couldn't remember the wife's name. It had too many consonants and needed to be read out syllable by syllable. Without any evidence, Eva guessed she was a piano teacher. On warm days when her windows were open, she sometimes heard the tinkling of a piano, and the music might have come from any apartment, but she attributed it to this woman, perhaps because she lacked a tag. Everyone called Severin by his surname, to his delight, though he was no relation to his idol. He insisted on being overtly corduroy-clad and bookish, and perhaps it was his name that overshadowed his wife's.

Her question had been, Has there been a fire? but everything smelled fine. Ibsen smelled provocatively luscious, to tell the truth, and he was smiling at her in a way that not even the looniest madman could do following a fire.

I thought I heard a noise, said Eva, cursing her resourcelessness.

He would be one up on her now. He had posed some politely critical questions at the AGM last year, which had ended with him joining the board of residents. She was sure he had his eye on her position. He had done nothing to help all year long, but he seemed exceedingly pleased with himself. He didn't seem ambitious, nor especially responsible, which were, Eva would readily admit, the driving forces behind her own position on the board. This man just seemed to think he knew better, that his way of seeing things was the only reasonable way. He also seemed a bit hard up, in that annoying way that intellectuals can make you feel little for earning a good salary. He wanted her position on the board for the paltry salary. It didn't cover all the hours Eva spent, but this guy would do less, so he would get a better hourly rate. He would congratulate himself on simplifying their affairs and claim his predecessor had been overly bureaucratic. Now her seemingly pointless agitation had given him ammunition, at least on a personal level. She began to dread this Friday's AGM.

All quiet in here, he said. Perhaps a window slammed. It's terribly draughty today.

Eva had left her own door open behind her in her haste, and her neighbour looked over her shoulder now as the noise of a dog barking came through the gap, inexplicably loud.

I thought you were against pets, he said.

The window's open, she said, and I'm not against anything. I simply require that rules are followed and consideration is shown at all times.

Back inside, she regretted snapping, but he hadn't thanked her for her concern. He was probably scoffing at the strict and jumpy woman next door, who runs over in a frenzy when she hears a noise.

In her bedroom, she took photos of the wall from various angles and wished there was someone she could complain to. At the top, you could only receive complaints. She decided to send the insurance company an email straight away. It would be impossible to sleep in here with the wall like this. She would make her bed on the sofa, or perhaps on the balcony.

The balcony door was ajar. She jumped at the sight of the great Rhodesian ridgeback out there and jumped again when he barked at her. A lion had roared at her in the zoo once; the great feline had laid sunning himself behind a thick Perspex barrier, opened his jaws as if to yawn and let out the most blood-curdling roar.

She pulled herself out of that relatively safe memory and looked again at the dog out on her balcony. She tried to close the door on it, scared by the size of the creature, scared by its closeness, but the door must have expanded, or warped, because it wouldn't fit back into its frame. She pushed a chair against it and held it in place with her foot, but the dog didn't charge against her as she expected. It simply stood there, with a nodding understanding about its huge head. It didn't look dangerous or aggressive. It was a beautiful dog. Its coat gleamed like polished walnut.

Eva filled a plastic bowl with water and filled another bowl with oat puffs, which were the closest she had to dog food. She slid the chair away with her foot, nudged open the balcony door and dropped the two bowls as far from his jaws as possible on the limited space of the balcony. If she was going to deal with this gigantic dog, she wanted him to be content and compliant.

He lapped up all the water at once. This was her big, orange mixing bowl, containing over a litre. The poor dog must have been there all day. He turned his attention to the oat puffs, slicking up a few, then nosing them and looking up at her.

You want milk? she said.

The milk helped. He ate the full bowl of cereal as well as two crusts, which she tossed at his feet.

Right, said Eva.

She took hold of his collar, and he moved in response to her tug. There was a brass label hanging off the collar, impressed with the word *Rocky* and a telephone number.

Come on, Rocky, she said, and she led him through her apartment. He was so tall she hardly needed to crouch to hold his collar. He seemed to be limping a little.

When she was out in the stairwell and halfway up the flight that led to Fritjof and Frida's apartment, she faltered. Her intention had been to pound on the door and demand an explanation, but she couldn't fathom what that explanation could possibly be. They had come into her apartment yesterday and left a revolting dog poo on her balcony. They had come in again today and left their dog there. If it had been a chihuahua or even a terrier, she might have entertained the possibility that they had somehow lowered it down onto her balcony from theirs. That had been her working hypotheses regarding the poo, but by no stretch of logic could this enormous beast have been manoeuvred down a floor along the façade. The only way in, it followed, was through her own front door.

The dog, Rocky — an ill-fitting name — was eager to get up home, so she released her hold on his collar. With an elegant lope, the Rhodesian ridgeback ascended the remaining stairs and stood outside his own door. After a moment, he sat on his haunches and fixed his gaze at human eye level.

Eva left him there for now and went back home. She checked the keychain where she kept one of her three keys. The other, she found, was in the cupboard in the hallway, though she had intended placing it with a friend in case of emergencies. The third key was with her cleaner, Ellie, a pleasant young Filipino woman whom she suspected was also an au pair.

She phoned Ellie, who answered promptly and, after much fumbling and mumbling, assured Eva that she had her key right there.

When were you here last? said Eva.

Friday, she said. I always come on Friday. It was morning, ten o'clock. Is everything all right? You want me to come sooner?

Yes, said Eva, surprising herself. Yes, I wondered if you could come tomorrow. I need a proper spring cleaning. If you could wash the windows, the oven and the fridge, that would be great, and there are some stains on the grout in the shower that you might give a scrub to.

Ellie agreed to come the next day. She said she could stay between eleven and three, and she should be able to do all that Eva asked in that time.

Eva hung up, realizing she had just enlisted a spy, but the work needed to be done anyway, so there was really no harm. She heard the dog whining in the stairwell and decided, even if it peed on the landing, she would leave it there.

The doorbell rang. Eva painted intolerance on her face and walked with footsteps as audible as she could make them.

It was Linda, slightly out of breath. The great Rhodesian ridgeback stood beside her.

Linda, come in. Are you all right?

Eva shooed the dog away and ushered the old woman inside. Linda looked significantly withered, her sun-damaged scalp visible through thin hair. Even her feet seemed small in her shoes.

Don't worry about me, said Linda. I just had to tell someone about the poor dog, and the owners are not home. I saw them outside earlier, without their dog.

What is it doing running loose in the stairwell? Are you sure they're not there?

Too many questions, said Linda. Might I sit down?

Eva led the way to the kitchen and had to consciously slow her pace, lest she leave the old woman behind. She wondered how long it had taken Linda to mount the stairs.

If you're afraid to come out in the stairwell any time, she said, if anything untoward is going on, you can phone me, you know that, Linda. You have my number.

Oh, the climb did me good. I lived on the top floor over at the other side for many a year, and I have plenty of time for going up and down stairs. I only moved so I could have Knut and his family near me. Did you notice that Une put up a flag on my birthday? I could see it from my window. We tried to buy Hildegunn's flat, the one below mine, but she refused, out of spite. He's a property shark, that nephew, and he'll have it on the market as soon as he gets old Hildegunn shipped off to a nursing home. There was something I wanted to ask you, but it's gone.

Eva spooned coffee into the filter and filled six measures of water.

My little Flink – that's my little terrier – he's probably barking his head off down there right now, just so you know. I'm sure someone will complain, but this is hardly my fault.

Of course not, said Eva.

She put a cup and saucer in front of Linda.

I was putting the washing on when Flink went mad barking, just inside the door to the stairs. He's usually such a peaceable dog. I thought someone must have knocked and I hadn't heard on account of my being inside the bathroom putting on a wool wash.

Wool? The central heating is still going, Linda, if you want to turn on the radiators in your apartment. We can leave it on until the end of the month if you like.

My windows won't close. That's it. There was something else too. What were we talking about, just now? said Linda.

The enormous dog outside the door.

Oh, that's right, that's right. Well, I went to answer the door, and there was no one there, only that big dog that belongs to Frida and Fritjof. I meet them when I'm out walking Flink, and they're a lovely couple, very considerate. They always keep their dog on the leash, even coming down the stairs. I appreciate small gestures like that, though I'm well able for a dog of any size. I was telling my old neighbour in 14A – the artist woman, Irish – I was telling her when we were last talking – it's been a while now since I've seen her. Does she still live there?

Do you mean Sonja Flynn? I think she works in advertising.

That's the one, said Linda, looking into her empty cup.

Yes, Sonja lives right opposite you now, said Eva, your mirror image so to speak.

Linda laughed. You're flattering me, she said. Anyway, I was telling Sonja, when I met her the last time, and this must have been back when I lived in my own apartment, I was telling her that I grew up with an Irish wolfhound. Can you believe it? They were very unusual back then. Amazing animals: take you back in time, they would.

Coffee? said Eva, and Linda nodded.

Linda raised the cup in her hands and blew off the steam. She didn't drink.

Yes, so I'm not afraid of a big dog, not at all, said Linda. I may be dwindling in size, but I was smaller, I can tell you, much smaller when I was a little girl ordering an Irish wolfhound around like I was the queen. What breed of dog is it Frida and Fritjof have? They told me, but, you know, old age and all.

It's a Rhodesian ridgeback, said Eva, a fabulous creature, really. I hope it's all right out there.

Don't give her anything to eat, or she'll be sneaking down to you all the time, said Linda.

Do you want to wait here, Linda, and I'll go up and see if they've come home?

I knocked and rang the doorbell, but there was no answer. They are architects, the two of them. They work all hours. I knew an architect once from Germany, a greatly talented woman. I can't remember her name now.

I'll phone them, said Eva, putting a plate of biscuits in front of Linda and picking up her phone.

That's it, said Linda. There's a pane of glass missing in my kitchen window.

It was no wonder the poor woman was cold. Eva would have to speak to Knut. First, she scrolled to Frida's number.

On the phone, Frida claimed she had no idea how the dog got out and suggested they must not have closed the door properly. Eva told her that the door was closed all right.

I don't know how this happened, said Frida. He must have slipped out somehow, without us noticing, before we left this afternoon. Eva, I'm hopping on my bike right this minute. I'll be home in fifteen minutes, max. Will you give him a bowl of water for me, please? He'll be parched. I'll wash the stairs too, she said. I'm so sorry about this, Eva, and thank you so much for calling.

Eva sat down opposite Linda and poured a cup of coffee for herself. Frida was a good liar, but her motivation still fazed Eva – the practicalities too.

The dog slipped out, she said.

She dipped a biscuit in her coffee, submerged it exactly halfway.

It must have happened when I saw them leave a while ago, said Linda, but that was before you came home. Didn't you notice him when you were coming in? You hardly walked right past him.

The biscuit dissolved in her coffee, rendering the mixture undrinkable, inedible. The wise old woman had caught her out. None of this was her fault, but, still, this guilt ...

He must have been waiting upstairs, said Eva. He must have been outside their door.

Linda pointed at the wall beside the fridge. This was the other party wall, and so it was with great dismay, but little surprise, that Eva saw it was subject to the same puckered waves on the paintwork. Most of the wall was concealed by cupboards, but the incomprehensible pattern could be seen on the stretch of wall between the counter and the fridge.

Wrong paint, said Linda. You can't use oil paint on any of the walls here. I had a painter who did the same up in my old apartment one time. He insisted I should have oil paint in the kitchen. It was meant to keep the steam out of the walls, but all it did was peel off.

That's it, said Eva, opening a cupboard to see if the wall behind was in a similar state, which it was. Well done, Linda, she said. That's another mystery solved. You must come up to visit more often.

# Knut

He's asleep, said Bibbi, as she padded barefoot into the dining room.

Do you know what happened to all the teaspoons? said Knut.

He was on his knees, elbow-deep in an awkward corner of the good sideboard.

No, I was looking for one earlier. Have you seen my flip-flops?

We'll use the silver. We should use it more often, while we have the chance.

Treasure, said Bibbi.

Knut rooted in a velvet-lined box, taking out bunches of ornate knives and forks and dessert spoons.

I was sure, he said. What's that box there?

Bibbi opened an empty cardboard box that smelled of candles.

No, said Knut. We must have given them to my mother. The dessert forks too. You might go down and have cake with her tomorrow, Bibbi, he said. Bring back a few spoons.

Damn, I forgot. I was supposed to have lunch with her.

You were still asleep at lunchtime.

Poor Bestemor.

We'll call on her tomorrow. She'll understand.

You're right. Have you seen my flip-flops?

What colour are they?

They're gold.

Indeed.

Not real gold, silly. They're Havaianas, you know, rubber flip-flops.

Haven't seen them, I'm afraid, and I always notice when there's gold lying around.

He pulled out a few more boxes and watched Bibbi walk barefoot over to Une, who was tidying up Teddy's Lego on the living-room floor.

You haven't seen a pair of gold-coloured flip-flops lying about, have you?

Is the pool open at this hour? said Une.

Not that kind of flip-flops. I'm going out, remember? Or, I mean, is it still all right for you to mind Teddy? I'll stay in if you want.

Oh no, you go out. Teddy's no trouble to us, the little prince.

He's asleep now anyway. He doesn't usually wake unless he has a nightmare. You didn't see the flip-flops then?

Were they out in the hallway earlier, or on the floor of your room? I'm sure I saw them somewhere. Have you checked under the bed?

Under the bed was where Une always told them to look for things, and she was rarely wrong.

It's all right, said Bibbi, I'll wear something else.

You might be better off, said Une. It's cold enough tonight. I was out with the rubbish earlier.

He liked listening to them. He could hear Bibbi better when he wasn't talking to her himself. Une was pushing all the loose Lego pieces into a pile, separate from the free-form structures Teddy had fashioned out of parts that were meant to make a house.

Is that more new Lego? said Bibbi, picking up the box.

She had the uncanny ability to laugh and moan in the one breath.

He lost the previous lot, said Une. Honestly, I don't know what he does with it, short of flushing it down the toilet.

Wouldn't it float?

Well, I haven't tried, Bibbi. Your father got him that new box anyway. It's a lovely thing, a haunted house.

Maybe we should go back to Duplo.

Knut came over, dusting off his sleeve.

You can't go back to Duplo, he said, once you've gone over to small Lego. Why did you have him playing on that sheet of plastic? It looks like a crime scene.

It was left over since we painted, said Une. I just wanted to see if it made a difference.

I don't see what difference it could make, said Knut, the Lego is hardly seeping through the floor.

There was a pause before she replied.

I know, she said, but it might help him to contain it.

As long as he doesn't smother in it.

I taped it down, and it's a flat sheet, not a bag.

Dad, you don't have to keep getting him new stuff. You'll spoil him.

I'm doing my best to pamper him, he said. I won't be happy until he behaves like a little emperor.

Are you sure it's all right if I go out tonight? He might wake up.

You go out and enjoy yourself as much as you want, said Knut. I wish I'd gone out more when I was your age.

I'll tell him a story if he wakes up, said Une. He makes me sing too, the little darling. No one else would listen to a voice like this.

You've a lovely voice, said Knut.

You've a lovely storytelling voice, said Bibbi.

Thanks for your honesty.

Bibbi didn't seem to receive this compliment, these thanks. Her head was turned towards the living-room window. You could see all the way to the sea and to a glass lift tower that used to bring tourists up to the top for a view. You couldn't get out of the lift. It only stalled a while to let you look out, then came down again. There had been long queues when it opened, but interest wore off, and it was no longer in operation. They still lit it up at night. It was blue now, like ice or moonlight. Perhaps it was meant to symbolize something.

What's on tonight, said Une, a play?

I'm just going out with a few friends. There's a vernissage.

Anyone I know?

Miro Johansen.

Is that your friend or the artist?

That's the artist!

They both laughed. They did it together like they were sharing it, and Knut was unsure who had given it to the other.

Will you be eating out? said Une. I can make you up something quick before you go, if you like.

No need, I'm fine. There will be finger food, and we might go for a bite somewhere afterwards.

Lovely, I'd say the town will be quiet tonight, on a Tuesday.

Have you seen her golden sandals? said Knut. They've gone missing. I bet they were stolen. A thief can sniff out gold like that from way down on the street.

They're here somewhere, I'm sure, said Une. You can't keep losing things.

I'll have another look around.

Something with a closed toe, I'd say, might be better for tonight, though the gold would match your outfit all right.

I feel like Midas, said Knut. Give me whatever shoes you want, and I'll have them gold for you in no time.

You will all right, said Bibbi.

The lift tower changed to purple as he listened to Bibbi sneak into the bedroom, and he waited for the sound of Teddy waking, crying, but it didn't happen.

Leave her alone about her clothes, he said. If she catches a cold, she'll have to stay at home.

Une went and turned on the washing machine she had already filled. Bibbi came out to the hallway wearing a pair of high black boots, and Une looked pleased.

They're lovely, she said, in her night-hallway whisper. Where did you buy them?

London.

Bibbi turned to look out the living-room window again, and Knut wondered if it was the sea she was looking at, or that gaudy tower, which was now glowing crimson. Why did Une have to bring up London?

I found our old baby-carrier, he said, down in the basement. We must stop storing things down there, Une. There's an awful stench.

Your back isn't able for that baby-carrier, said Une.

I could carry Teddy in it, said Bibbi. He'll probably want to get down all the time, but just in case he wants to sleep. Will we go on a hike this weekend?

Yes, they said together, a bit too enthusiastically. Une was beaming, and Knut wanted to tell her to tone it down a bit. She wore the kind of astonished look a bird might have when her egg finally hatched.

Bibbi, she said, I just put on a wash, and I must have pressed something wrong because it says it will be three and a half hours before it's done. I wondered if you could hang it up when you get in, if it's finished. We'll be gone to bed by then.

That was a lie.

No problem, said Bibbi.

But just leave it, of course, if you get in earlier. I'll give it an extra rinse and hang it up in the morning, but just in case you get in late – though I suppose it won't be too late now on a Tuesday. The city will be dead in a few hours, I'd say, not that I'd know.

I'll hang it up if it's finished, said Bibbi. It's no bother. It's just towels.

Bibbi rooted in her pockets and picked her brown leather bag off the floor. She still had the child's habit of dropping her things on the floor whenever she came in. She scrambled in the bag.

I can't find my keys, she said.

When did you have them last? said Une. She shuffled through the few things on the hall table, then opened the wardrobe and went through the pockets of the coats.

I'd say they're with the golden flip-flops, said Knut.

When did you use them last? said Une. On the way out or in?

Bibbi handed Knut her handbag so he could check it too. I told you, she said, they were in this bag, I'm sure of it.

Here, you can borrow mine, he said.

She accepted his keys, let him zip them into her handbag and hang it over her shoulder. Maybe she felt she owed it to him, thanking him by receiving his care.

Don't lose them, said Une, or we'll only have one set left.

# Wednesday

*Our power of reflection casts off your image. This is the clearest we will ever be. You see through us, but we see through your warbling sounds. Your noises make weak waves through time.*

*'open close open close a draught don't let in the rain polish draw the blinds light will bleach nice fresh breeze it will slam put on the latch not so wide lovely view but neighbours' eyes the building's eyes putty loosened leak in storms rain blows in stains on the sill paint next summer this autumn next spring open close rattle with thunder so much pollen open close polish slam crack'*

*If you were heated like we were, you would blacken to dust and blow away, but we are clear when warmed so much then cooled. Transparent, we can appear to disappear, but we will last forever – a long ever – some time; we will become shards. The dust we are crushed into will not be the same corns from which we began, though that was no beginning. The sand was rock and shell; the shell was home around crustaceans who ate of the seabed, which ate of the algae-made oxygen, and it's the same at the other end. When we smash we will be swept up, carried away, divided further – but we can never be crushed so small that we completely disappear.*

# Linda

I must bring out Knut's old tricycle for him, she said, and then she remembered she had given it away years — no, decades ago, more than half a century.

On the alarm clock, which she never needed to set, it was just gone six o'clock, and that was enough of a lie in for a Wednesday. It didn't take much, but it was important to distinguish between night and day, and between weekdays and the weekend. Clocks and calendars were so artificial that she could only tell what was what if she let herself be ruled by them.

Linda had given up on trying to close the windows, and the weather seemed to be taking a turn towards the better, so she just left them open, if that's what they insisted on doing. She had complained to Eva, but maybe she should ask Knut to get her a repairman. Windows were tricky. The board took care of repairs, but, if you wanted new windows, you had to buy them yourself. She simply wanted them to close.

The railing at the French windows felt rough under her fingers, and she saw that the patches of rust were now bigger than the flecks of black paint.

Flink was stretched out on a sunny patch of lawn, but he jumped up when he spotted her. He had something in his mouth, and, as he trotted over to her and stopped on the path beyond the bed of roses, she was dismayed to see it was her nice leather handbag, a present from Bibbi, protruding from either side of his small jaws and giving him the look of a hammerhead shark.

She looked up to her old apartment, and she had to grip the railing more tightly, for, though she had spent most of her life up there, it now seemed precariously lofty. Bibbi had forgotten to call on her yesterday, or maybe she was busy – or ill. Linda should have kept the macarons in case she came today, but last night she was angry. She had eaten them all, giving one to Flink.

She put on her shoes and a cardigan in the hallway and searched for her keys. They were not on the hook or on the dressing table, and she realized they must be in the handbag, which she had used the day before, and which was now covered in drool.

She left her own door ajar. There was a pump at the top that held it almost closed for fire safety. They had put in new doors the year before and, while Linda had never been overly worried about fires in the night, these doors were a better barrier to noises and smells – and bother.

She used some junk mail to keep the outer door open, because she didn't trust that Flink had managed to keep the contents of her handbag in place, and she might need to get in without a key. If she could avoid it at all, she didn't want to ask those architects to let her in again. They were lovely people, both of them, but they just seemed so bothered. She wondered if they felt their burden lightened each time they met her, because a small fraction of their woes had been transferred to her.

This was terrible nonsense and Linda knew it, but it was what came of having only a dog to chat to all day. Quite often, her neighbours passed without a nod. They would only stop to talk if something was the matter.

The low garden gate creaked with greater purpose this morning. Flink pattered over to her with the handbag in his mouth like he had found it for her or saved it from some terrible fate. Linda looked towards her apartment with its windows and balcony door wide open, and she was inclined to fear someone had been in there: a burglar in the black of night who had stolen, for want of greater treasures, her good bag. She imagined old Flink giving chase and latching his half-toothed jaws around an ankle.

He dropped the bag at her feet now, and it looked relatively unharmed. Her keys and her purse were inside. Flink sat before her with a tilted head, and she wondered if he expected a reward.

I'm not throwing it, she whispered, if that's what you have in mind.

Her keychain was heavy with the keys to her flat, the front door, the storage room, her bicycle lock and the keys to her old apartment, which Knut insisted she keep. They didn't want her to feel like they had taken the apartment from her entirely. They hoped she would drop in often, they had said, and they would call on her all the time too.

Linda believed this had been everyone's honest intention, but, somehow, as the weeks went by, she had hardly seen her family. She hoped Bibbi was all right.

Looking up in that direction now, she thought she saw a movement on the terrace, though it may simply have been the creepers rustling in the wind up there. In any case, she decided to pay them a visit.

Flink started growling on the front steps, so she left him tied to the railing there. She took it easy, pausing for a breather on each landing. As she passed Hildegunn's door, she averted her eyes, then shook off this habit to examine the door. It did not look like it had been kicked in. Hildegunn had broken her hip. She heard it from Nora — or was it Stella? That was the problem with lesbians: they matched so well, she couldn't tell them apart. Hildegunn's door looked fine.

When she got to the top, she looked down through the opening at the centre of the stairs, along the railing which spiralled through four stories. She wondered how she would ever get back down again.

Flink's low whining could be heard all the way up here, over the sound of snoring, along with the odd crash or bang. It was too early, really, to call on Knut and his family, but Linda needed to sit down more than anything in the world, so she put her key in the lock.

She imagined a whiff of coffee washing over her. She remembered how Leif always hummed over the radio. Instead, she opened the door to silence and a smell she recognized but could not quite place, apart from the vague feeling that this was an outdoor odour.

She closed the door with muted puffs and clicks, and watched her step as she came inside, afraid to stumble over a toy car as she had done the last time. She sat down on a stool to take off her shoes. The hallway was impressively tidy, considering four people, including an infant, lived here. There were no toys on the floor, nor anything else, not even shoes, and she thought they must have vacuumed the evening before. The mat inside the door was gone too and it looked nice and tidy without it, but they would have to get a new one before the winter. Perhaps they were washing the mat, she thought, as she went into the living room and sat down on a good armchair. She felt she might never get up again and vowed to go up and down the stairs in her own block twice a day, because she had clearly lost fitness living on the ground floor.

The living room and dining room were spick and span too. At least, there was nothing lying around. She presumed this must be Une's doing. Knut had always been messy. Perhaps they were getting the floor sanded and varnished. She had only got it done once herself. That was around ten years ago and the first time it was ever needed. The timber did look a bit run down. It was off-colour here and there, and the man she got in to do it must not have done a good job. She would tell Une to use someone else this time.

The clock on the wall said just over half past six, and she wondered how long she should wait, or if it would be better to come back later.

Linda used to keep a little set of hammered-brass kitchenware by the fireplace. It was gone. They had belonged to her own grandmother and had no real value, but she hoped little Teddy might use them as a tea set. She remembered how she used to pretend she was making food for her grandmother. Perhaps Teddy had taken them to his bedroom.

The brass fire set was gone too, but those she didn't mind losing. She had bought them cheap somewhere to match her grandmother's brass, and they were worn out by now. She made a mental note to get them a new set for Christmas if they hadn't replaced them by then.

If she stayed any longer in the armchair, they would have to pull her out of its deep sag. She stood a moment before she took to walking. She had an unsteady feeling, as if she were standing on uneven ground. Something was different. Her ankles were swollen, her bodily fluids sucked downwards, but that was not all. As she walked to the kitchen, the familiar ill will that came through the floor didn't pinch and poke her feet like it used to, but seemed rather to nibble at them greedily.

At the sink, she tilted a glass under the spout and filled it without letting the water run cold first, to make as little noise as possible.

She sat on the stool in the hallway and looked around her on the floor for her shoes. She looked under the stool: nothing. She stood up again. Scanning the floor, she turned and turned until she felt dizzy.

Teddy, she said, eyeing the gap at the door to the room where Teddy slept with his mother, where Knut had slept as a child.

Teddy, she whisper-called, what did you do with my shoes? Teddy?

She heard a bed creak and the scurry of small feet, and Teddy's sleepy head peeked out.

Oldemor! he exclaimed, and Linda heard Bibbi groan and rise. There was movement in Knut and Une's bedroom too. She had woken them all.

Get my shoes, Teddy, she hissed.

The boy looked at her feet. He crouched in front of them. With a finger, he traced the lines of her protruding veins.

Where did you put my shoes, Teddy?

The boy lay face down on the floor, his forehead against the floorboards as if he were trying to look right through it.

Hi, Bestemor! said Bibbi. You're up early.

Knut and Une emerged from their bedroom, propping each other up like the co-dependent constructions Leif used to design.

Is everything all right? said Une.

I can't find my shoes. I think someone hid them.

Oh dear, said Knut.

He looked at his own bare feet, and at Une's.

Did you hide them on me, Teddy? said Linda. Get them for me now. Don't be bold.

The boy showed her his empty palms, and tears bulged from his eyes.

He was with me, said Bibbi, are you sure you were wearing ...

You're not in trouble, said Linda. Just find them for me now, won't you?

More tears.

Bibbi picked the boy up, saying, It's okay. She stroked his upturned palm and said, We'll find them together, Teddy. Oldemor's shoes are playing hide-and-seek.

Une gasped.

Our slippers! she said.

Shoes have been going missing around here, said Knut. It's not Teddy. They're just disappearing. Don't worry.

I took them off just now.

I know, but don't worry about it. It happens to all of us.

Une pinched him in the arm and it must have hurt, but he only stroked the pinching hand. There was something they were not telling her. Maybe they thought she was going mad.

That's right, said Bibbi. Just yesterday I couldn't find my favourite flip-flops. My outfit was ruined without them.

Bibbi tried to laugh, but Linda had heard the girl's real hiccupped amusement too often in the past to be fooled by this fakery.

Honestly, said Une, it's nothing to worry about. We'll get you a new pair.

Linda could see how it pained Une to say this. She was a kind woman, but frugal.

I had them just now, said Linda.

We know.

I didn't forget to put them on. I didn't walk over here barefoot like a crazy woman.

Of course not. We're not saying that.

I remember taking them off right here. It was Teddy. I'm not angry with him. I just want them back.

The boy wiggled down from his mother's arms and clawed at the floor, big teardrops puddling below him and slipping through the cracks. He put a soft palm on her swollen foot, and she wanted to give him anything he desired then, wanted to cajole and comfort him and tell him everything would be all right.

I'm sorry, Teddy, she said. It was my fault. Silly Oldemor forgot her shoes.

This settled it for them. They wandered into the kitchen, talking of breakfast. They all spoke at once, like a synchronized troupe of actors, and they seemed to understand each other, but Linda did not hear distinctly if she was invited to join them.

Flink was whining for her, so she slipped out of the apartment and back down the stairs. She wanted to be gone before her old neighbours came shooting out to work. As she stood on the cold stone steps and unknotted Flink's leash, she realized she should have asked to borrow a pair of shoes. She walked home barefoot, an official madwoman.

There was no difference between real madness and the madness others decided you suffered. Madness meant that you were convinced of something and everyone else disagreed. There was no more to it. They had may as well lock her up now, but she would go one better, she would lock herself up.

# Raj

A soft line squirmed flat under the thin sole of his sock, and an owl's screech flew from Raj's mouth. He shook the soiled foot away from his body. The creature left a grimy stripe on the floor, but it clung for the most part to the weave of his sock.

He pulled it off inside out, which was the best way to remove it without touching the offending creature. He could not identify it directly, but he saw its comrades all over the floor, the penis-tip coloured, back-to-back rings of soil-engorged flesh.

Raj tiptoed a jagged pattern out of his bedroom and into the hallway, where earthworms lay in greater numbers. Kindly adjust, he said, as he found a stepping-stone path through them to his slippers, which hung on the wall hooks by the apartment door – or the door's flimsy replacement. They kept nothing on the floor anymore. Their shoes and slippers hung over one hook each, with their cavities opening downwards, in case some creature might scale a wall, take a leap and in such a pouch make its cot.

Raj stood like a water skater, afraid to skid on his first slippered step and land in a mess of worms.

He undid the two bolts and opened the makeshift door, trying not to squash an arc of worms as he pulled the plywood panel inwards. He expected to see a trail of the creatures trickling down the stairs, but there were none at all out there, not even on the tiles right outside the door. He pushed the panel back and bolted it in place again, his own prison warden.

Guys! he said.

He was answered by a non-human noise from Pradeep's room.

I'm in here, said Krishna, in slow syllables.

Raj joined him in the kitchen.

I threw one out the window yesterday, said Krishna, but there was only one then. I thought I'd brought it in on my shoe somehow.

There are so many, said Raj. Do you think this is why the mice and the rat were here? Do you think they were feeding on the earthworms?

It depends, said Krishna, on which came first, and we don't know for sure that they were eating one another. Not everyone wants to eat each other.

Krishna held onto the kitchen counter as he spoke. He had turned towards Raj from the waist, without moving his feet, so he was contorted into an awkward pose. Raj held onto the back of a nearby chair and wondered why it helped to have some solid object in his grasp.

I suspect the rat ate the mice, said Raj. Remember, we caught no mice that morning the rat was in the trap, and mice can hide away in any small hole. They might have been here for some time, feeding on earthworms we never saw, because they ate them up each night.

They surveyed the floor: so many.

We must get rid of the full ecosystem, said Raj. We must sterilize everything and seal off every hole. Then we'll be rid of them. Then we'll be left in peace.

Pradeep's door opened, and Raj could hear he was barefoot. His steps came towards them in slow slicks, and when he turned into the kitchen his face looked green.

There was one in my Wellington boot, he said. Call the landlord, Raj. Get our door back.

They didn't come through the door. There are none on the stairs. They came through the floor. I'm certain.

Someone has cursed us, said Krishna.

Raj pointed to the one chair which was already pulled out from the table.

Pradeep sat there, cross-legged and safe. Krishna reached for a glass, filled it with cold water and passed it to Raj, who passed it to Pradeep. They watched him gulp it down, the oesophageal muscles of his gullet kneading the water down to his stomach.

Are they dead? he said.

They will die soon, said Krishna, if we leave them like this.

I couldn't sleep, said Pradeep. All night I listened out for mice and all I heard was the silence of these worms. Why are they here, Krishna? Raj, where did they come from?

They came in some hole, said Raj.

But why?

I think it might be something to do with the water table, said Raj. Did you two study biology in school?

No.

Well, when the soil is waterlogged, earthworms come to the surface. They need to breathe air. They have enough in well-aerated soil, but after heavy rain they must come to the surface so they don't drown. Have you never seen earthworms on the path the morning after heavy rain?

I have, said Krishna, yes.

Me too, said Pradeep, and I heard rain last night.

That's right, said Raj. You see, there's a perfectly logical explanation.

So, we'll be all right, said Pradeep, as long as it doesn't rain.

In the silence, Raj could hear raindrops falling from leaf to leaf on the bushes outside.

We should take turns keeping watch at night, said Pradeep. I'm not sleeping anyway.

Mice are nocturnal animals, said Krishna. What about earthworms, Raj? Are they only active at night?

It doesn't matter, said Pradeep, since we're away during the day.

Earthworms come to the surface at night to mate, said Raj. Our teacher thought it was the most romantic page in the biology book. Something about a warm, sultry night. They do it by sixty-nining, you know. They're hermaphrodites.

Drink more water, said Krishna.

Pradeep looked greener than ever.

They were mating on our floor, he said, these hundreds of worms. No wonder I couldn't sleep.

Raj walked on the balls of his toes to the cutlery drawer and paused with his fingers on the handle, counting with his breath. He pulled the drawer open, finding nothing but cutlery inside.

Here, he said, holding out three forks. Let's clean them up.

Pradeep and Krishna looked intently at their forks, and Raj wondered if they too were happy to have something inanimate to focus their gazes on. Armed with the fork and an empty fruit bowl, Raj crouched down. The fork hovered over the slowly undulating middle of an earthworm. They had may as well get this over with fast, but his hand would not let the prongs sink to pierce the flesh.

If you chop them in two, both ends survive to crawl away, said Pradeep.

That's a myth, said Raj, though all their essential organs are up at one end, so they can survive without their tails.

There is a better way, said Krishna.

Raj folded the fork back into his palm and stood up. Do you think they would come apart, he said, if we brushed them into the sweeping pan?

You're the expert, said Pradeep.

Chopsticks, said Krishna. There are some takeaway chopsticks in the back of the cutlery drawer. If you help me collect them into brown paper bags, I will bring them to the park.

Raj pulled the drawer further out along its stiff wooden rails, with the same irrational wariness. The back of the drawer held only the usual mess of utensils. He found three sets of chopsticks and passed them around. They each pulled a pair from its paper glove and snapped the bamboo apart. There was something ceremonial about this.

In less than an hour they had collected them all in three paper bags, which they placed in the middle of the kitchen table. This was no longer a room to eat in.

Raj fingered a gap between the skirting board and the door frame.

I'll stop at the hardware store, he said, and get a tube of silicone and a few rolls of strong tape like the plumbers use. This will all be fine again soon.

The floor's dirty, said Pradeep.

Perhaps it's the drains, said Raj, leaning over the sink. It didn't smell any worse than the rest of the room.

The smell had improved since they got rid of the rat, though they might just be getting used to it. If they remained here long enough, they might begin to accept these conditions. This place might change them, drag them down.

Look at that dirty patch by the fridge, said Pradeep, and that huge one under the table.

Raj got down on his haunches. The dark-brown grains of dirt he rubbed between his fingertips were some of them coarse and some of them soft. They were slightly moist but not wet.

Pradeep went out into the corridor. Here too, he said. I told you it was dirty.

Raj listened to doors opening and closing.

Guys, did you not notice in your rooms? said Pradeep. There are big patches of dirt. Where did it come from, Raj? Was it the earthworms?

Raj moved to the worst patch, under the table. I don't understand, he said. It's a little wet, but mostly just dirty. There must have been a leak.

A lot of leaks, said Pradeep, and they all looked up. The ceiling showed no sign of harm and, anyway, the worst one was under the table.

It doesn't make any sense, said Raj.

He folded a piece of kitchen paper and slid it into a gap behind the skirting board. It's dry here, he said. I should check all along the edge.

I'll help, said Krishna.

But the spots are in the middle of the floor, said Pradeep. I mean, I know nothing about buildings, but it must be leaking through those spots.

They might be low points, said Raj. This might be the result of ponding. He put his cheek low beside the floor, and he looked along the surface. Do we have a marble? he said.

Don't get it on your face, said Pradeep. It could be anything. It could be sewage.

It is not the smell of sewage, said Krishna.

They looked at him. Raj knew it was unfair of them to gaze at him like this and realize that Krishna was poor because he knew the smell of sewage better than them.

I know the smell of sewage, said Krishna, and this is not it. This is the smell of, I don't know, the ground. It is the smell of a cave, you know?

It must be a leak, said Raj. The dirty groundwater must have found some point of ingress and then ponded in these lower parts before —

Evaporating? said Krishna, and he offered Raj a hand up.

It was too much to have evaporated in just one night.

No, said Raj, I think it soaked between the floorboards.

All three of them stood with legs slightly apart and held one another's gaze like a rope.

We're on a raft, said Pradeep. He lifted his heels and bounced on the balls of his feet, making the floor creak. This is cheap parquet, he said. I bet it's rotting. That's the problem.

Raj examined the parquet up close. It hardly looked like wood at all, more like a picture of wood, printed too pink onto plastic. He knocked on it, and it was wood that sounded and wood his knuckles recognized, but Pradeep was right about the quality. The varnish was peeling away around the edge of the dirty patch under the table.

The floor must not be sealed properly underneath, he said.

Everyone was quiet for a while, and Raj could almost hear the trickle of water under their feet, the splurge and suck of wet and rotting wood, but he knew these were imagined sounds.

There was a rattling knock on the door and the tread of shoes in the stairwell.

The pace quickened, receded, as Raj unbolted and cast open the plywood door. He took a few steps after the hard leather footsteps, but whoever it was had by then disappeared, and the main entrance door had already slammed shut. Turning back, Raj saw a folded sheet of A4 paper on his doormat.

It was a second notice, dated, and written in both Norwegian and English so there could be no cause for misunderstanding. The recent sound of footsteps enforced a rhythm on the words. He felt low, like something underfoot.

# Sonja

Sonja brought the insurance assessor to a halt on the asphalted garden path directly outside her apartment. A deep bed of rose bushes lay between them and the offending wall.

The assessor lifted his phone and tapped a few photos. She waited for him to make some comment or, even better, some discovery, but he was silent. The wall looked as ordinary as ever, so there was nothing he could conclude from here, from this distance. He let his phone fall to his side, and she saw on the back of his hand that same tanned, sinewy movement that appeared on his face when he smiled. It made her want to touch his skin – more than that, it told her precisely what his skin would feel like, even without touching it.

She had smiled when she found this man on her doorstep. There was something funnily Humphrey Bogart about his camel suit. Perhaps it was that the waist was unusually high on the trousers. When he smiled back at her, she almost forgot why he was there.

Though the draught was strongest in her bedroom, and her bedroom was the closest room from the front door, it seemed improper to lead the man straight into her sleeping quarters without preamble, so she brought him into the living room and let him examine the wall there first. That's when she noticed the skin over his cheekbones and temples, which seemed delicate in a way that would last. She showed him which spots on the wall she was most concerned about, and, when he let his palm hover upright by the painted plaster, she wanted to place her own hand on top of his, turn him and lead him to her bed.

Their slow examination of the living-room wall before they moved into the bedroom seemed a sort of foreplay. The quiet movement of his stockinged feet over the oak floorboards, her subtle utterance of, that spot there, yes, all seemed quite erotic as they stood in her bedroom, though, of course, she did nothing about it. Another woman would have him naked by now, but she was not that woman. She would make a nice pencil drawing of the back of his hand later.

A sense of camaraderie, at least, lingered between them as they went outside, as she led the way around the block and he held the low garden gate open for her and closed it behind them, while gushing about buildings from this era, how they were solid and firesafe, and well designed.

The garden is lovely, he had said. There's so much space between the blocks here. A new building would be two floors higher and only have eight metres between the façades, and nothing like this would grow in a place like that.

He touched the two horse chestnut trees with his gaze and told her that he and his partner were thinking of buying something from this era themselves, now that they had another baby on the way.

This movement from bridled flirtation to chivalry to *I'm taken* left Sonja somewhat taken aback. It was in silence she stood beside him now, his phone hand dangling beside her still. If there had been sex, he seemed to be saying, then it would only have been sex, nothing more, but he might not be suggesting this at all. There was a good chance she was the only one thinking along these lines, and he was thinking about property and homemaking. That's what most people were preoccupied with.

Sonja tried to remember the time before she owned or rented anything herself. Even back when she had nothing to do with the acquisition and maintenance of house and home, she had assessed the differences. She had weighed up a wooden house in the north of Norway against a terrace house in an Irish village and the dream of the ivy-covered cube of a home, which she passed on the school bus.

The wall of my apartment, she said, stretches around two metres to the left of the French windows and a metre past the balcony there on the right. The bottom is, well, you see the level of the balcony there, that's a step lower than the floor inside, and my part of the wall stretches up to the next balcony floor there.

This was as precise as she could be about her own section of external wall, but the fact that she had to describe it in such detail said it all. There was no visible difference between her part and the rest. The whole wall looked fine.

The cracks are most likely in the brickwork, she said, under the plasterwork. I was advised of this by two architects.

The insurance assessor nodded to himself, or possibly to her, with his lips drawn into his mouth like he was trying to stop himself from speaking.

We must take a closer look, she said, looking for a gap in the rose bed that might provide their path to the wall.

She pressed into the bed, and the bushes reached her upper thighs: wet petals and jittery leaves, soil with too much give under her thin soles. Thorns caught on her skirt and on the skin of her calves. When she reached the wall, she turned, triumphantly, and was about to say something like *I won*, but she now had the full expanse of bloody bush between her and the insurance assessor who had no intention of following her.

He looked at her a moment, and then he checked his phone, scrolled. She examined the wall herself. If she found something noteworthy, she could point it out to him and insist he press his way in. He was, however, wearing that fitted camel suit. It was not her action which was problematic. His clothes were unsuitable. He wore that suit to intimidate his customers, or to get out of any real work. What she needed here were craftsmen, a bricklayer or plasterer, not some paper pusher. He probably didn't know the first thing about external walls – but she needed him to approve the work, to cover the cost. She couldn't continue accumulating unpaid bills. Her business must appear solvent.

Sonja walked along the wall, tapping with fingertips, taking close-up photographs on her phone.

I'll send these on to you, she said.

She was too low down. That was the problem. The earth was a metre below the level inside, so she could only reach up to the lower section of her own exterior wall. She heard no rumble wherever she knocked, felt no give and only made her knuckles sore.

She turned and found the imbecile walking slowly along the path, nodding a low, mumbled conversation on his phone. This expert was letting her do all the work and not even paying attention.

I should have brought you out on the balcony, she said, when he took the phone away from his ear and thumb-tapped it off. If you won't come in here, she said, you can examine the wall close up from the balcony.

Have any of the neighbours around you complained of the same issue? he said.

I haven't actually asked them, she said, but that's a good idea. We'll knock on their doors when we go inside. I'm sure one of them works from home.

He looked at his arm and, finding no watch there, looked at the face of his phone.

As far as I can see, he said, there seems to be nothing wrong with the wall itself. These blocks are solidly con-structed. It's not the same on the east side of town, where they're built from whatever they could find after the war. The blocks on this street were designed, and the building commenced, before the war, so they're composed of proper materials, good concrete and bricks.

He gestured with his phone-holding hand to her French windows.

If you've a problem with draughts, he said, it's almost always the windows that are to blame. That taping you have inside won't be enough. Get them replaced or repaired at least. That should do it. Windows are not something we cover, incidentally, but not to worry. I'm happy to come out to put your mind at ease.

No, said Sonja, halted by a tug at her skirt, causing her to look down for just a second, because the smug assessor was starting to move away. No, she said, it has nothing to do with the windows. The windows are fine.

Well, that's my conclusion, based on what I've seen. I'll send you on the report. I have your email address.

Just come onto the balcony. Have a look there.

He looked at his phone again.

I must head off now, he said. Do get the windows checked, at least. I'm quite sure that's the problem. Goodbye now.

Sonja stood in the middle of the thorny rose bushes like a fool and watched the brisk swish of his pressed trousers pass through the open gate. Looking down at her bloody fingers and the crimson trail of a thorn down her calf, she saw that her blood was exactly the same colour as the loveliness of ladybirds that had swarmed here in their thousands. She imagined similar back spots floating around in her veins.

She crouched, eye level with the ladybirds. To live like that: to land on your home and eat your neighbours.

# Eva

Everyone in these three adjacent conference rooms agreed that climate change and biodiversity were matters of urgency, yet they had spent most of the day strolling from canapés to display stands to panel discussions, taking time to chat and linger, everyone bored but happy to get some time away from the office.

Eva's phone vibrated and the name Ellie Cleaner pulled her aside.

Eva Holt speaking.

It is Ellie. Sorry to disturb you at work.

Not at all, said Eva. You must always feel free to call me, Ellie, if anything's the matter.

She offloaded her pile of brochures on a display table and loosened the lanyard at her neck.

Do you want me to clean already the paint dust? And I can wash the clothes and the dishes if you like.

Paint? said Eva. Do I hear barking in the background?

Yes, said Ellie, but …

The poor girl paused, and Eva wondered if it was cruel to send her into an apartment which potentially contained a vicious dog, though, as a cleaner, she was probably used to pets.

Is he in the apartment?

No, Eva. He is outside.

On the balcony?

He is on the balcony downstairs. Is he your dog?

Oh no! It's just so loud.

Nora and Stella, the healthy-looking lesbians who lived downstairs from Eva, were allergic to dogs — or one of them was, at least. She hoped they hadn't felt compelled to bring Rocky in from the stairwell. It sounded like his hollow-barrel bark.

I can't close the windows, said Ellie, or the door to the balcony.

Oh, have you washed them already? When did you get there?

No, said Ellie, and Eva could hear her breathing.

What's wrong?

I just arrived. The windows are all open. Is it because of the paintwork?

The paintwork? What happened?

That is why I am ringing, said Ellie, and she must have gone into another room now, maybe the windowless bathroom, because there was more of an echo but less barking.

Oh, that's much better, said Eva. What did you say about the paintwork?

Just, if you want me to brush it for you and vacuum, I can do that first. It's up to you, of course. I am only asking. I can clean the closets too.

This was getting out of hand. The paint must have begun to peel right off the party walls. It felt wrong to ask Ellie for details. Eva was the owner, the employer. She should know what was going on. Still, she wondered if she could hire this master sleuth full-time, if she could steal Ellie from her au-pair family. She would be better off with Eva, not having the responsibility for children. For now, it was important not to scare her off. If Eva felt a note of terror about paint peeling off her walls, that was the natural reaction of an owner, but she couldn't risk Ellie getting frightened. A white lie was required.

Eva, are you there?

Could you please take some photos of the paint and send them to me? You can tidy afterwards. I had someone in to do some work, as you can see, but they were told to clean up after them. I'm disappointed they left such a mess behind.

Oh, workers! said Ellie. Oh, Eva, they did good work on the walls, but the mess is very bad. It is on the bed, the pillows, inside the wardrobe on your nice clothes, on your plates and food too. But I will clean it for you, Eva. Don't worry anymore. Maybe there is no time for the refrigerator and oven today.

That's fine, Ellie. Send me the photos first, on your phone, if you can, and see how you go with the other jobs.

Then they spoke at the same time with almost the same words.

You can do the rest on Friday, said Eva.

I can do the rest Friday, said Ellie, like a true ally.


An SMS came through while Eva was in the taxi:

*See, nice and clean!* ☺

Attached were photos of the wardrobe and a kitchen cupboard, both cleared out and clean looking. There was also a picture of her pillows, looking a bit blue, and a picture of eight plastic bags with prickly contents in the hallway. She would get the paint tested. She texted back: *Leave bags in hallway: special waste disposal. On my way.*


Ellie was gone when Eva came home, along with the bags of paint.

The party walls were perfect.

She had expected a messy surface with bits of paint hanging on loosely, but these walls looked like they had never been painted. They had a trendy, industrial look about them, and she thought she might leave them as they were.

The bedclothes were changed. Her washing baskets were full of blue-dusted sheets and unworn clothes. Knitted fabrics clung onto flakes of paint. She managed to pull off a few crests, and she put them in a ziplock plastic bag to bring to the paint shop. She had to know.

The dishwasher was already going, and piles of other plates and glasses were drying on the counter. The entire contents of the dry-foods cupboard were arranged on the kitchen table. Eva was amused to see how many jars of cinnamon she had accumulated.

In the living room, the blankets and cushions Eva had slept on the night before were arranged into a civilized pile at one edge of the sofa, and Eva felt her fear of sleeping in the bedroom had been approved on some level. It was sad, she knew it, to appreciate such care.

She heard voices from the direction of her bedroom. This reminded her of yesterday's email from that petulant accountant, Blix, over in 14A. The neighbours, he claimed, were noisy. Their children ran about like small elephants — little girls as lithe as Eva had ever seen — and Blix himself had teenage boys. Who was he to complain? They held late-night parties, he said, and had loud sex in the early hours of the morning. He seemed a bit too persecuted to believe. Eva told him to approach the neighbours in question directly, knowing he would never do it. It was easy to complain to the board, exaggerating one's grievance, but quite another matter to stand face to face with those you accused of a misdemeanour. This was Eva's chalk circle. These were good, solid buildings of brick and concrete, and if a little bit of noise bothered that man, it was nothing Eva could possibly fix. She rather suspected he was suffering a psychosis, but it was not within the remit of the chair of the board to psychoanalyse the residents, fortunately. Eva's position had exposed her so to the nasty and paranoid tendencies of her neighbours that she would have sent half of them off to the madhouse. Before she took this position, which coincided with her promotion to general manager at her firm, she had thought that people, by and large, were reasonable. Now she wondered how they managed to live together in any kind of harmony. There was such a thick layer of loony right under the thin skin of everyday.

She sifted through her post in the hallway.

I know it was you, said a man's voice.

She put a half-opened envelope aside, because this voice was too loud. The back garden, lying as it did between two parallel blocks, was something of an echo chamber, as she had been forced to inform quite a few neighbours. Conversations on the balconies, she told them, were reflected back and forth, causing an unintended disturbance. The neighbour in question always expressed regret and claimed ignorance. It was easy for people to apologize, Eva found, when their misdemeanour was an accident. If someone did something wrong by intention, they almost always denied it.

I understand that you're angry, said a woman's voice, but it's hard to fathom why the anger is directed at me.

This was too much, too clear. This was not a voice that had suffered the dishevelment of ricocheting across the back garden. This voice was closer than any neighbour's balcony. It was an indoor voice.

Tell me why you did it, said the man.

How can you even imagine it was me? the woman replied.

The bedroom door was half open, but Eva could not see in. She had been in there just now. Her guiding sentiment shifted from surprise to fear, but there was something about the voices which seemed to hold too little of a threat to her. Rather, they seemed a threat to each other, and she felt empowered. She took hold of the long umbrella with the wooden duck's head, and she held it like a baseball bat as she approached the bedroom and kicked open the door.

She was ready for gasps and apologies, even a gun, but she found her bedroom empty of anything but these people's voices.

I never even go past there, said the woman's voice. I walk in the other direction to work.

It's because of the piano, isn't it? said the man.

You're insane.

The voices swirled around Eva in the empty room and, in a fit of the spooks, she entertained the idea that she was witness to a pair of ghosts, a couple who had died in this bedroom, only to come back now for a final marital flare-up. The voices, however, had direction. The party wall was free of paint now, the plaster fully exposed. It was through this wall that the voices came.

Eva looked out the French windows to the empty adjacent balcony.

Tell me again what bushes you found them in, said the woman – the pianist next door.

Don't play innocent, said the man, who had to be Ibsen. It doesn't suit you, he said. Don't pretend you're trying to figure this out. You planned this sick vengeance.

If something bad happens to you, then it's automatically my fault, is that it?

Now that Eva could put her fear aside and listen more closely to the words that came through the wall, it was obvious that these were the voices of her neighbours, though she had never heard them use this tone. Ibsen especially, was always so pointedly restrained.

We have clearly been burgled, said the pianist.

Nothing was stolen, said Ibsen. The door was locked.

Someone must have a key then. I bet it was that woman from the board. I always knew she was too sensible to be true.

Leave that poor old woman out of it. This is between you and me.

It was unsettling to be referred to directly and even more so to be considered old when she was only in her early fifties. She moved closer to the wall, though there was no need. She could hear them perfectly well, as if they were in the same room. She wondered if they had been communicating by notes the whole three years they had lived there, and finally this great dispute had erupted to break their silence, because she had never been bothered by them before.

She moved a pillow aside and sat on the bed.

Someone threw them from the balcony, said the pianist, or the window.

They couldn't, said Ibsen. The books were nowhere near the balcony or the window, as you know very well. They were right in by the wall, in the bushes, right down there.

There? Bit of a coincidence.

If you think you're going to drive me mad, you're wrong.

You found the books right below the bookshelf, at the wrong side of a thick brick wall, three floors down? It is a bit crazy.

Eva wondered if they might be rehearsing a play, but they were too convincing. This was real.

I'm not sure if breaking my sanity is the point of your trick, but it's really not working. These were good books, signed first editions. Look at this one, look at it: Olga Tokarczuk, signed before she got the Nobel prize. It's ruined.

Not my fault.

How could it not be your fault? I know what this is about. It's quite clear.

Enlighten me.

It's about your stupid piano, isn't it? It's revenge, isn't it? You're teaching me some sort of lesson not to mess with your sacred piano.

How could this have anything to do with the piano?

I only moved it to make way for the bookshelf. You're not supposed to put a piano along an external wall. How was I to know it would be such a big deal for you? I didn't know you'd have to get it retuned, and you retune it all the time anyway.

They paused, but they were still there. Eva could hear their breathing, especially Ibsen's nasal fuming.

You've flipped, Severin.

I only moved your piano. I didn't throw it away. These books are by authors I have met, writers I have a great respect for.

Yes, the books are signed, I get it, and it has nothing to do with me. That's what's insane: your reaction, the blame.

You could at least have sold them to a used bookshop or put them in the recycling bin. Why in the bushes, for heaven's sake? What if a neighbour saw me climbing in there? What if someone saw you throwing them in there? They'll think we're insane.

They'd be half right.

A single piano key sounded. It was quite loud, close.

Without any proof, said the pianist, you blame me. You have all the world to accuse, but you choose me, because all the failings in your life are my fault, is that it? All your lack of success, all your measly book sales, are my fault. That's what you think, isn't it? What are you doing?

Eva was going numb in her left leg, but she dared not move, in case they could hear her as well as she could hear them. She wished she had a glass of wine, a side of olives.

Don't expect that piano to be there long, honey, said Ibsen. It's going right on the buy and sell.

You'll do no such thing.

I've already posted it.

It's not yours to sell.

I'm giving it away.

It's mine.

Those books were mine.

They still are. I didn't throw them in the fucking bush, you insane idiot.

If that isn't the pot calling the kettle black.

If you get rid of my piano, I'm getting rid of you.

What have you planned? Will I be thrown in the bushes too?

Eva shifted her weight slowly, until she lay back across the bed, propped up on her elbow so she could continue to gaze at the wall. She longed to cheer the pianist on, but the woman didn't seem to need any encouragement.

I own 65 per cent of the apartment, said the pianist. I'll buy you out.

I won't sell.

You'll have to. You can't afford the whole place yourself. We can put it on the market if you like, but I'll be bidding.

You wouldn't. You know I can't afford anything this close to the library by myself.

Move to the suburbs.

My leg.

Your leg: your problem. Your lack of income: your problem. I'm finished bailing you out.

There followed a silence, and Eva put a hand on the wall, afraid it had stopped working, ceased transmission. If they sold their apartment, the threat to her position on the board would disappear. She felt ungrateful not to remember the pianist's name. Dobro-something with too many consonants. It was difficult to remember a name you couldn't visualize.

Now wait, honey, wait, came Ibsen's voice, faltering now. I'm sorry, right. I'm sorry. Things have got out of hand, snowballed. We're both saying things we don't mean.

I've never been so level-headed.

Look, the books ... it doesn't matter. I can put it behind me, forgive you or whatever. I was exaggerating. You can put the piano back where it was, okay? I'll help you move it, or I'll ask Jon to help us. I know it's important for you to look out the window when you play, for some reason. I know that now.

For some reason? Even your apology is tainted. You can forget it.

Just listen.

You don't get it. There's nothing to forgive me for. I've done nothing wrong, apart from a rash choice in spouse, perhaps.

You know I love you.

The pianist laughed. I know you need me, she said. It's not the same.

What are you doing? Put that away.

I've applied for an evaluation. We'll have it on the market in no time.

Slow down.

I'm quite fast when I don't have to carry you.

Don't you dare use that. That's low. I wouldn't have this injury if it wasn't for you.

I'm not responsible for the misdemeanours of any man, even members of my family.

You might have warned me, defended me.

It's not my fault, and even if it were, I've surely paid my debt by now. I've done a seven-year sentence. They give less to a rapist.

What are you talking about, a sentence? I didn't know …

Our marriage, you blind fool, and that's right, I'd better call that off too. Thank God for prenups.

Eva heard silence, leaned an ear against the wall, almost expecting her head to pass right through, like in a ghost movie. The plaster was rough and crumbly, and she thought perhaps it wasn't the paint itself that had been faulty, but the plaster underneath. That made more sense. The scale of destruction was too much to be blamed on a bad mix of paint. Something more fundamental, more structural, had to be at fault.

She heard a door slamming and she jumped back, off the bed and away from the wall, as a rage of piano music flew over her. The piano must be right at the other side because the wall seemed almost to come alive with the sound. She stood back and waited for the whole partition to crumble away, but nothing happened, no visible change.

The boom and clang, though of artistic merit, drove Eva from the bedroom, and she brewed the tea she had been wishing for since the idea of wine became overwhelming. The piano continued to sound as she brought her cup to the balcony, a thundering crescendo, and then silence.

At first, Eva thought a rug or shawl lay on the floor of the balcony. It was something rarer: a mat of velvet red, a rug of petals.

She bent down and picked up a fistful. They were soft as chickens – not that she would know – and light as the finest silk. They covered the whole surface, which had previously been a glossy, grey-painted epoxy.

Her flower boxes were filled with these strange red petals too, each the size and tilt of a thumbnail. She poked a finger through them to find the earth underneath.

Her nose twitched, searching for the old remembered scent of smoky incense, but she only smelled sweetness. The air was perfectly still, just as it had been all day, and Eva looked across the way and to the balconies on either side of hers, where her neighbours had planted giant white daisies and multicoloured pansies in their respective boxes. She saw no match for these petals, no flush of red on any of the other balconies.

It made no sense, but there was something peaceful about her balcony now, something that told her all was well, though she felt bad stepping on the petals.

She fetched the sweeping brush and the dustpan from its corner in the kitchen and swept the lot into the bin. She used her hand-held kitchen vacuum cleaner to suck the petals out of the flower boxes, sucking away the top layer of earth too, making sure not a single red mark remained.

*This tripping down my flights and tapping my steps: my nosing is worn thin with the dust they kick off, salty shoes squeaky scratching my treads, and all the small things they drop. Oh my diagonal, my rising can hardly hold out with all their ascents, the press on my handrails: I'm not a slide. My pitch has had enough. My baluster cannot take much more of their tug, the incessant passing of feet, the wimpy groans of the mounting weak, the bum pat descent. I am home to no one; I am liminal space for their up and down but not forever, for even Sisyphus will come to an end when no one tells his tale.*

# Gunnar

He hoisted his hard-shell suitcase up the stairs, ensuring it didn't rub against the brushed wool of his suit.

Hildegunn's apartment door had been successfully transplanted from his rental in the basement and looked just the same as her door had always done. It even smelled the same – something which had been a genuine worry. It was slightly disconcerting, a feeling of minor exposure, to know that his tenants now had a set of keys to Hildegunn's apartment, but they didn't know this.

The door looked fine on the inside too, though there were some scratches on the paintwork in the niche. He put down his suitcase, turned on the lights and took a photo of the marks. He would insist the insurance company cover the cost of a painter. He knew a good one.

Stepping backwards, he tripped on, almost fell over, a flip-flop. There were two of them, one in the middle of the mat and one by the wall. They were golden Havaianas. This was just too much. For one thing, he couldn't understand how he had overlooked them earlier. More importantly, he would have to insist that Hildegunn wear sensible indoor shoes, something sturdy, something that would cover up her feet. Even the thought of her vein-heavy toes and dumpling skin threaded around these thin rubber thongs was unbearable. Here was the reason for Hildegunn's broken hip. The marbles she insisted she'd slipped on were nowhere to be seen. He could not rule out mental-health issues.

He flung the flip-flops out of sight on the hat shelf in the cloakroom. He filled the cat's bowls with water and meat and brought his suitcase into the guest room. Hildegunn, ever the gracious hostess, always had the bed made up so she could say to her dinner guests, Gunnar included, Have another glass of wine, for the guest room's made up if you want to stay over.

His father, Hildegunn's brother, had been dull as they come, and his mother had been a total frump, so Gunnar often mused that it must be from Hildegunn that he had inherited his sense of style.

He opened the impossibly narrow teak door to the built-in wardrobe which Hildegunn had instructed him to use.

Push my old furs aside, she had said.

He remembered playing hide-and-seek among her mink and fox-fur coats as a child, jealously imagining his cousins had access to Narnia, but now the wooden hangers clacked against each other in the empty wardrobe. She must have sold them and forgotten about it. If she was in financial need, he had a sound suggestion at the ready.

He followed his rumbling stomach to the kitchen. The two bowls on the floor were empty again, though he had not seen the gluttonous feline. The oven clock said it was just past five, and he decided to wait for the ambulance down on the street. There was no point in keeping his good deed a secret. All these neighbours were potential customers, as were their friends.

Seeing the ambulance had already arrived, he rushed down the stairs, but he took care to keep his pulse below the level that brought out sweat.

The paramedics lifted Hildegunn up the stairs in a wheelchair, which she quite understandably hated. No one wanted to be seen weak like that, and it was rush hour, with neighbours returning home, sucking air through their teeth at the sight of her.

Put that cushion there, said Hildegunn, I have to sit on a slope.

She lowered herself into a chair that resembled the Michelin Man in a nice way. Gunnar sat opposite her, on a matching armchair, and he hoped she would appreciate his solidarity.

These are Bibendum chairs, Gunnar, she said. I met Eileen Gray once.

Bibendum, he said, yes, really quite comfortable.

I'm thirsty.

He came back with a glass of milk and a plate of biscuits on a tray and asked if he might move her book from the little coffee table.

My book? she said, picking it up and fixing her glasses to look at it better. Did you get this for me, Gunnar?

He hummed to himself. He did not, of course, get her this book. It was one of those books with women's shoes on the cover. When she came off the tablets, she would forget all about this, so there was no point in making an issue of it.

You really mustn't, said Hildegunn. I've awfully particular taste in literature. You're wasting your money buying me books, though I appreciate the gesture, I really do, Gunnar.

Well, he said, just let me know if there's anything in particular you'd like me to pick up for you.

These painkillers ... I'm so tired. Here, you had better read all these instructions they gave me. I can only sit for so many minutes. There's more. It's all in there.

Gunnar scanned the discharge summary and leafed through diagrams of exercises and daily tasks.

You can do this, Hildegunn, and I'm here to help. I'm a free man now.

He smiled at her, but she wouldn't laugh.

I always got on fine with your ex-wife, as you call her, but I'm almost envious of you, Gunnar, getting divorced.

He left the leaflets fall to his lap.

You wanted to?

I never found divorce quite available to me.

You would have been free, he said.

I've always wondered how long it would take, if I left my home, before it would fall into disrepair.

Now, Hildegunn, don't worry. I'll take care of everything, if it comes to it. You can count on me.

If I got a divorce, the floors would not be waxed every second year, she said. Small spillages would not be wiped up promptly and would stain the wood. The putty in the windows would not be repaired at the first sign of cracking, and rain would seep in and form watery patches on the teak windowsills. The grout between the tiles in the shower would turn black with mildew.

Was my uncle so useless?

Doors would be scratched bringing things in and out without care. The radiators would be left off in unused rooms, causing hairline cracks to appear on the walls.

That is an issue. I've seen that.

Light bulbs would blow and lamps burn out. Cheap alternatives from IKEA would be plugged directly into the wall sockets, their cables trailing across the floor. Dishes, not stacked in order, would crack and be thrown out. Hot pots would burn dark rings on the dining table, which would be replaced by a green-tinted glass table with chunky, stainless-steel legs. Everything, everything that was so well composed, would be ruined if I divorced. It was not such a hard decision really to stay, considering all this.

I never knew you felt that way. All these years. I would never let your home fall apart, I promise you.

I had a lot of time to think, while I was in hospital. I had time to think about legacy.

Now, Hildegunn, you weren't dying.

An artist would call this his masterpiece, she said.

It is a perfectly choreographed home, Hildegunn, an interior delight. Wait, how long have you been sitting there? It said no longer than forty-five minutes.

I'll go and lie down in a moment, but first there's something important I need you to do for me. You must be good on the phone, given your profession.

Well, I don't mind admitting it.

I would do it myself, but this medication is clouding my brain. I don't want to phrase my request badly. Do you know Frida Kross in 14B?

The architect?

She works for the folk museum. At least, she used to. Can you call her for me?

What do you need from Frida Kross?

They have a collection of buildings on their compound, Gunnar, I don't know if you're aware. They have representative buildings from all areas of the country and all eras.

Indeed, yes, I've been there, Hildegunn.

I want you to ask her to take my oeuvre when I die.

Take it? Now, Hildegunn, you can't just give things away. What do you mean?

Do it for me, Gunnar.

He tried to put her off. He told her he would do it later, that he would call over to Frida one day, that there was no rush, but Hildegunn, who now had the end of her days firmly in sight, refused to delay a moment, and he found himself looking up Frida's number on the website. He rose and stiffened into a posture of authority for the phone call. Frida was a good-looking woman, prudishly architectural and married, but ...

He hovered on the neighbourly preliminaries: Hildegunn's hip, the approaching AGM, until Hildegunn poked him on the knee with a walking stick and told him to ask her.

I'm actually calling you in your capacity as conservator, on behalf of my aunt. As you know, her apartment is a beautifully preserved example of mid-century architecture, and she's considering making a bequest to the museum.

What would she like to donate?

Just a minute – Hildegunn, what exactly would you like to donate?

The whole thing, the ensemble.

The entire contents? Are you sure?

Walls and all.

He brought the phone back to his ear.

She is toying with the idea of possibly donating the entire contents, he said, and he hated saying it, but he wasn't promising anything, and he could surely talk Hildegunn out of it when she came off the pills.

We're not specifically looking for 1950s objects at the moment, said Frida.

Oh, well, that's all right. Sorry to bother you.

But I suppose I could come and have a proper look. What kind of contents are we talking?

What kind of contents, Hildegunn?

The lot: furniture, crockery, light fittings, fabrics: the full set.

Did you hear that?

Yes, well, let's see. I could come over some day next week after work. How about Monday, around six? Fritjof and I need Hildegunn's expert advice on a skylight too.

Gunnar looked around him as he pocketed his phone and sat back down.

I don't know about this, Hildegunn, but we'll see what she says, right? I'm not sure you should separate the contents from the apartment, if you know what I mean.

Oh, you're right. There's no point. I imagined my whole apartment out there, cut away from the rest of the building, a box of floor slabs and walls, transported out to the headland, but even then it wouldn't be the same without the view from the balcony and from each of my windows, without the mirror-image block at the other side of the garden, nor without the garden itself.

It's a beautiful dream, Hildegunn.

It would be better to have public viewings right here: open days. I want to preserve my whole life, she said, pickle it all.

# Fritjof

Fritjof deposited three plastic bags on the mat, and bottles of detergent and packs of microfibre cloths spilled onto the floor. He opened the umbrella to dry, though it had not been raining heavily, and leafed through the post. There was nothing important, just newsletters and magazines from the innumerable charities Frida subscribed to. He handed her a panda-decorated package from the WWF and a magazine from Future in Our Hands. She also supported the Rainforest Alliance, Greenpeace, and other less memorable do-gooders.

Don't you think all this junk mail defeats the purpose? he said.

Frida unhooked the leash from Rocky's collar, and the dog looked up at her and then at him. Fritjof had the distinct impression that Rocky thought them fools to let him loose.

He inspected the door once more before he closed it.

It must be something to do with the latch, said Frida. She ruffled Rocky's jowls. Are you some sort of genius dog?

Fritjof steadied the door leaf between his shoes and checked what happened when he twiddled the latch and the key. The latch on the inside was a small, oblong brass knob, three centimetres in length. It was a little loose in its attachment, so you had to get a good hold of it to turn it. If it had been a door handle, then Rocky might plausibly have pawed it open and gone into the neighbours' downstairs, if they had simultaneously left their door open. But this knob was difficult enough for a person to use. Many a departing guest had struggled with it.

There's not enough leverage, he said. He can't have opened it himself.

We must have left it open then, said Frida. It's the only possibility.

And Stella and Nora did the same, on the same day?

They insisted they found their door locked, but it must be that.

Fritjof closed the door and shook it by the latch, to see if it somehow opened itself. It didn't. He opened it again and looked closely at the lockset, tried to push the lock bolt in.

They probably put their key in the lock to open it, without realizing it was already open, said Frida. I think we must have done the same.

Fritjof tested this, stood outside the unlocked door and put his key in, but the door swung in with the pressure of the key moving into the lock. He would have noticed this.

Close it now, said Frida, so he doesn't slip out again.

She let out a sneeze.

I'd say Rocky snuck out when we were leaving, said Fritjof, without us noticing. Remember you went back to get hand cream?

Sunscreen, said Frida. Maybe.

She sniffed, more in the way of smelling than snuffling.

It smells damp, said Fritjof.

Frida kicked off her shoes and went into the living room.

The floor's all wet, she said.

No, I mopped it up really well, said Fritjof, struggling with his laces.

It's drenched, said Frida. Come on, we'd better dry it off quickly, before it damages the wood. Get those cloths out. Why did you open the windows?

She was right. Fritjof's soles were damp through after just a few steps off the hallway mat.

I closed all the windows before we left this morning, he said. I'm quite certain.

Frida went and got the new cloths, throwing one of the packages at him to open.

You were the last one out, said Fritjof. You went back to get hand cream.

It was sunscreen, said Frida, and it was on top of the chest of drawers in the hallway, so I certainly didn't open the windows then.

It doesn't matter, said Fritjof. I probably opened them and forgot. I hope no more birds got in.

He attached a new cloth to the mop head, and before he had dried a few square metres he needed to wring it out. Frida tore sheets of unread magazines from the stapling and cast them on the floor, an insufficient spread of endangered species dampening quickly.

The sofa, she said. Oh no! Look at it, Fritjof.

Their cognac-coloured raw leather sofa, soft as silk, sponged clean with a special detergent four times a year: it was ruined. Frida stood over it with a ball of damp paper in her hands.

But we didn't wash the sofa, he said.

Frida's face turned to the window and the balcony door.

Do you think the rain blew in? he said, but he didn't believe this theory himself, so his words held an unintended tone of irony.

Not at that angle, said Frida. It's wet all over.

He touched the leather and looked at his wet fingertip.

Don't get ink stains on it, she said, though she was the one with the magazines. Frida stiffened. Someone was in here, she said. Check.

He took the mop with him, for something to hold onto, and snuck from room to room. The apartment was equally damp and empty in all its corners.

He found Frida on the balcony with Rocky, looking down to the garden, and Fritjof imagined someone sneaking out that way with a rope.

The flowers have died, said Frida, resting her palms on the barren stems.

They had planted red geraniums all along the five metres of new copper flower boxes. Now, there were only a couple of petals left on the earth. The rest must have blown off.

He also noticed that the copper had gone over to green awfully quickly. Usually it took years. When Fritjof had worked on the renovation of a church steeple, someone suggested using horse urine to make the replaced copper green to match the rest. He looked for Rocky, who had gone off again, and wondered if a dog's urine could do the same. He could hardly have peed upwards.

With their softest bath towels, they swabbed off the damp leather of the sofa.

We'd better leave it to air dry a while before we oil it, said Frida. Come on, let's get back to the floor.

Have a look in the bedroom first, said Fritjof. You're not going to like it.

The bedroom floor was as bad as the living room, but the bedclothes and the books on the bedside tables were also damp.

It's pure vandalism, said Frida.

Someone was in here with a watering can or some kind of mister, said Fritjof.

We'll have to install a burglar alarm, said Frida, though I don't see what anyone could have against us. Nora and Stella are angry at us because of Rocky, and they were already annoyed when we said we couldn't help watering the plants, remember?

Blame the lesbians? said Fritjof. It's probably some random nutcase.

A lock-picking nutcase, said Frida. That's a new industrial lock – oh, no!

What?

It's Eva Holt, has to be. She has a spare key for here.

No.

She's the only one who has a key, and she's the one who ordered the doors.

She seemed so trustworthy, said Fritjof.

You can never tell, can you?

Fritjof wiped something off the top of his head, and he saw Frida do the same.

The roof's leaking, he said.

Shit, it is, said Frida, but —

The two of them walked around the apartment, with their eyes on the ceiling and their palms up to catch rain-drops. The light but steady patter was the same no matter where they were in the apartment. Frida folded out the step-ladder, climbed up and started pawing at the ceiling.

It's not wet, she said.

She took another step upwards, tilted her head and looked along the surface.

There's more now, said Fritjof, bigger drops.

Frida moved her palm up and down under the white, painted surface.

Watch your step, she said, pointing at the floor.

It looked like a forest-green stripe of oil paint, squeezed straight from the tube.

Shit, he said.

He heard a screeching noise from above. Frida rushed out to the roof terrace and appraised the skies.

Geese, she said, a whole flock of them. They're going towards Frognerkilen.

Fritjof was about to laugh at this detail. Now they knew which nesting ground to go to for revenge.

He was, of course, looking at the ceiling, and so he saw it with his own eyes: a slimy dash of green angling through the ceiling in a flash and landing, with more of a split than a splat noise, on the leather couch. He looked from the gooey stripe to the spot on the ceiling it came through and back again, to and fro until he could not say for certain where exactly it had traversed the ceiling. It was dark-green shit, but it left no mark on the white paint.

They're gone, said Frida, coming back inside.

It's coming right through the ceiling, said Fritjof. I saw it. It's as if the ceiling, or the roof, isn't there at all. Frida, the geese didn't fly in here and out again. They shat right through the roof. I saw it go through. I saw it falling. Look at the couch!

That's what I said about the rain, said Frida. You wouldn't believe me until you saw it with your own eyes.

She had not mentioned this, but he didn't care. He was just glad he was not alone in his observation. He moved to hold her and knew it was not the time to curse the goose dung he trod on.

Frida, no one would believe this, no matter who told them about it, because it is completely insane. I'm not even sure I believe my own eyes.

It can't be happening.

To be honest, my main theory is I'm going mad.

But I saw it too. We can't both be mad.

You might be humouring me. Tell me the truth.

He stood back from her and measured her reaction in a manner that was supposed to elicit an honest response, but he couldn't help feeling comical when he tried to talk seriously about this.

If I'm imagining this, he said, I would prefer to know. I could get psychiatric help and pills. Just tell me if you didn't see what I saw. I'm ready for the truth.

These sounded like foreign words in his mouth, and Frida's expression was uncharacteristically vacant. He held her by the shoulders and stared at her to make her see he was serious, though this laboured action made him feel like a cheesy replica of some film-noir hero.

Madness, said Frida, is something that already exists in the world. It's treatable; you could tell someone about it, and they would understand, but this ...

She went up the stepladder again and tapped the ceiling with a forefinger, jabbed it repeatedly, and it seemed as solid, as normal as ever, but then, just once, her finger went through. She screamed and pulled it out, scrambled down the ladder, away from danger, and stood stroking her hand.

Did it hurt?

No, I felt nothing at all. Did you see it?

I think so. Do it again.

You do it.

It could get stuck. I'm not touching it.

I don't understand it, she said. I can't even find the right question to ask about it. It's just happening, or we perceive that it is happening, and I just don't know how. Can you see it, Fritjof, the ceiling?

Yes, of course. It looks just the same. You could never tell from looking at it that there was anything wrong, that it was porous – is that it?

That would just give us leaks, said Frida. The thing about this ceiling, this roof, is that it's not there at all.

It's there visually, said Fritjof, wondering if it might just be a memory they were seeing. Do you think someone would see it, he said, if they had never seen it before?

You mean, if they saw it for the first time, would they … see it?

I don't know if there's any point trying to make sense of this.

We have to, she said.

Say it's just the memory of the roof we see, he said, and it's actually gone. Then a stranger, or someone who had never been here before, they would just stand here and look right up at the sky. We should invite someone round, to check.

Fritjof thought this might work, though it would have to be someone who was not important to them, someone people didn't trust, in case they told anyone else about it.

Whether they see the roof or not, he said, they'll think we're mad.

None of our friends, then, though maybe Ida? She's a bit loopy.

I thought she went abroad.

That's right, and she was actually here once, at a party.

We'll have to think of someone else.

The Indians in the basement flat, said Frida, the tenants: no one likes them, though they've probably never spoken to them, pack of racists.

Are you going to invite them round under the guise of integrating them into our culture?

Come on.

Or is it a curry sauce you're going to ask them to taste?

No, but my idea was a bit prejudiced all the same.

You're going to ask them to give you private yoga lessons.

He was enjoying this a bit too much, like some sort of therapeutic comic relief.

I'd like to remind you, said Frida, that these are all your ideas, your prejudices. My particular prejudice persuades me to believe that surely one of them works in IT, and I might ask him to have a look at my laptop for me. Is that so awful? I'll pay him. I'll pretend I heard one of the other neighbours mention one of them worked in IT.

You're sly.

They both looked upwards.

We'll meet them if we walk the dog at the right time of day, said Fritjof. I'd say they get home late.

Rocky, said Frida, something to make up for the trouble you cause us. Rocky! Where is he? Don't say he's gone off again.

Rocky! said Fritjof. Oh God, is the door closed?

Frida was out in the landing already. They put on their trainers, and a look between them was enough of an agreement: they would not call out for the dog.

They slipped downstairs, nudging each door to see if it was open. There were no nooks or corridors for their large dog to hide in, so when they reached the bottom, they knew he was not in the stairwell. Out on the street, Fritjof took off at a jog, but Frida stopped him by the sleeve.

Try to look normal, she said, in a bored voice. We're in work clothes, not sports gear.

And so they walked, swiftly, around the block, smiling vague normality at each other, displaying disinterest at everything they viewed, though they scanned the street with all its hiding spots behind cars, trees, bins and bushes.

They looped the block twice, and, not finding him on the street, they went into the back garden, though the gate was closed and they didn't see how he could have got in any other way. Their hunch paid off.

They saw no sign of Rocky in the bushes where they first checked, but a troubled whimper pulled them over to the garden-level balcony that belonged to Linda. A metre above the level of the garden, and with a wired glass balustrade all around, Rocky seemed to be trapped.

They stood on the path with a deep border of rose bushes between them and the balcony, thinking that if what goes up must come down, then what goes in must come out. At least, that's what Fritjof was thinking. Frida looked confused, but her brow was working on it.

Fritjof patted his thighs in a come-here-boy manner. Rocky only whimpered in reply.

He has a point, said Frida.

We could get the stepladder.

Even the thought. Imagine what the neighbours would think if they saw us climbing into an old lady's apartment with a ladder. It's out of the question.

She was speaking in her lowest audible tone. Rocky looked forlorn, disappointed that they would let him suffer this situation and not come to his aid. The thought of Rocky jumping out of the balcony, landing in the thorny bushes and bounding over to them was so far from possible that Fritjof could not even visualize it.

Come on, said Frida, we'll knock on her door. At least this way there will only be one old lady who knows we can't take care of our dog. That's surely better than the lot of them thinking we're burglars.

She was right. Balconies like these, on two facing blocks, were like theatre boxes. One was always on display.

I think we should say you twisted your ankle, he said. It happened while you were out walking the dog, and he got away from you and must have jumped into her balcony.

Why do we have to lie about this? The dog escaping is the most normal thing that's happened to us, unless —

Do you think the balconies are like the roof?

No, look at all those plant boxes and parasols. They're not sinking. It's just the roof. This is just Rocky being a little sneak. Don't complicate it.

I'm sorry, Linda, said Fritjof, as soon as the door opened, it seems Rocky has somehow —

Go through, said Linda.

She stood in a pair of oversized slippers with the small terrier in her arms and pointed to the balcony that opened off the living room. Fritjof was almost proud to see that Rocky was staying outside where he could do no harm.

We're really sorry, said Frida. We don't know what got into him. He's usually so predictable.

He admired Frida for her ability to talk at length without giving anything away. She should have been a politician.

Rocky whimpered in place before setting off at a canter through the mismatched furniture and porcelain distractions that filled Linda's living room. Fritjof grabbed him by the collar as soon as he could.

Sit, he said, and then, Bold boy! Bold!

I don't know what to say, said Frida. It's not like him at all.

Fritjof noted a pause in her apology, as if she were waiting for the old woman to tell her precisely what it was she should be sorry for: that Rocky had jumped into the balcony from the garden, or that he had snuck in when she opened the door. The kind old woman might even have found him out in the stairwell and brought him in to give him a bowl of water.

Fritjof noticed a big bag of keys on the hall table and even some on the floor. He wondered if it would be too demanding to ask her to keep a key for them, so she could shove Rocky back into their apartment if he ever got out again.

I'm an old woman, said Linda.

Her dog squirmed in her arms, stretching to get down to Rocky, though he seemed scared by him at the same time.

It won't happen again, said Fritjof, edging towards the door.

Linda scratched her dog's head.

It's Flink here, she said. He can get a bit overexcited, and the vet said it's bad for his heart. My husband got him for me many years ago, and I don't mean to be morbid, but Flink's all I've got left of him.

We'll send Rocky to stay with my parents for a while, said Frida, looking at Fritjof for approval. It came in the form of a vigorous nod, more automatic than weighed.

That's right, he said. It will do Rocky good to be somewhere quiet for a while.

They live in Asker, said Frida. They have a garden, and their own dog passed away recently, this guy's mother.

It's for the best, said Fritjof, not sure who he was trying to convince.


Let's do a walk around the park before we go in, said Fritjof. The IT guys might be coming home around now.

The size of the little park across the street from 14A precluded much of a walk, but they looped around it a few times and threw a stick for Rocky.

Come on now, said Fritjof, time to close the computer and come home.

I admire people who work hard, said Frida, people who can keep going until late at night, like we did in architecture school.

I admire roofs that keep the rain and bird shit out, said Fritjof. What's happening, Frida? I'm not sure it's safe.

We must have imagined it. The power of suggestion or something.

When I admire people for working hard, said Frida, there's the presumption that people work hard because of their innate vigour, but people work long hours because they're poor or they need to pay off debts, and they probably wish they didn't have to work so much.

There goes socialism.

There's a limit to how much pride you can expect people to take in their work. That's what I mean.

How can you even think about issues? There he is.

Frida threw the stick underarm in the direction of 14A, so she had reason to dash after Rocky and raise a hand to the young Indian man who was coming down the street. Fritjof intended to follow her, but he couldn't bring himself to move from the spot. He didn't recognize the man. He might not live there at all, except that he fit the bill, ethnically, and in terms of his laptop-sized backpack. It would be embarrassing if it turned out he was not who they thought he was. Frida was shaking his hand, and they were both looking at the dog. Fritjof was ashamed of himself. He took out his phone and jiggled with it a bit, to give the impression that he had been waylaid by an important message, though his efforts were wasted, as neither of them looked his way. As he walked over to them he added the title *Roof* to his notes app. He made a list: *visible? memory? schizophrenia? when did it start?*

# Thursday

*It's all I can do to keep them apart. I'm the go-between. Those I bear have no idea of the forces the ground asserts, forces I deal with alone. I land right on the rock, we touch, and heave! and up you go! I am the lowest, the first poured and hardened plane. Underneath my reach it's rock and lava all the way to the earth's core. I have held back the push of the earth; I've kept it all on the level, allowed no settlement, tilting or sinking. I strengthen their corners and underpin their walls, but I am old. I am tired. They wouldn't know what happened to them if I let up.*

# Raj

He crawled through the tangle of duvet and switched on his
bedside lamp. It was not enough. He turned on the torch on
his phone and shone it along the floor. There were no mice
or earthworms there, but something about the carpet troubled Raj. There was something unfamiliar about it, a sense
of déjà vu, like this was a carpet he remembered from some
other lodgings. He had rented ten or twelve different flats
all over the world, or in a few countries in different parts of
the world at least. At first sight, this place had not seemed
the worst. Once he had shared a bedroom with three others,
but he had never been so troubled by an apartment, by the
building itself. A building had never attacked him, or even
confounded him quite so much.

He stepped barefoot onto the carpet and remembered
that the floors here were timber. He could feel the cheap
parquet under his feet through the earth.

He turned on the ceiling lamp to confirm what his soles
already felt: this was no mysterious substance strewn about
his bedroom. This was soil.

It was spread in a thin, even layer all over the floor. It was deep enough to conceal the parquet underneath, but shallow enough that he could clear away a patch using the spine of a book. This was not the result of any leak. The earth particles adhered to one another in little clumps, just like in any garden or tilled field. This earth was the same depth in the middle of the floor as along the edges. It lacked the sloped flow of a landslide. Furthermore, the earth was relatively dry. It was not in any way possible that this was the result of a flood.

There was only one solution: the answer he had been looking for in building technology was in fact to be found in the field of psychology – or criminology. Someone had been in here. Someone had intentionally done this. Someone had crept in here with hostile intent while he slept. This person had, this night, carefully spread this earth all around him. This person was a stealthy saboteur, because Raj had not woken. He had not slept well at all. He could not fathom that he had slept through this intrusion, but he had. It had happened. It had happened to him.

It was the same out in the corridor and in the kitchen: soil that collected between his toes. He found Pradeep asleep, fully clothed, on top of his bedcovers, with a digital reflex camera still clutched in his hand. Raj woke him with a whisper, ready to save the camera if Pradeep should let it go in fright when he woke.

What is it? said Pradeep, sitting upright on the bed, looking over the edge. What happened? he said. What's that on the ground?

Did you hear anyone in the apartment, Pradeep, anyone moving around?

That's earth, said Pradeep, pulling his feet underneath him. Raj, that's earth. You're standing on it.

Someone was in here during the night, said Raj. Someone came in here and did this. It's the only logical explanation. Were you filming?

Pradeep looked at his camera. He seemed surprised now to see it in his hands.

I fell asleep, he said. I was ready to take a picture if there was any flooding or any creatures, but I must have slept.

He checked the camera all the same.

Nothing. I didn't capture anything. Where is Krishna?

Take pictures of it now, said Raj. We need to document this if we're to complain.

Pradeep took photographs in his room and in the corridor.

There are footprints, he said, look.

Those are mine.

Raj crouched and searched for other footprints, but there were none. Whoever did this was shrewd, working backwards, painting themselves out of the apartment. Quietly, he unbolted the plywood door to the stairwell, expecting to find a trail of dirty footprints, but there were none, even if the floor tiles on the landing at their level did look grubby.

It was the same in Krishna's room. Krishna was awake, lying on his back, his lips murmuring something at the ceiling. His eyelids were puffed and glossy.

Did someone come in here? said Raj.

I have not slept at all.

His voice sounded strange, like he was struggling. In fact, he seemed quite out of breath. Raj put a hand on his forehead. He did not have a fever. If anything, he was cold to the touch.

You're not well, Krishna, he said. Can you sit up?

Is it gone, Raj?

Did you see something?

Has it stopped?

Raj pulled the blanket down from Krishna's chin. He took a plastic bottle of water from the bedside table and opened it for him. Krishna refused to drink.

Is it still here? he said.

The floor is covered in earth, said Pradeep. Raj says someone was in here in the middle of the night, spreading it around. Did you see or hear anyone, Krishna? You were awake.

Someone did this to us, on purpose?

They must have, said Raj, but we're going to catch them. Pradeep, your camera gave me an idea.

Raj has a plan, said Krishna, and his smile seemed almost to sink into his pillow.

What if we set up every video camera we have tonight? said Raj. Laptops, phones, webcams: we'll conceal them and stream directly to the cloud. If we spread them around the whole apartment, one towards the door to the stairwell, one in every room, we'll catch whoever this is, I promise you. They won't come in here unnoticed.

It might be that angry man next door, said Krishna. He hates us.

He's a divorced alcoholic, said Pradeep, so I imagine he hates everyone.

There is the question of how he's getting in, said Raj. Maybe one of our predecessors gave him a key so he could water the plants while they were away – but the door was bolted. He must have come through the window.

We have done nothing to him, said Krishna.

We can report him to the landlord and the police, said Raj, as soon as we have proof. We should start clearing this up. The landlord will be here at nine.

No way, said Pradeep. We need to show him the evidence.

He'll say we did it, said Krishna.

He will, said Raj. Until we have proof someone else is to blame, he's going to pin it on us.

I need my deposit back, said Pradeep. I'm not asking my father for help. He's just waiting for something like this to happen.

Then we must keep the place nice, said Raj, so the landlord can show it to new tenants. If he can't get anyone to replace us, he'll hang onto us and our money.

If we don't tell him, the same will happen to the new tenants, said Krishna. It probably happened to those before us. It will go on and on. It will never be fixed, and the tenants will always be blamed.

# Linda

Without raising her head to look, she knew where Flink was. She could feel the small weight of him on top of her feet, and the pressure made her legs stiffen, but the warmth was good. The sentiment was good too.

She could smell dog pee, but the smell was faint and not from here in the bedroom. It was Flink's own particular odour, not some other dog's dribble wafting in from the garden. He must have done it in the hallway, or somewhere further away in the flat, maybe even the bathroom. Of all the faculties that are, one by one, stolen from the elderly, it was not her sense of smell she wanted to retain longest. She would have chosen reason or memory, if given a choice.

Flink had been trying to coax her out of bed all day yesterday. He had jumped repeatedly from her bed to the floor by the French windows, where he would whinge a while before jumping up on the bed again. He had kept this up all day, this to and fro, apart from interludes where he lay beside her and let her stroke his wiry coat. If he had eventually succumbed and done his business indoors, then she had only herself to blame.

You're better than any family, Flink, she said.

Flink had been exceedingly loyal to her since it happened. Whereas every morning recently he had leapt to freedom through the windows, this morning and all yesterday he had stayed with her. He was a good dog, a good companion.

Yesterday morning, when her shoes had gone missing, when Teddy hid her shoes — what else could it be? — and her family concluded so lightly that she had gone senile, Flink had stayed true to her. When she came inside with cut soles and throbbing ankles, Flink licked the sores. He stayed with her as she washed her feet in the bath and took to bed, where she had been ever since. There had been knocking on the door, but she didn't answer. She left the phone off the hook.

Flink's weight, though small, was too much on top of her old feet, and it was a bad sign, but she wanted to itch the sores.

Flink, get off, she said. Down now, Flink.

She attempted to kick Flink off, but then she heard his whimper from the floor. Two paws and a muzzle appeared on the edge of her pillow. He stretched his snout, his tongue, towards her, but he couldn't reach the skin of her face, sag though it did. She heard the round-the-bed patter of his paws, and now he was on the blankets, barking down by her toes.

She tried to pull her legs up towards her, to start the process of sitting up, but she must have lain there too long, for her feet refused to move. Flink was busy tugging at the blankets down at that end of the bed, and he would make a right mess of the duvet cover if she didn't intervene soon. She felt cheated by this, that it might be concern for her bedclothes that tugged her out of her slump.

She managed to prop herself up on her elbows, and it was a difficult enough manoeuvre when you didn't have your feet for traction and eight decades had laid waste to your arms.

Flink was not pulling at the duvet at all. He had his pink jaws slathered around a bramble.

Linda reached for her glasses from the bedside table, falling back onto her shoulders in the process. Propped up again, she saw it was a creeping rose plant which had, in this one day of lassitude, stretched its thorny tendrils through the window, across the room and up onto her bed. How long had she been asleep? She had a momentary fear that this was the claw of some witch, some creature whose presence should tell her, loud and clear, that this was a dream. Her doctor had warned her not to let her sugar levels drop too low. She didn't have diabetes, but she needed to eat or she would get weak. Her appetite had waned with years of cooking for one. She had never gone so low as to cook a portion of stew for Flink along with her own, but now that she was officially in her own nuthouse maybe she could do crazy things like that. No one would know. She had long been her own sentry.

She adjusted the glasses on her nose. This was not the original species of roses which she had advised the gardening committee to plant. This was a dusty-pink, romantic folly, a plant that was intent on covering over the plaster and brickwork on the façade like ivy, a plant that had come for her, perhaps in revenge. She laughed at that.

Don't be so sore, she said to the rose stem.

Flink gave another tug and fell off the bed with the stalk in his mouth. He spun in circles, with bloody drool hanging out the corners of his mouth.

Linda breathed deeply towards the overgrown stretch of floor between her bed and the French windows. We'll be back for you, she said, and she did everything in the correct order now.

Supporting herself with a hand on the wall all the way, she walked to the kitchen. She poured herself a glass of milk, which she drank in small sips. Flink trailed her into the bathroom, and, when she pointed into the tub, he only protested with a single whine before he jumped in. She rinsed his mouth under the slow-streaming tap, telling him he was a good boy, and he was. She was afraid he might snap her fingers when she held his skull against her, opened his jaws with splayed fingers and removed two thorns, but Flink was patient. He trusted her.

She knew she had hand pruners somewhere, but all she found for tools were sewing scissors and wire cutters.

She might have been sleeping for days, but, even then, this growth seemed too much. If it grew a metre a day, this was three days' worth, but no plant grew that fast. She was reminded of a science-fiction film she had seen in the 1970s. If Leif was here, they would understand this together.

They would tease out strands of truth, make sense of it all. Alone, there was little difference between real and imagined.

The stems that stretched into her bedroom, up onto her bed, were thin and green and easily cut. She reached a hand through the railing and clipped them back, as far down as possible. She chopped the tendrils into manageable lengths and flung them to one side out the French windows. She leaned out to see if her neighbours on either side were suffering from the same problem, but she couldn't see past the protruding balconies. The climbing roses had extended up the plasterwork on either side of her window, and she feared that they might grow so tall and confident that they would stretch in along her ceiling, attacking her from above. She was ready for them now. There was that difference.

It was still early for the young, though she heard a child crying somewhere. It sounded like Teddy, but she always thought that.

On her balcony, she used her wire cutters and a screwdriver to remover some copper clips from the flower boxes. She pressed them into the shape of nails, as sharp as she could make, and put them in her pocket. She put on a pair of rubber boots and hardy trousers and went out to the garden.

She passed easily through the rose and hibiscus bushes, though her feet dug a furrowed trail.

Maybe it was unnatural to live high up on the fourth floor for so many years. She had done nothing to deserve elevation. She grew up on a farm and now she could smell earth again. Her parents were slaves to the soil: tilling, fertilizing, cultivating. This required respect. It was her turn now, and it would not be long until she decomposed into soil just like this. Was this why everyone was so opposed to dirt, afraid of the future, dirt to dirt?

Not yet.

On either side of her French windows and beside her balcony, she drove a copper nail into the base shoot of each climbing rose plant. From a carrier bag, she brought out a large bottle of weedkiller. It had been lying at the back of the cupboard under the sink, unopened for decades, so she could only hope it would still work. She poured a good measure over the roots of each offending shoot. She had recommended which roses to plant, and they should have listened to her — though, in fairness, she had relented, told them to go ahead with whichever planting plan they felt most strongly for. I'm just an old-schooler, she had said. Don't listen to me.

# Sonja

While the builders were setting up in the bedroom, Sonja went to her desk at the living-room window and looked up to Eva's apartment as she phoned her again.

I tried to call you yesterday, she said. Did you get my email?

Sonja, hello.

The insurance assessor didn't find anything, didn't do anything to find the problem, so I've got a couple of builders in to find out what's wrong. I'll take pictures of whatever they uncover, and we can send it to the insurance company.

No, said Eva.

But Eva, you said –

I didn't sanction this.

I know, but you agreed that maintenance of external walls is explicitly the collective responsibility of the residents. It says so in the house rules.

For someone who's in arrears with her contributions, you're demanding unreasonably prompt action. I only want to pursue this through the insurance company. Otherwise, we could be stung for the costs ourselves.

But the builders are already here.

That's on you, Sonja.

Eva rang off, and Sonja rested her forehead against the windowpane. Right now, she had no way of paying for this herself. She would have to let them do as little as possible and owe them.

It was awkward telling them they should fix the one wall only. The older man, Dovydas, traced his trowel down along the corner between the exterior wall and the party wall and said something in Lithuanian. The younger guy, Matas, said, Corner not good. Need to paint the whole room.

One wall only, she said, her palms circling parallel to the wall she wanted done. Do the best you can with the corners.

This was not an aesthetic project, after all. She would have done it herself, as well as she was able, but she was afraid of what she might find under the paint or behind the plaster. It was better if someone else saw it, told her what they observed and why it happened. She did not want to stand alone inside a perfectly fine brick wall, with a mess of plaster about her feet, and confirm to herself that she was wrong. What she needed was a professional opinion, the sanity of numbers. These tradesmen were perfect for that reason. They could be trusted to tell her what they saw, to give her the plain, abbreviated truth. Neither of these two could ever be accused of imagining a draught.

She returned to her desk and listened to the decisive tapping and scraping from the adjacent bedroom.

173

They were under instruction to call her if they found a crack or anything wrong. It hadn't seemed problematic for them to start in the bedroom, and this too was a sign of the trust they engendered. She remembered the unease she had felt at bringing the insurance assessor in there. Perhaps it was all right this time because there were two of them, an insurance itself against any funny business.

She put her hand on the external wall and imagined that she could feel it jolt with each whack of the chisel, silently chastising herself for imagining things about this wall, when all she wanted was cold facts. There was a pun there that she could not laugh at. She swept her palm over a known trouble spot, and she felt it for sure: that same draught, air pushing against her skin.

Lady!

Matas appeared in the door from the hallway.

Come and see, he said. We found the problem.

Sonja followed him into the bedroom, where the thick layer of felt along the exterior wall was already covered with crumbled plaster and dust.

Dovydas was tapping with his chisel beside the problem, though it was not difficult to see.

Brick missing, said Matas. Very strange.

There was no doubt about it. At one of the spots where she had noticed the draught, there was one brick missing clean out of the wall. She ran her palm along the wall until she found another such spot.

Try here too, she said.

It was the same there, and Sonja wondered how the wall had not fallen down. There was enough left over, she supposed, to keep it standing.

Dovydas dusted out the new hole and tapped it into certain existence with his chisel. He said something in Lithuanian, and Matas replied, in accents so beautiful that Sonja wondered how their families ever let them stray.

Builders cheat you, said Matas. Stingy fifties, after the war, was a shortage of materials. They trick you, he said. They cheat you, but we fix, no problem. We fill with mortar.

Do you mind, said Sonja, and she took photos of the two missing bricks on her phone and sent them directly to Eva.

She thought she might stay and watch them work, to see the full problem and how, precisely, it would be fixed, but they stood there, looking back at her, nodding and repeating their diagnosis and cure, until she admitted she would have to get out and let them work.

She refilled the water that loomed around her paintbrushes. Work was once again possible. Her art required a functioning world as its background. The only thing that did not make sense was why she or the previous occupants had not noticed the draught before now. She had been unobservant, and so had they.

Sonja began to mix a palette, forming a scale of greens. Her neighbours: she had to tell them about this. It must be happening to them too.

# Gunnar

Gunnar took a cup from the overhead cupboard and stood, slightly baffled, in front of the empty coffee machine. He could have sworn he heard the noise of percolation just now. He was sure, too, that he had smelled freshly brewed coffee. The smell was still in the air. He wondered if Hildegunn had drunk the lot, but the coffee grinds in the filter were dry, from yesterday.

A cafetière, he thought. She must have brought it into the bedroom with her. It was positive that Hildegunn was up and moving about so early in the day. He put on a brew for himself.

He heard teenage music start and stop underneath him — those punky twins, Blix's sons — and footsteps from above. He heard a meow below and Blix's nasal voice: I told you not to bring that cat in here. The cat screeched. A door slammed. A drawer opened and cutlery jangled, or so he imagined. That noise came from above. In Blix's apartment, a chair scraped along the floor. He heard the nudge of chair legs on wood that prompted an image of someone sitting down, just below him. He was almost certain that person sniffed and rustled paper – a newspaper?

In what sort of cardboard abode had he taken up residence? He always had the impression this was a sturdy building. It certainly looked so from outside. The façade was partially fair-faced brick, partially plastered, and the plaster showed no sign of cracks or discolouration. Hildegunn had never complained, though she might have kept silent about the building's faults out of pride. He couldn't ask her about it now, given her state of mind.

The public health nurse insisted Hildegunn's confusion was a temporary effect of the painkillers, but if Hildegunn was indeed going senile her wayward offspring might consider selling to him directly. He wouldn't even mind putting it on the open market for them if they preferred. He would get a good commission on it. A place like this would go well over the average for the area, well over the asking price, he was certain.

These noises were disconcerting when he considered the valuation of the property. Although the other apartments in these blocks must be the same, and they sold well, on the few occasions they actually came on the market. They tended to pass down from generation to generation.

He heard a low thump and the scratchy rumble of bread being sliced in the room above. He had to remind himself that there was a concrete slab between them. They had commenced building before the war, but the certificate of completion was dated 1950. This might mean that the load-bearing walls and floor slabs were left waiting during occupation. They might have been exposed for years, corroding away. He held onto the counter.

Gunnar had been spoilt in terms of acoustic absorption, living in a detached house, but he had also presided over countless viewings in apartments, so he was quite familiar with the array of domestic noises one might be subjected to.

Problematic noise was almost always due to bad behaviour: parties, loud music, the refusal to give a baby a soother. The sounds he now heard were low, nothing you could even complain about. His neighbours were not producing excessive noise. It was the building that was at fault, transmitting excessive amounts of sound. Someone hummed above him. A spoon clinked off the side of a cup below. He heard it quite distinctly when someone right under his feet slurped his coffee. At least, he presumed it was coffee. He could now smell his own brew.

His imagination must be filling in between the lines. He was not used to having people stacked all around him, like goods on a shelf. He turned on the radio, which was sufficient to drown out the neighbours' activities.

Gunnar!

He found Hildegunn propped up in bed.

Gunnar, darling, she said, do I smell coffee? I wouldn't mind a cup in here before I get up. I hate to bother you, but I'll be steadier on my feet if I just get a small measure of caffeine inside me.

Coming up, said Gunnar, trying to believe it was his own desire for coffee he had smelled when he rose. There was no sign of a cafetière by her bed.

When she was noiselessly sipping her coffee, he told her he was going out for a short while.

He hurriedly ruffled his hair in the hall mirror and took his shoes from the rack where he had left them to dry after polishing. He had arranged to call on his tenants downstairs at nine and wanted to go out first so he could ring the door-bell from the street. If he could manage it, he didn't want them to know he was living upstairs. Not that they would tell on him, but they might start coming up with their complaints. Better if they thought he lived far away and any visit was a bother to him.

Gunnar! called Hildegunn, before he reached the door. Have you seen Gertrude?

She has eaten and drunk her fill, he called back, and has gone off now to clean her fur in the sun.

The latter, of course, was pure speculation. He had fed the beast and, though he had not actually seen her, her food was gone. He liked to help, but there was no point in going overboard. He brought the recycling with him on his way out.

Down on the street, he regretted the lack of a tissue. The bin was covered with dirt. He had a mind to complain about it, but someone else was sure to do the honours. Also, Hildegunn might be stung with higher water and heating rates if they got wind of his living with her. He was only staying to care for her, but he had, at Hildegunn's request, made sure that Knut and Une paid extra for their daughter and grandson. He had every reason to be wary of retribution.

He nudged up his sleeve with the back of a knuckle and saw it was already past nine. One of his tenants looked out at him through a window as he rang the doorbell from the stoop. He could have keyed his way in and knocked directly on their door, but respect generated respect, and he was willing to offer this small gesture to make them feel they were welcoming him, rather than the sense of intrusion that might otherwise have taken hold. People skills.

They buzzed him in, and he could smell the apartment as he descended. Raj was holding the temporary door open, and one of the others was standing further in along the corridor, his eyes flitting between Gunnar and the floor like a guilty child.

Can we turn on the lights? said Gunnar.

They were standing there in the dim glow that came from the worktop spots in the kitchen, and he decided they could save electricity on their own time. He flicked on the switch by the door, and, just as he was about to chastise himself inwardly for presuming this freedom in their home, he congratulated himself instead for cutting through their tricks with such speed. The floor was filthy, absolutely mucky. He could see the brown swirls where they had made a sorry attempt at mopping up.

He walked past them, into the kitchen, into the bathroom, opening the doors of their bedrooms. One of them had not even bothered to get up. He cast aside any remaining sentiments of politeness and respect, along with their protests. He photographed it all. Absolute filth. It was like a stable.

This is the worst I have ever seen, anywhere, he said. How did you even manage to accumulate this amount of dirt? It's unbelievable.

Mr Lofthus, said Raj, do not worry. We will fix this.

I can't believe my eyes, said Gunnar. Were you growing something in here? Cannabis?

Nothing like that, said Raj. I promise.

It's not our fault, said the other guy. It's the apartment.

Gunnar watched the two glare at each other, but, whatever beef they had between them, he was not getting into it.

You have the audacity to call me down here, to invite me for a viewing, and you have not even cleaned, said Gunnar. What kind of ...

I think there is a leak somewhere, Mr Lofthus, said Raj.

This is no leak, this muck!

We will clean it.

I was quite clear. I made myself quite clear. You can move out early if I find new tenants to replace you, but I'm only going to find new tenants if they can view a clean apartment. No one is going to want to move into an apartment that looks like this. No one, no decent ...

I promise, said Raj, next time you come here it will be spick and span. You have my word.

I was so considerate, said Gunnar, as to place an advertisement online already.

We'll be out of your hair in no time, said the other guy, holding out a sheet of paper on which he seemed to have drawn up some sort of contract.

You'd better not think I'm signing anything, said Gunnar. You can forget it.

He looked down at his shoes. He had managed to scuff the toe of one in his flurry, in his absolutely reasonable rage.

We slept in, said Raj. I'm so sorry. We meant to get up early to clean, but we've been working so hard that we slept in, all of us. It won't happen again, I promise.

I'll give you one more chance, said Gunnar. Can you open …

He was dismayed to see that the windows were already open, all of them. He could hardly breathe, though that might be the fury.

My plan, he said, was to have potential tenants round next weekend.

Do, said Raj. We'll be ready for them then, I promise.

It's in your hands now, said Gunnar. If you want to exit your lease early, you'll have to pull your weight.

We will, said Raj, absolutely. You can count on us.

Have the apartment spotless, I mean absolutely shining, and be out of here at midday next Saturday and Sunday.

No problem. Right, Pradeep?

The Pradeep guy just scowled at him.

I'm going to come back tomorrow, and that's the last time I'll be checking up on you. I want this place absolutely shining, said Gunnar. Otherwise, you're out, all of you.

It would be one thing if these were students, but these men were in their late twenties or early thirties. They were professional academics. He thought he had played it safe.

What date can we end the lease? said Pradeep.

Gunnar looked at him and wondered if he understood English.

I don't know where you …

He had to stop himself before he commanded the boy, who was of course a grown man, back to the slum he came out of, because he had to admit that Pradeep did have a certain dishevelled poise, which the others lacked. It was not for Gunnar to compare them to one another, nor was it up to him to figure out which one of them had made this mess, or if they were all equally to blame. They had signed a lease together, so they could take responsibility for it together. They could sort it out among themselves.

At best, he said, you'll leave your lease when I've found someone to replace you, and not a day sooner. I have evidence. I can have you thrown out today for this mess and use your deposit for cleaning. I'm well within my rights to do that.

No, please, don't, said Raj.

It's not our fault, said Pradeep. You'll see. Someone's breaking in. We're sure of it. We don't even have a proper door.

I just ordered you a new door!

He cut through them to the stairs.

You'd better get cleaning, he said.

He didn't give them the satisfaction of looking back as he left. He went right up the stairs and heard the temporary door rattle closed behind him. Fresher, better air filled his lungs as he climbed the four stories to Hildegunn's apartment. He had already turned the key in the door before he remembered that he had planned to leave through the front door, so they wouldn't know he was living here, but they were hardly in a position to complain about anything now.

He wanted to sit down to take off his shoes, like an old man, but the stool that was usually in the hallway was not to be found. Hildegunn must have moved it. How, with two crutches, he couldn't say.

Directly underneath him he heard a string of mumbled curses that matched his own mood. He could hear the precise, whispered words: all this junk, where does she get it?

Hildegunn appeared at her bedroom door in a dressing gown.

On your feet, Hildegunn, he said, that's good, but listen: ask me if you want any furniture moved around. Don't try to do it yourself.

All right, she said, I'm just going to freshen up.

Lovely, I'll put on some breakfast for us. I could do with another cup of coffee.

In the kitchen, Gunnar became aware of the characteristic sound of plastic wheels on wood, a child playing overhead. Hildegunn turned on the tap in the bathroom. Gunnar was ready for an experiment. He spoke at regular volume, high enough for someone in this room to hear him, but not loud enough for Hildegunn's ears.

Would you like some chocolate? he said, and waited.

Who wants chocolate? he said, and a clear reply came from overhead.

Teddy have chocolate! Teddy have chocolate!

Gunnar heard the sound of stockinged footsteps above, the repeated exclamation, and then an older man's voice — Knut's, he presumed.

Well now, said Knut, chocolate, is it? I suppose I may as well give in straight away. We'll make some nice hot chocolate to drink, and I think I've some chocolate spread in the cupboard for your toast. Would you like that?

Gunnar didn't hear any reply, only the thud of a bare-footed toddler jumping and the slow shuffling of older feet. Gunnar smiled and looked around him for some other use to which he might put this newfound benevolent power.

# Knut

This was the first time Knut had experienced vertigo. It felt heavy, like the air was laden with a fine cloud of leaden dust. He flopped into one of the purple armchairs that had belonged to Une's mother. He was not a particularly heavy man, but the legs of the chair creaked under his weight. Une winced, and he wondered if they were both coming down with something, or if she was worried about the splaying teak of this heirloom.

Teddy was on the terrace, brum-brumming his new tractor and trailer, which was full of pinecones, wherever he'd found them. Knut would continue to get the boy all the toys he wanted, as long as they were dinosaurs or vehicles or anything that led him to make a noise. He couldn't keep an eye on him all the time, so the sound of him was reassuring.

Une closed the door to the hallway and spoke in a low voice. There's nothing anywhere on the floors, she said. Are you certain it wasn't you?

I would remember tidying, Une. You don't think ... It must have been Bibbi.

Do you think she cleans when she gets home, in the middle of the night?

It wasn't you? said Knut. I thought you'd hidden every-thing away wherever you hid her golden flip-flops. She's still looking for them, you know.

I did no such thing. Why would I hide the girl's shoes — all our shoes?

Why did you order those carpets?

Une was massaging the back of an armchair, too restless to sit. Yesterday, she had ordered wall-to-wall polyester car-pets for the whole apartment.

I rang them again, she said. The fitters are coming this evening at six. It took a bribe to get them to come so soon. I went for a standard colour they had in stock: wheat or sand, I can't remember which.

Do you really think it will help? If you believed it, you would have ordered linoleum.

It's impossible. It might give us peace of mind for a while but, there's some real explanation. Knut, do you think it's Bibbi?

What harm if she's tidying up?

She might be selling things off to make money for — you know.

She's clean.

She's out every night.

That's drink. She was addicted to painkillers, not party dope.

Well, do you think she's selling off our stuff to buy drink then? I can't find the ironing board or the vacuum cleaner, and that pedal bin from the bathroom's gone.

Who would buy a bin, for heaven's sake?

She's been through a lot. She might be doing it at night, cleaning up.

She hates housework.

I don't mind about the stuff. It will cost a lot to replace everything, but I don't care. I'm only worried about Bibbi.

If it's her.

It might not be her at all, said Une. It was uncanny that the hall mat and the shoes out there went missing the same morning Linda was here.

She slowed down at these last words, and Knut appreciated this hesitation.

You're onto something there, he said. She wasn't wearing any shoes.

Your mother might be going senile.

She might be sleepwalking. She's always sleepwalked. I bet that's it.

She has a key.

Do you think we should ask for it back?

Christ, no. We don't want her locked out on the street, Knut. She probably wanders back here out of old habit if she's sleepwalking outside.

I'll call over to her.

Do that, but first let me go down to the basement. I think we have old summer shoes down there. There must be a box of toys too.

See you in a few hours then, said Knut, and he laughed and winced.

Une put on a pair of rubber boots to go out. I'll bring us rain, going around in these, she said, but there's not much to choose from.

Knut closed the door behind her and gave Linda a ring straight away. There was no answer, which must mean she was out, because she was certainly up at this hour. Old people hardly slept – and when Linda slept, she went sleepwalking, so she basically had the whole night to raid the place. He would not even be too downhearted if it turned out Linda was going senile. He just hoped the problem was Linda, so it would not be Bibbi. He had heard her come in last night, but he was too tired to check the time.

Teddy's voice-engine continued on the terrace.

From Bibbi's room, a clunk was followed by a groan and the clod of boots as she came out into the hallway.

Morning, she said.

She was a purplish-grey colour and smelled like something marinated.

You had the right idea, sleeping in your boots, he said.

She looked down and said, Shit.

They weren't as strict as most people about it, but they didn't usually wear outdoor shoes indoors. Knut was almost impressed she hadn't noticed she was wearing them.

All the rest of our shoes have gone missing, he said. Une's down in the basement if you want her to get anything for you.

He looked for guilt on her face, and he saw something there. She stretched her upper lip over her teeth, but he didn't know how to interpret this.

What do you mean, missing? she said.

Teddy was crying on the terrace, and they went out to him.

Are you hungry? said Knut.

Hay-bays gone!

Say it again.

Hay-bays gone, said Teddy, and he lifted up the empty trailer to show him.

Your hay bales. Oh dear, that is serious, but don't worry. We'll go out and find some more hay bales for you, lots and lots of them.

Teddy lay down on his belly and looked through a thin gap between two concrete tiles, sad but still singing, never silent.

An' a one two three, they a' gone, gone, gone.

Slow down, Teddy, said Bibbi. That's a Christmas song you're singing. It's only May.

She crouched down, and drove the tractor around the terrace, twisting and turning it so Teddy couldn't catch up, even at his top speed. His laughter never sank to anything under a giggle, until Bibbi finally let him have it.

How was last night?

Good. I don't know why I stay out so late. Did you say Mum's putting stuff down in the basement? Do you know if she took the heels and make-up from the floor of my room? I mean, fair enough, the place was carpeted in my junk but ...

We're getting wall-to-wall carpets.

Carpets?

Your mother thinks it would be cosy. We've a beige carpet picked out that would be nice in all the rooms. They're coming to install it this evening. What do you think?

Bibbi lifted Teddy inside and put him on the living-room floor. She stroked the wood with her palm.

I don't know what we did with the sample, said Knut, but it's a nice tight weave, not too fluffy.

Bibbi looked around the floor without getting up. The carpets made no sense, aesthetically. He had to explain it somehow.

Your mother's afraid Teddy will slip on the wooden floor and knock his head off the bricks around the fireplace. She had a pile of cushions stacked around it earlier. She should have left them there.

She's right, said Bibbi. Teddy will have more of a grip when he's dashing around. He's only going to get faster.

Exactly, said Knut.

Bibbi walked around the edge of the living room, examining the floor and the skirting boards.

What is it? said Knut. What are you thinking?

Oh, nothing at all. I'm so spaced out these days.

Teddy was scratching the edges of the floorboards with the claw of his digger.

The carpet will be lovely, said Bibbi.

Une came back an hour later, with two bags from the shoe shop. She said there was something wrong with the door and she couldn't get into the basement.

I got something for everyone, Linda too, she said, passing the bags to Bibbi.

Now who's extravagant? said Knut. Was it the padlock that wouldn't open? Why didn't you come and get me?

No, I'm talking about the main door from the stairwell to the basement. I could turn the key, but I couldn't push the door in. Something must have fallen down behind it. It's completely jammed. I sent Eva a text about it. You know what else, it absolutely stinks down there. It's not a foul smell, but it's really strong, overwhelming. There must be damp.

I have a pair just like these in our storage room, said Knut. There was no need to buy a new pair, exactly the same.

We can't go around in rubber boots.

There was a pattering on the roof right overhead, and they all looked up.

That's heavy, said Bibbi. Lucky you got back in time.

All four of them looked out the windows and the door to the terrace. They looked alternately up at the ceiling and outside. Knut could not remember hearing rain on the roof before.

That's some downpour, he said.

The windows remained completely dry. This was a new, more decisive form of rain. This was a heavy rain, which understood gravity only, and would not be swayed by wind.

# Fritjof

The conditioner smelled like icing. Fritjof sponged it into the sofa cushions with a circular motion, spreading it evenly. The mark from the goose droppings rose up in contrast to the leather around it. He wondered if the shit had a conditioning effect or if it blocked the conditioner. They would have to send this tender piece of furniture away before any more damage was done.

He was working from home to keep an eye on things, but he found himself incapable of sitting in a damaged home without repairing it. It was he who insisted they leave everything the way it was until the insurance assessor came next week, but here he was, making fruitless attempts at reversing the damage. They had already cleared away the goose droppings and wiped up after that spell of rain, so the evidence was gone.

He and Frida bought this apartment, one of the best in the development, because their grandfathers had designed it together. The people who lived here were second and third generation. If they sold this apartment, they would not be likely to find a replacement here. Fritjof was almost ready to cut his losses, but he wondered if they would be better off anywhere else. If the roof over his head had changed beyond what had previously been possible, then the same must be happening to roofs all over the place. There was nothing special about their roof. It could just as easily happen to someone else as to them. It might have been happening for years, in buildings all around them, for all they knew.

There was a spattering of white droppings over by the bookcase. On the top shelf, he saw a small pile of sticks. He went closer. It was a small circle of twigs, knitted together and hollow in the middle. He pulled over a footstool. If he was in any doubt, then the eggs settled it for him.

They were small, the size of the sugar-coated marzipan eggs they had eaten at Easter. Light blue and speckled with yellow, they were delicate and beautiful. He had learned as a schoolboy that if you touched them, the parents would pick up your scent and abandon the nest. He put on a pair of plastic gloves and brought it out to the roof terrace, but he could see no obvious place to put it down and it was starting to fall apart in his hands.

Across the void over the communal garden, he saw that his mirror-image neighbours were out on their terrace too. He could hear the squeals of a child behind the parapet over there, and Knut and his daughter were smiling and chatting. They did not seem worried about their roof. Every now and then a peal of laughter caught on the echo that only seemed to work on utterances over a certain volume. Their eyes were cast ever downwards, towards the presumed child on the terrace tiles. Even when they went inside, they did not look at their ceiling at all. They sensed no danger overhead.

A dark circle appeared on a concrete tile close to him, and he felt the cold shock of a large raindrop on the thinning patch on his crown.

Inside, he deposited the tangle of twigs back on its shelf and flung the leather cushions into a heap on the couch. Gathering the painter's plastic that he had laid to one side, he stretched it over, found he had rotated it incorrectly, pulled and turned it, tugged it down over the edges. The rain came heavier on his scalp and his bare, outstretched arms, and in dark trickles on the couch, under the plastic.

Fritjof had always considered these floors as perfectly horizontal, but now he saw there were high and low points, depressions enough to create small ponds. The rain made a cheap sound on the plastic and droplets bounced merry and disrespectful on the floor. It was a beautiful nightmare.

This rain was coming down with a completely vertical trajectory, so none was blowing into the books on the shelves – apart from his grandfather's *Case Study Houses* book, which stuck out, too deep for its shelf. He pulled it out, too late, the pages already wavy at the edges. His grandfather had little sketches and notes in the margins. He shoved it under the plastic on one of the armchairs.

Grabbing all the towels on the clothes horse, which were damp themselves already, he spread them out on the floor in a pattern somewhere between chess and Tetris. He took out what other towels and sheets they had stored in drawers and in the wash basket and scattered them around too.

The first towels he had laid out already needed to be wrung dry, but he took the time, all the same, when he found himself by the living-room window, to spy on the neighbours opposite. The Klevelands stood in their own living room. He noticed that they did look up now and then, but even that seemed to rule out a permeable roof. Fritjof could not look up without getting rain in his eyes. They seemed to notice it was raining but were not rushing about with towels. It hardly seemed fair. He wondered if it would be worth approaching them to ask if they wanted to sell. He and Frida could sell on this apartment at a loss – if it didn't rain the day of the viewings.

He heard the door opening, Rocky whining, Frida cursing, and he ran out to them, as if he had done nothing but run about since the rain started and it was about time she came and lent a hand. The rain came to a sudden halt as he squelched over the towels on the living-room floor. In the hallway, which had remained uncovered, the surface of the water steadied into a mirror. With the light coming in from the stairwell, it looked almost picturesque, and he remembered that artist who filled the floors of exhibition spaces with black oil, creating the illusion of double-height rooms.

Frida had her hair tied back like a dishevelled ballerina, severe but crooked. She rattled and splashed a huge yellow bucket on wheels into the hallway. A mop stuck out of it and whacked her in the face. She didn't even react.

It has a wringer, she said.

Not a moment too soon, he said.

Rocky was out on the street again.

He'd noticed the dog's absence a couple hours before but didn't want to abandon the apartment in search of him.

We have bigger problems, he said, and started the exhausting task of wringing and re-spreading twenty towels.

He dashed to and from the kitchen sink with dripping towels as Frida worked radially out from the entrance door with her industrial-style mop. She toppled it on the door saddle going into the bedroom and managed to do the same on her way out. The darker patches, where water had seeped between the floorboards, started to smell of wet woodland, and Fritjof knew that under the tightly packed oak boards there was a layer of softer wood that would hold this water till it rotted.

Frida stood in the door between the hallway and the living room and said something inaudible. He went and took her hands.

It won't last, she said. It can't.

I called the estate agent we bought it off, he said. The first fine week we get, I think we should put it on the market.

Our home.

I know, but ...

We'll never find anywhere like this again, anywhere that's so perfect for us. It's part of us, this apartment.

I'm more the indoor type.

Frida wiped the rain off her forehead with a rubber glove. The deep frown line that used to appear in moments of surprise was now a permanent fixture.

We need to think about it properly, she said.

We don't have time to think, and it doesn't even fathom logical thinking.

So just sell it?

Fritjof led Frida by the elbow to the living-room window.

I was looking at them just now, he said.

The Klevelands?

I was looking at them when it started to rain. It's not happening to them.

How do you know?

They didn't look up.

So, it's just us, just this apartment, this roof.

We should ask them to swap.

Frida touched the windowpane with a rubber fingertip.

The apartments are the same, said Fritjof, just mirrored, and they'd be closer to Linda.

We can say we prefer the orientation of their apartment, said Frida.

Yes, said Fritjof, and we'll offer them a payment to compensate. They'll think they're getting a great deal.

Let's do it, said Frida, but wait until we test it on Raj first. He's coming up tonight.

# Eva

The letter boxes were no longer on the wall. Theft? She was aware they needed to be replaced. It was on her spreadsheet for maintenance, though not at the top of the list. Surely neither Une nor Ibsen would have ordered new boxes without her leave. They had a budget to consider. And they should have kept the old ones until the replacements came. What about privacy? Security?

Ellie had texted to say she could no longer work for Eva, as her host family needed her. She said she put Eva's key in the letter box. Had they taken them away full of post? Now she would have to get the lock changed. She sent a quick email to the cleaning company asking for a replacement cleaner as soon as practically possible, and texted Une and Ibsen asking them what was going on with the post boxes.

Ellie, she thought, I need you now more than ever.

Eva opened the door to her apartment slowly, expending particular care to ensure that the first rush of air did not destroy her trap. It was more a test, really, but it bore the shrewdness of a trap, so that's what she called it. On the sand-coloured doormat, she had sprinkled a layer of flour. The wholemeal flour was the same colour as the mat, but if you crouched down, as Eva did now, with the door firmly closed behind her, you could see if anyone had stood there.

She recognized her own footprints. It had been impossible to leave without pressing her own prints into the flour, and that was the beauty of this trap: no intruder could step over the mat because it was too big. She saw her own footprints, but no others.

She stepped out of her shoes and smelled that high-up smell of summer which could only be perceived at a certain altitude. She wondered now if fumes from that bad paint had prevented her from sleeping properly. It was two days since she had found the Rhodesian ridgeback on her balcony, and the shock had now dissipated.

Look at the facts and examine them closely, she told herself as she moved into the bedroom to study the party wall. On Monday, there was dog shit on her balcony; on Tuesday, the neighbours' dog was there. A feeling of persecution held sway those first two days, but now, cooler, distanced from the alarm of the discovery, she considered it possible that on both Monday and Tuesday she did not close the door to the stairwell properly and the dog had got in that way. On Monday, he must have done his business on the balcony and wandered up home again. On Tuesday, he stayed for some reason. Perhaps he had only just arrived when she found him. In any case, the whole theory hung on whether the door to the stairwell had been open or closed. She could have sworn she had found it closed on both occasions, though she might have sworn more vehemently to this effect on the day it happened. Now, after the passage of time, she considered it most likely that she had, under the influence of paint fumes and bad sleep, locked the door in an open position and caused this whole problem herself. Of course, there should not have been a Rhodesian ridgeback wandering the stairwell, and it was their fault, really, but at least this theory made some sort of sense. She found, with some distaste, that to form a logical conclusion she would have to accept that she had been sloppy.

Well, she thought, if I was sloppy then, I'll be thorough now. She called the locksmith who installed the locks on the new fire doors. She told him that her lock was not closing properly, that it was faulty. He said he'd come and have a look at it the next day.

Great, she said, one of my keys has also gone missing, so I'll need a new set.

That's a different story. I'll have to order a new lock. We're talking one or two weeks at the least.

She reminded him of who he was speaking to and threatened to report him if he did not prioritize this case. He agreed to come the next day just to have a look. She considered whether she should get him to check all the locks, or at least Frida and Fritjof's, but she decided to see what he said about hers first.

As she spoke on the phone, she examined the plasterwork. She might, quite plausibly, not have looked at either of her party walls for weeks or months. There was no reason to look at something she knew was there. She rubbed an indentation into the plaster at eye level on her bedroom wall. The plaster was quite loose.

She called the painters she'd employed to paint the stairwell a few years back and told them she might need some replastering along with painting, but it was a small job. Of course, she also asked them to prioritize her, though she had nothing to threaten them with. They could fit her in, they said, in two weeks' time at the earliest. Accepting their offer, she decided to call around in the meantime and see if she could find someone else sooner. She owed them no loyalty.

Eva took a pen from her bedside table and bored some way into the wall with it, to check whether she came to concrete or brick. The plaster was so loose and chalky that the pen slid easily inwards, and she was holding it by the tip, the whole pen inside, when she halted in fright. What would the neighbours say if they found a peephole? She consoled herself with the fact that her bedroom backed onto the neighbours' living room, so she might claim it was they who had been spying on her.

She carefully extracted the pen and looked into the hole. She was relieved to find it dark inside, so she had not bored all the way through. She would tell the painters to put on a thick layer of screed before they painted, or she might even tell them to mount plasterboard for soundproofing. The antics of her neighbours the day before had been of great amusement to Eva, but she saw how she could become distracted by them over time. She had not turned on the television or the radio since she heard their fight. She kept her own apartment free from chatter and music so that she would hear the least noise from them, and, while this might be fun for a while, it was not healthy in the long run. In any case, all she had heard from them since their fight was footsteps – quite clear – the scraping of a cup on a table, and the piano, which was nice, well played, but which sent her from her bedroom every time.

She would get the repairmen to excavate a section, to find out what kind of a wall it was. The floor plans she retrieved from the planning office when she first moved in gave only the dimension of the wall and nothing about its composition. The party walls might be concrete, for stability. If it was a brick wall, she might have managed to bore her pen through the mortar between two bricks. The mortar, in that case, must not be all that strong. She would get the decorators to put up a stud wall with a double layer of plasterboard towards her. For all she knew, this was a fire hazard.

In the kitchen, she could hear her neighbour slicing carrots ... and crying. She took a plate of cheese crackers to the balcony for some peace, but there she found none.

Someone had been here again. She made to put down her snacks on the small table which she kept beside a narrow wooden bench, but she found that both were gone. She put the plate on the glossy epoxy floor.

She rang the locksmith once again and left a message telling him to put a temporary lock on the door tomorrow.

A padlock or a bolt or something, she said. Someone broke in. I can't live with my home unsecured. Do you understand?

The missing balcony furniture was not the only problem. It was, all in all, the lesser problem. Eva slowly approached the copper flower boxes that ran along the top of the railing. Someone had come in here and planted some sort of bushes.

This was not anything that had grown from blown-in seeds. The plants were too ugly – too barren, at least – to be a parting gift from Ellie. A few buds were about to open, but, otherwise, the plants seemed to be devoid of flowers. More specifically, the petals seemed to have fallen off.

She felt the hardy leaves, the concentric rings of alternately dark and light green. She noted the curved serration at the edges of the almost circular leaves, how it all seemed to radiate from the point where it joined the stem. She brought out her phone and did a search for red flowering plants. These empty-stalked plants, and the petals that she had found the day before, were geraniums, but this knowledge did not help her in any way.

She stepped out to the edge of her balcony and saw that there was a marked difference between the upper balconies, like her own, and those down at garden level. The lower balconies were full of flowering plants and terrace furniture. One from the top, she had always desired to be further up. Now she was not so sure. Perhaps it was too warm and dry on the upper balconies, and plants thrived better down low.

She heard a crash from the bathroom. Sound was no longer a criterion by which Eva could tell if something was happening in her own apartment or next door. The pinging crash-smash continued to issue from the direction of the bathroom, and Eva might have presumed the noise was coming from her neighbours' were it not that the tiles on the wall of the shower had appeared a little loose that morning, the grout between two of them broken away. In the steam of the moment, she had attributed this detail to Ellie's over-zealous cleaning.

As she traversed her own living room, Eva hoped against overriding doubt that she was hearing her neighbours' bathroom fall apart, in increasingly frequent crashes. She opened the bathroom door and watched, like one perceiving something uncannily beautiful, as all the tiles on the party wall cascaded in near musical sequence to the floor.

All was still and hushed, the only movement a low cloud of dust above the mound of tile fragments. All the tiles from that one wall lay on the floor. The grout had fallen off along with the tiles in places, revealing patches of bright blue waterproof membrane. Eva stood completely motionless in the doorway.

She heard footsteps in the bathroom that lay back-to-back with hers and the mouse-squeak of a voice at the other end of a telephone call.

My heart, said the pianist, it must have been my neighbour. That's the last thing I need. I've three estate agents coming for evaluations next week ... Well, I hope so, but, if he insists, we can put it on the market. I'm not too pushed either way.

Eva tried to make out the mashed words of the other half of the phone conversation.

No need, said the pianist. She's head of the board, so she'll take care of it herself, whatever happened ... I know, but it's just she's a bit of a nutcase. I'm going to pretend I heard nothing ... I'm serious. She gives the term highly strung a whole new meaning. If she was an instrument, you couldn't play her ... Yeah, yeah, I know ... No, I feel good about this, actually. I don't know, I think I've only kept him this long because having someone needy around me made me feel capable, if you know what I mean ... That's it, nail on the head.

Eva's own phone rang in the living room, and she crept away from the bathroom, closing the door after her, but she noticed a silence like the pianist was listening.

The locksmith was cancelling on her, and she could hardly believe it.

I will hold you accountable if there's another break-in, she said.

I'm sorry, I just can't fit you in. Things are hectic, like I said, and we had an unforeseen delay on another project. I'll get to you next week sometime, I promise, and I've ordered your new lock.

You will have my complaint in writing, said Eva, and I will be in touch with the consumer association if you don't prioritize this. Somebody broke in!

I'll be round as soon as your new lock arrives, next week, maybe, or the following week at the latest, all right?

No, that is not all right.

It's the best I can do, I'm afraid. I have to go now. Bye now, he said, and he hung up.

She flung the phone onto the sofa and growled. She balanced her forehead between her thumb and middle finger until the pumping stopped. Then she went out onto the balcony and looked around for her plate of crackers.

It was gone.

The plants, if they had ever been there, were also absent.

She ran to the apartment door, which was closed. She crouched down to inspect the flour on the doormat. It still held nothing but her own footprints.

*And hurry — back and forth — make haste — get on now — to and fro — and come back quick — push on — electrons, motion — this way mostly, that direction, this one, move in one direction, back and forth — a buzz — a whizz — there is resistance — bring on change — and charge to resist change — charge quickly now — the switch is on — and all is flow so all is pull — or push — ampere a volt forced through an ohm — at fifty, sixty times per second, alternate — charged waves — assembly, wires — the skin effect: the surface keep to — shielding, with coaxial geometry of the corona discharge — bundled, cable harness — feel resistance to this haste which gives off heat — which generates — which dissipates — the stealthy flow — the stream of charged so particles — resist the power of V is I by R.*

# Fritjof

Fritjof decided it was a good idea to be changing the light bulb in the hallway just as Raj arrived. He put the stepladder in place and balanced a light bulb in its cardboard box on the top step.

Frida, do you think ...

Don't interrupt me, she said, and continued into the dining room, talking to herself like a madwoman. She had been talking about her computer the last twenty minutes, as if there were actually something wrong with it. She had a 3D render going in the background, and, on a laptop of that capacity, anyone could have told her it was going to slow things down.

He climbed up and gave the lamp a little tug, but it stayed in place. He climbed up further and stroked the ceiling gently with his palm. He could feel it. He rubbed his hand along the adjacent wall too, for comparison. It was exactly the same sensation. He took the bulb out of its box and tapped the screw-in end off the ceiling, lightly. It made just the noise he expected. The resistance too was ordinary.

Then he jabbed the ceiling with the bulb, and it went through. He gasped and let go, and it fell right out again, landing in his palm. It didn't leave a mark.

Both ways, he said.

Holding his sleeve over his hand, he screwed out the hot light bulb, ready for its replacement. With the hall lights out, he noticed there was a peculiar blue glow coming from the ceiling. One point seemed to glow white.

He went to the living-room window, stepped up to the glass and away. He put his head out the window and pulled back inside. He was certain. The glow he saw on the ceiling was the full moon. He walked around the apartment with his eyes on the moving disc of lunar light, guided by the moon.

At the sound of the door buzzer, he returned to his ladder and climbed up.

I'm drawing his gaze upwards, Frida, he said.

Frida buzzed Raj in.

They waited for him to make his way up the four flights of stairs.

Raj came in and looked up at Fritjof, and from Fritjof to the ceiling lamp, and Fritjof, of course, was none the wiser. His connivance had ruined the possibility of interpreting whether Raj's gaze was drawn upwards on entering. Still, Raj didn't say anything about the lack of a ceiling. He didn't seem shocked.

Raj insisted on taking off his shoes, even though Frida told him there was no need. She was probably afraid he would find the floor damp. He did look down at his feet as he walked, but he didn't seem bothered by the floor.

Frida led Raj into the dining room where she had her laptop set up, and Fritjof padded after them.

I've no idea what it is, said Frida. It's just slower than usual.

Fritjof interrupted, Can I take your jacket, Raj?

The guy looked frightened. He even seemed to edge away.

No, it's all right, thanks, he said.

It is a bit cold, said Frida. We've all the windows open.

Raj was sitting in front of the laptop, clicking, but now he looked around at the dining-room window and through the open double doors to the living room. There was nothing particularly upward about his gaze.

It is nice and airy up here, he said, the opposite of our apartment. We're having problems.

Fritjof was uncertain how much he should read into the use of the word *airy*. They had always thought of it as airy themselves, even before the roof started non-performing.

Strange to think it is the same building, said Raj, or the same development. We rented our apartment unseen. Do you know who lived there before us? Did they discover anything strange?

Various students, I think, said Frida. They were pretty young, all of them, and it was empty a good while before that, before it was rented out. It used to be the maids' quarters.

Were there any complaints? said Raj.

Frida looked at Fritjof, and he could tell she was worried she had said something wrong, worried Raj was insulted she had called his apartment the maids' quarters. He had every right to take offence.

I doubt there were maids here that long, said Frida. Could you imagine having a maid in an apartment like this, so close. I mean, it can't have been comfortable for the maids. It was mainly single, male engineers who lived here in the beginning. It was built by a company for its employees.

So, our apartment has always been in use? said Raj. It was never a store or a coal room or something?

Don't let her bore you about the building, said Fritjof. Our grandfathers were partners in the architectural firm who designed these blocks, you see, so we're a bit over-informed.

A bit over-interested, said Frida.

She was laughing in an unconvincing manner, making a noise she didn't normally make, though perhaps Raj wouldn't notice this, not being familiar with her habits.

No, that is good, said Raj. I was wondering, actually, if you know anything about what's under the building.

You mean the basement? said Frida.

What's under our apartment?

Oh, no, that's the lowest level. And don't worry, you're on solid ground. It's built on rock.

So, there's no soil underneath?

No, I wouldn't say so, said Frida, maybe a layer of gravel.

Fritjof went and dimmed the lights in the living room so the lunar glow could be seen through it at an angle from the dining room. He noticed that Raj had isolated the rendering program and would soon be concluding his examination of the perfectly fine computer.

Sorry I couldn't come earlier, said Raj. I was at university all day.

That's a long day's work, said Fritjof, trying to sound impressed.

I'm doing a postdoc alongside my research position.

He said it as if it was nothing, as if he had just told Fritjof he was interested in motorbikes.

Do you mind if I interrupt this application? he said to Frida. It's using most of your capacity.

Be my guest, said Frida. I didn't realize that was still running.

Is it long since you restarted?

Ages. Is that all it is, do you think? I'm such an idiot when it comes to technology, Fritjof too.

Fritjof nodded eagerly, and it would have looked fake, but Raj did not look up.

Let's see, said Raj, yes. There's not really anything wrong with the computer. No bugs or anything, as far as I can see. Maybe do visualizations remotely on a stationary machine, if you can. It uses a lot of memory.

Frida reddened, and he couldn't tell if it was intentional or not. She asked how much she owed him, but Raj refused to accept anything, even when Frida insisted it was her own fault and said she felt bad for bringing him all the way up here for something so silly.

It's no problem at all, said Raj. This is what neighbours are for.

Well, said Frida, thank you then, and our architectural services are at your disposal if you should ever need them.

Fritjof could feel the visit coming to a premature close.

Will you stay for a beer, Raj, he said, or a glass of wine? It's almost the weekend, after all.

A beer would be lovely, said Raj.

It was easier than expected.

Out in the living room, he handed Raj a bottle of IPA. Frida was pulling plastic off the armchairs, explaining that they were about to have the place painted. They hadn't discussed this excuse, and Fritjof didn't know if Frida planned it or came up with it on the spot.

Actually, Raj, he said, maybe you can help us settle this: we're not sure if we need to paint the ceiling. It's such an awkward job. What do you think?

He watched as Raj squinted at the ceiling.

I can't really see it, he said.

Frida's eyes were wide, flitting between the two of them in a manner sure to divulge their secret.

Is it possible to turn up the lights? said Raj.

There was a strange landing feeling in Fritjof's chest, that could be either disappointment or relief. He went and undimmed the lights, ridding the room of its lunar glow.

It looks fine, said Raj. I don't think you need to paint it. It's lovely here, so high above the ground.

Fritjof sat down in an armchair and tipped the neck of his bottle toward Raj by way of cheers.

Do you know my landlord? said Raj.

Well, not personally, said Fritjof.

His aunt lives in your building, said Frida, on the third floor. He comes to our AGMs on her behalf sometimes. He's an estate agent.

Frida shivered at her last words.

You don't like him? said Raj.

I don't mean to be rude, said Frida. It's just that architects and estate agents, well, we don't usually see eye to eye.

He does not take good care of our apartment, said Raj. There is a smell and a leak somewhere, but he will not fix it. He insists it is our fault, but it needs investigation. There is soil all over the floor. It could be a structural problem with the ground slab. You two would know what's going on if you saw it. The landlord just tells us to clean it up.

That's completely irresponsible, said Frida. I knew we shouldn't have sold him that apartment – though it's nice to have you as a neighbour, Raj, a silver lining.

We are trying to move out, said Raj. The conditions are so bad, and we think someone must have a key. We think someone comes in when we are not there and in the night. We don't have a proper door.

That's terrible, said Fritjof.

You know what we should do? said Frida. We should bring it up at the AGM tomorrow. You have a right to come, Raj.

But we only rent.

You can't vote on anything, but you have a right to be there and to speak your mind. It's actually in the rules, and we'll support you, won't we, Fritjof?

215

Of course, said Fritjof, though he wondered if they should really be getting involved.

It's in everyone's interest that the basement apartment is well maintained, said Frida. It's the foundation that everything else is standing on.

I should probably tell you something, said Raj, tilting his beer bottle from side to side. We got two letters of complaint about the smell, but it is not our fault. We don't know where the smell is coming from, but there is all this earth on the floor and it seems there is some kind of leak, maybe cracks underneath the floor.

I'll bring it up, said Frida. They'll listen to me. Those Lofthus-Lunds are total snobs. They already have a big feud going on with the Klevelands who live upstairs from Hildegunn, that's Gunnar's aunt. Anyway, don't worry, Raj. We won't let him get away with this.

Will you come down to have a look, said Raj, putting his bottle on the coffee table. You know about foundations, don't you?

Sure we do, said Fritjof. Can I get you another? I've a six-pack cooling in the fridge.

No, thanks, said Raj. Why don't you call down to our place, meet my flatmates? They'll be delighted to hear that you can help us. They're at home now.

What are their names? said Fritjof.

Pradeep and Krishna.

Frida apologized and consoled Raj with the information that they had been living here for years and had hardly got to know anyone yet, not properly.

Will you come down to meet them and maybe you can make some sense of the leak?

Absolutely, said Frida. Are you home tomorrow?

Tomorrow? Yes, we can arrange a time.

Great. We'll come in the afternoon if that's all right. Better to see it in daylight and before the AGM.

They waited until they could no longer hear his footsteps.

Nothing, said Frida.

Did you notice that he used the word *airy*?

He's a polite guy, but he would have commented on the lack of a roof. He told you it didn't need to be painted.

Don't you think he gave the impression he felt he was kind of outside, said Fritjof, that the sky was open above him?

He saw the ceiling. It's visible.

Why did you get involved with Gunnar Lofthus? I know we owe Raj a favour, but we have bigger problems to contend with.

He pointed at the ceiling.

You can't see past your own nose, said Frida.

You're not making sense.

Listen then, Hildegunn and Linda are, as we know, arch-enemies.

Rivals and fiends, yes, go on.

We want to swap apartments with Knut and Une, and it might even still be in Linda's name, so, well, we must choose sides.

I don't get it.

On the one side, said Frida, you have Gunnar and Hildegunn. On the other side you have the Klevelands and Raj and his flatmates. We're with the Klevelands.

We should pay them a visit now, said Fritjof, launch our idea.

Tomorrow morning, said Frida. We'll have to bring them in here too.

They looked around them at the water-stained furniture. Despite their feverish airing out, there was still a smell of damp. The walls, which had recently been the clearest shade of white available, now had smudges of grey in places. They would have to wash them too – or dry them – both.

# Friday

*It gives you comfort to see the craftsman's hand in our arrangement, but the hands that laid us lie deep in mud. We were won from beneath the surface of this great sphere and moulded cuboid to fit your courses. We were baked at temperatures you reserve for your dead. We were transformed forever by this heat, and you thought this would prevent your own degradation. You did not anticipate what burning us would do to you. You made from us a crust, stacking us so we might never sag, adhered with a concoction of rock stronger than us. This is your innate condition, you told us. Endure, was your refrain, stay this way forever, so that we may live on in your fair-faced layers.*

# Sonja

Sonja could smell the garden, weighed down with dew, the chilled beginning of a green-spiced day in May.

She was convinced that what she smelled was green, that it was alive, growing, moving at a pace invisible to the naked eye. Sonja's eyes were closed, but her nostrils ticklishly identified earth, twigs and leaves. There was a slightly musky smell too, which, with brazen specificity, announced itself as the smell of feathers. She wondered how she could know what a feather smelled like, but every child picked up a crow's feather at some stage. She could recall teasing apart the barbs.

Roses: she smelled them — not the fragrant flowers themselves, which were only budding yet, but, if she listened carefully, she could appreciate the shuffling comfort of a bed of rose bushes.

Also, a gentle dripping: dewdrops falling leaf to leaf to earth. Tap, tap, tap, all in time, and then the silent tap, the one awaited, the one that was the dewdrop reaching the soil, and the soil made no splat of the drop, but rather absorbed it, soaked it up, divided the tight globe into its component molecules; and roots reached out, in an if-you-please manner, soaking up what moisture was available with the kind of thanks only a plant can express, a humble nod to water and nutrients, which are never stolen, only elevated from dark earth to bright leaf, brought before the sun. She was an idiot to put such trust in her own sensory understanding, but, in this moment, it felt true.

Overlaid upon these smells and sounds of a garden at its molecular level, Sonja was aware of larger movements, not initiated by the plants themselves, but by nestlings – her skylarks? – snapping twigs and repositioning wings.

She heard a leafy branch splat-tat against the painted plasterwork that covered the bricks outside. It ruffled insistently on the wall, smacked, seemingly at will, gave up and recommenced without any notice, without any logic Sonja could make out.

She could not see the windows properly, but they were more than closed. Dovydas and Matas had sealed them with continuous strips of springy rubber between the sashes and the frames. Her wall, too, was fixed, the missing bricks replaced with mortar and a thick layer of plaster. They would return in a few days to apply the screed. Sonja told them she would do the painting herself, to save the cost. Wasn't she a kind of painter, after all? She didn't give in when they insisted she was getting a good price for good work. She wondered if she should tell them she would take care of the screed herself too, or just paint the plaster directly – but she wanted this done properly. Maybe, she thought, her position sliding along a mental see-saw, maybe it would be better if she let them do everything, paint and all. Then they would be responsible for it. They had offered an under-the-table no-tax arrangement, but she turned that down. She wanted a certificate of completion, stamped and signed with someone else's name on it. She wanted everything out in the open.

Sitting up, she could feel it on her cheeks. It came in puffs, on and off, but she was sure of it: there was live air in this room.

She switched on the bedside lamp and approached the exterior wall at the pace of one nearing a horse that might shy. The smell of the plaster had not lingered, though it was not yet thoroughly dry. She could see where it was dappled darker, giving off its wet load at its own pace.

Clothed in only a singlet and underpants, her skin was amply exposed to the rush of wind. She stood by the walls and moved her arms like scissors, noting that over here there was more of a gust than over there. She isolated one of the worst patches, and it didn't correspond to any spot where a brick had been missing. This was a new patch, a bigger patch, and she would have noticed if it had been like this before now. Dovydas and Matas would have seen it. They hacked off all the plaster on this wall and showed it to her. They counted the missing bricks and told her the total: nine.

She wished that Eva had come over to look at it then. Sonja had sent her slightly blurry photos, and Eva said she couldn't make it out properly, but they would bring it up at the AGM. She planned to take another picture when Dovydas and Matas were gone, but they plastered faster than she imagined possible, and all was fixed and covered up when they left. Eva would have to sanction paying for the work, just as soon as the others realized they had the same problem – if that was even the case. It might just be happening to her.

She wondered if Dovydas and Matas had played a trick on her, just as the original builders had done. She was not quite upfront about how much she wanted to do herself. Maybe she had left them with so little work that the job was a loss to them, including travel and set-up time. They could have said so if it was a problem, but perhaps they had. A job that took them one hour would take her ten hours, they told her. It was not possible to guarantee a good result if they did not do everything, they said, but she held her ground. She thought she was being assertive, but perhaps this was self-sabotage, and there was revenge behind their smiles which she failed to translate.

She winced at the cold pain of metal underfoot: her largest palette knife. Lacking a hammer, she found a wooden clog she couldn't recall purchasing that would do the trick. She hesitated a moment, with the utensil poised at the windy spot, and then let the heel of the clog swing.

It took no force at all. Soon she had cleared away the place where five bricks were missing in a jagged hole. She leaned her face in closer. The hole was large enough to fit her whole head inside. She could see all the way through to the external layer of brickwork, outside the wall cavity. Putting her hand into the cavity, she pawed around, felt cold, rough bricks and mortar, and a strong draught.

Her fingertips touched the outer brickwork gently, not wanting to break through this last shield.

It was impressive that her builders had managed to plaster so flat and clean over this sizeable hole. It hardly made sense, but, true to their own words, they were skilful. She could not report them without any decisive proof of what they had done. Call them off, that's all she could do, and get a local firm to fix it up and document the damage to present to the insurance company and the board of residents for compensation. Five bricks! And that was only the first spot she examined.

The clear tones of a goldfinch sounded at the other side of the wall, and she backed away, retreated all the way to the kitchen on the opposite side of the building, up against a whole other external wall.

She closed the sliding doors between the kitchen and the living room. Isolated like this, the kitchen seemed a different place entirely. The living-room wall was still intact, visually, but she felt its secret offence. She knew what the plasterwork might be hiding. She closed her bedroom door too, and the door between the living room and the hallway, so that the apartment was now divided in two, partitioned into the good half towards the street and the bad half towards the garden.

It was easy now to regret the hole she made in the wall, but she was afraid she might succumb to something similar again. This was the same compulsion that always made her squeeze a pimple, even though she knew it would get infected. She could not entirely trust herself, especially in the middle of the night. She would wait to go in again until she was certain she had fully shaken off sleep.

The shrewd course of action would have been to remove the plaster and expose the hole in front of someone or, better still, to record while someone else did it. She needed proof.

She rang around to builders, names she had seen on scaffolding in the area. Builders rose early but it took a while before anyone answered. When she got through to someone, he said they might have an opening in two or three weeks. She wanted to tell him there would be nothing left by then. It made no difference that she pleaded impending visitors. The wall is going nowhere, he said.

She would have to call the insurance assessor again, and Eva – but it was already Friday. She could bring all this up at the AGM that evening. For now, she sent Eva a text: *Please call in to see my wall before AGM. Bricks missing! One patch left open for inspection.* A compulsive vision of Eva's forefinger pointed at her, with the words: you did this!

This must be happening to the neighbours around her too. They just hadn't noticed yet, because they didn't listen to the wind at night to the same extent as she did. She would call on them all before the AGM. Together, they could solve this.

The wind whistled in her bedroom, and she followed the sound like the Pied Piper's flute.

As she opened the door to her bedroom, she had the feeling of stepping outside. There was foliage on the ground, strewn all around.

She stomped about, making snap and crackle noises on the leaves and twigs she trampled on. She crouched to examine them and burst into a fit of her pollen-allergy sneezing. The floor was dusty. There was a mixture of fresh, light green, miniature leaves, only partly grown, and dark brown, crispy leftovers from the autumn. A bee was buzzing somewhere in the room, but she couldn't see it.

Approaching the hole in the wall, she wondered if a pressure difference between inside and out had sucked this foliage in. The five bricks were missing, as before, but, deeper inside the wall, three bricks in the outer layer were now missing too. Her hand reached in, but she stopped herself from touching the exterior plaster. She was not willing to upset it, this last covering, a brittle veil to the garden. It was less than a window.

Fear brought her two steps back, putting the wall out of reach. She closed her eyes, breathed, and looked again.

She was quite certain these three bricks had been there when she last inspected the hole. They must have fallen down the cavity, though the cavity between the two layers of brickwork was narrow and not a full gap. Stabilizing bricking crossed between the two layers, but there was some sort of aeration going on between them all right. It didn't seem enough of a gap for bricks to fall through. She craned her head inside the hole, but it was too dark to make anything out.

Sonja looked at her phone, overcome by the conviction that she should call for help but unsure who would come, who would understand.

She shone her phone lamp down the cavity, but it didn't reveal much. She took flash photographs down the hole, and to the sides and upwards too. It was impossible to make out any distinct pile of wedged bricks in the jumble down there, and she couldn't really tell what she was looking at.

That buzzing again: there must be two bees in the room, at least. She looked around to locate them. Up on the orange metal lampshade on the ceiling, a bird was perched. It jerked its beak, looked at her with one eye.

A skylark, said Sonja.

# Raj

Raj felt it in his bones, more specifically in his shins and his spine, this hacking, chipping. Soon it would crack right through some part of him. He was lying the wrong way in the bed, his head at the end closest to the door.

A faint glow of civil twilight came through the thin curtains, distorted by the bushes outside, making strange patterns on the walls like in an overgrown ruin. It sounded like the building was crumbling around him, though he could see no evidence of this.

The noise continued. His own walls transported the sound to him, but the hacking was taking place further away, on some other part of the block. Who was building, or destructing, in the middle of the night – and could it possibly be allowed? Tap, tap, tap. Someone might be knocking on the door, but this was not a wooden noise. This was the sound of metal on stone.

A yawn brought a musty taste to his tongue. It was Pradeep's watch. It was his turn to sleep.

The rapping continued. It was hard to tell if the noise was increasing or if he was simply becoming more alert to it. He tried to make a judgement on whether he was being shaken by each whack or if it was just a feeling to accompany the sound. Something or someone might be trying to get into their apartment from below, or from one of those basement storage rooms that lay wall to wall with the corridor and kitchen. Someone could be trapped in a storage room, had perhaps been trapped there for weeks, stinking and digging holes underneath their floor in an attempt to escape, only succeeding in creating a passage for mice, rats and earthworms to come through. Maybe she had been locked in that room by an evil neighbour; maybe they should help.

The hacking stopped. In the quiet that followed, Raj heard a siren outside, not on their street, somewhere further off.

His rubber boots, bought the day before and left beside his bed overnight, were submerged to the ankles in brown earth. The insides were clean, empty of soil.

He ploughed his way to his desk. He could have stepped over the dirt like one does when walking through shallow water, but Raj wanted to get a sense of this earth's resistance.

His phone stalled as he pulled the slider through the night's footage. He needed the others. He shoved everything into his laptop satchel and tramped sinking footsteps to the door – which would not budge. He kicked and scraped away earth until he could tug the door inwards.

They had left all the lights on the night before, to better illuminate any intruder and, as Krishna had argued, to keep the darkness from swallowing them. Raj was concerned the intruder might not come in if he saw the lights on, but Pradeep told him his thirst for knowledge was verging on self-destructive.

The floor in the hallway was the same: ankle-high earth spread neatly – so much. It smelled like farmland. All the lights were on, but it still seemed dark.

He knocked on Pradeep's door. The knock was absorbed like in a sound studio, and Pradeep didn't answer. He tried the door handle and found it locked.

Pradeep!

The word was confiscated by the soft earth as soon as it left his lips. He rattled the handle and pounded on the door.

Pradeep!

Raj! Come in!

The door is locked!

I'm coming. Wait.

The apartment smelled of the outdoors – not really farmland, something less cultivated. This was an improvement on the smell of basement and almost a consolation.

The door opened an acute angle and Raj poked his head in. Pradeep was digging and flinging the earth away, using his wash basket. He had taken the time to put on plastic gloves.

Did you catch anyone on film? said Raj. It's all over the apartment.

It's too much. How did we sleep through this? There must have been a whole team of them.

Raj came in and pointed to Pradeep's wide-open window.

They came through the windows – but let's look at the footage. Mine was stalling. Pradeep gave Raj his phone for inspection, while he opened the film on his computer. He had double widescreens on his desk. It was a clearer image, more detailed. Pradeep spooled through it at x24. It took fifteen minutes to play all the way through, and they both scrolled manually through their phones and Raj's laptop at the same time. It looked like nothing was happening at any time, the whole night long, but at high speed they saw the earth gradually building up.

You went too fast, said Raj. My screen's so small. We must have missed it. Krishna! Come here!

He's sick, said Pradeep. Let's do this again, properly.

They repeated, with all their devices before them, playing simultaneously at half the speed. Raj's eyes stung, and his legs ached from bracing on the soft floor. They did not look away for a full half-hour. Nothing.

It looks like it was building up for the whole night, said Raj. Here, look at this: twelve, three, five. Look at the edge. It got deeper and deeper over the whole night.

Do you think the floor's sinking?

No, the skirting boards and the door are the same. Unless the whole building is sinking. It makes no sense. Frida said the foundations were built directly onto rock.

Raj examined the wooden floor under the earth. It seemed intact. He thought he had figured it out. He had been sure it was some neighbour, some lunatic they could blame and report. Now they were back to square one.

This is a natural phenomenon, he said.

This is too much. Look, Raj ...

Pradeep pressed his boots into the earth an authoritative distance from him. This was a pose Raj had seen him do before. It had something of a peacock about it.

Firstly, said Pradeep, there is something totally wrong with this place. We have established there is no psychotic neighbour we can report, and, whether it's a curse or some force of nature, I really couldn't care less. Whatever it is, there's nothing we can do about it. We have tried all your plans and failed. This place is doomed.

There are no footprints, Pradeep.

The second weird thing that's going on is that we're still here. This, and this alone, is in our power to change, Raj.

There must be some explanation.

We must leave.

Pradeep pushed aside the dirty clothes he had heaped on his bed and sat down, sinking deep, any evocation of peacock feathers gone.

Look, he said, I checked, and all the hostels and hotels are booked out, at least any that are remotely affordable.

Krishna does not have enough money, said Raj. Neither do I. I have a huge loan, and I spent so much on flights my credit card is maxed out.

There was nothing available online, and when I finally got through the hotel receptionists all said they were having unprecedented bookings. I rang everyone I know last night, looking for someone to take us in, all of us.

Pradeep looked at Raj without pride. He looked like his own poor cousin.

I told them that we had a terrible leak and about the hotels being full, but they all said no. It's not their fault. I couldn't get them to understand how bad it is.

Raj didn't like to mention, but the walls were thin, and he had heard these calls, not the words, but the tone, which began enthusiastic and ended apologetic each time.

It's a matter of perspective, said Raj. They could not understand the gravity of our position because you could not possibly explain the weirdness of what is happening.

I told the truth to a senior colleague, and she told me to see a psychologist. Everyone else was just worried about my stuff, telling me to make sure we get compensation for anything damaged. It was like they were in a different world, where this could not happen. I even asked my exes, Raj, but they're both shacked up with someone new by now, and they didn't feel comfortable having an ex staying over, naturally enough, by their non-nightmare logic.

We'll figure something out.

The thing is, Raj ...

Pradeep's words trailed off, and his chest became increasingly concave.

The thing is? said Raj.

You see, one of my new colleagues, this intern, he said he'd let me stay a few nights, but, you see, his mother is staying with him at the moment, so he doesn't have room for you and Krishna.

It's okay. We'll go straight to the board with this, or the police. Look around you, Pradeep. No one will blame us for this. It's a natural disaster.

Do you have someone to call?

I know exactly who I'm going to call. I'll call the landlord, and the board of residents, and I'll either call the police or the fire brigade, I'm not sure which. What do you think?

I think we should leave. Krishna!

There was no answer, but there were no other sounds either. They were in a place beyond sound.

Do you think he has left? said Pradeep.

They tumbled out the window.

Stop crouching like you're hiding, said Pradeep. If someone sees us, they should help.

Raj broke his way through the bushes and fell in through Krishna's open window. Krishna lay on his back in bed, mumbling.

I can't move, he said. I'm sinking.

Together, they lifted Krishna to a sitting position and poured water from a plastic bottle into his mouth. He coughed and the water dribbled over his chin, and when they let go of his arms he sank down to his supine position again.

I'm too wet, said Krishna.

Raj put a hand to Krishna's forehead. It was cold and damp.

What's the matter? said Raj. Tell us.

I'm heavy. I can't move. The weight. It's rotting me.

I'm calling an ambulance, said Pradeep.

Raj took Krishna's pulse: it was fine. He pulled down his lower eyelids, not sure exactly what he was looking for, but he observed nothing out of the ordinary.

On the phone, Pradeep had the enunciation of a war correspondent.

He is extremely unwell, he said. He cannot even move … No … Do you have diarrhoea, Krishna?

Krishna's lips replied, No.

No, but he can't move, don't you get it? He's completely weak … Yes … Can you understand what I'm saying, Krishna? Can you smile? Raise your arms.

Krishna gave an unconvincing grin and seemed to try and move his arms.

He can't move his arms, or any other part of him, like I've already told you. He is too weak. But … What … But … You don't seem to understand. We need to get him out of here. There was a leak – or a landslide.

He looked at Raj, and Raj nodded his approval.

There has been a landslide in our apartment, said Pradeep. Okay, he said, and in a whisper, They're transferring me. There's been a major incident so they're hardly taking anyone in. They think it's just MS or something, told me to call his GP – hello!

Pradeep moved as if he was about to pace around, but his feet were stuck. His upper body leaned this way and that as he spoke, backing his arguments with vehemence that would remain unseen and ineffective. He put the phone on speaker.

Is anyone trapped? said the calmest of voices.

No, but my flatmate can't move, said Pradeep. You must come and help.

Okay, any idea how deep it is?

It's ankle high.

There was a pause on the line.

Look, my flatmate is terribly weak.

Is he stuck under the rocks?

No, it's earth.

What happened, exactly?

There is just all this earth, all over the place.

And your flatmate is not trapped underneath?

No, but ...

Any structural damage?

I believe the foundation is cracked, said Raj. It is not safe here. There is ankle-high earth covering the entire floor of the apartment. It was not here yesterday. Yesterday there were traces of earth.

You should ring your insurance company and stay somewhere else tonight.

My friend can't move. We are in need of assistance.

You should have called for an ambulance. I'm transferring you now.

Raj explained this time, in what he thought was a calm and rational tone, but it made no difference. They refused to come, told them to bring Krishna to his GP on Monday, to avoid the A&E unless his condition deteriorated significantly, if he had difficulty breathing or blue lips.

Pradeep sat on the bed, his head tipped low.

We'll bring you ourselves, Krishna, he said.

No, leave me.

Don't be so dramatic.

I'm ringing the head of the board, said Raj. Ring the landlord, Pradeep. He might listen to you.

Eva Holt did not answer but sent him a text saying she was busy with the AGM today and would be in touch in due course. He replied with an urgent but calm description of what had happened. She texted back telling him to phone Gunnar Lofthus, who she said was responsible for any internal damage.

Mr Lofthus, you do not understand, said Pradeep. Just listen ... But ... No!

Pradeep rang off.

He said he is going to evict us unless we get the place in order, and we can forget about ever getting our deposit back. I told him we would report him to the board. Is she coming over?

She said it is the landlord's responsibility, said Raj. There's an AGM this evening. Frida said we should attend.

We'll be gone by then. Get your architect friends to come now. Ring them.

Raj did as he was told, watching as Pradeep stroked Krishna's forehead. Krishna's lips continued their murmur.

Raj, how are you? said Frida. Lovely to see you last night. Sorry, we're still in bed. What time is it? Oh!

We have an emergency.

Just a second. Wait. Jesus. Right, go ahead, Raj.

The floor is covered in earth. It's a thick layer. I don't know how it happened. It makes no sense.

No way, that's terrible. Earth? Fritjof, did you hear that? There's a pile of earth on their floor. Did a wall cave in?

It is all over the floor, ankle-deep.

Do you think someone dumped it in the window?

I don't know. I mean, I suppose it's possible, but we filmed it and saw no one. We would appreciate it if you or Fritjof could come and have a look at it. You will understand what's going on. Can you come over?

We will, absolutely. This is horrible, Raj. I can't believe anyone could be so nasty. You didn't see anyone? I think you should call the police.

The police?

Absolutely, this is not on.

But you'll come over too?

Yes, we'll see you this afternoon, as planned, unless you want to postpone? You sound like you have enough on your hands.

No, please come over as soon as you can.

Come right now, said Pradeep.

Come straight away. We need your help, Frida. The landlord was horrible on the phone, and Eva is busy. We really have no one else to turn to.

Raj, listen, this is going to be fine, believe me. Fritjof and I fully support you. Now, we have a removal company coming this morning. We're getting the floors oiled. But we'll call over to you after that, all right? As soon as we can. Raj, this is going to be fine, do you hear me?

Thanks, Frida. Come as soon as you can.

239

An SMS pinged in Pradeep's hand, and his face fell as he read.

It's my colleague, my ... He can't ... He says ...

Pradeep seemed to lose the power of summary and proceeded to read out the message:

*Sorry mate, have to cancel on you. Brother and family showed up unannounced. Honestly, any other time. Sure you'll find something else. Sorry so last minute.*

I'm going to get help, said Raj. I will drag someone over here if I must. They have to see it to believe it. I don't have enough words to explain.

He climbed out the window and looked back at his friends.

I have no choice, said Pradeep, who was looking at the face of his phone like it might provide some sense.

Raj looked at the list of names at the door to 14B. He regretted running over without washing and changing, but reminded himself this was an emergency. Over here, at the opposite side of the block, it seemed like a different world or time. He pressed the buzzer beside the name Holt. Something was wrong. It didn't buzz.

Frida and Fritjof's buzzer also felt odd when he pressed it, loose. He waited. He pressed it again, and again. It didn't make a noise like it had done the day before. There was no answer.

He tried phoning Frida, but it cut off straight away. She rejected his call.

Standing back from the door, he looked up along the façade to where his only allies lived. Their windows were open. All the windows in the block were open, apart from a few which had been demounted.

He called: Frida!

Fritjof! Frida!

A man in paisley pyjamas stuck his head out a window on the third floor.

Do you know what time it is? he said. Get out of here. Some people are trying to sleep.

Frida! he called, again.

Romeo, she's not interested, said the man. Get out of here before I call the police.

A piano started playing inside, and the man growled as he turned away.

# Knut

Bouncy, bouncy.

Teddy was laughing like a happy hammer drill. Knut rose, too suddenly, and steadied himself with a hand on the wall. It felt like the ground was giving way underneath him. His feet were used to polished wood. Une had accepted all the shortcuts the fitters suggested, such as not bothering to remove and replace the skirting boards and only nailing a wooden bead along the edge of the carpet to keep it in place. Yesterday evening he had strolled around barefooted and felt like he was on holidays, or away at a business conference. He felt like he was in a hotel, especially in the bedroom.

He followed Teddy's voice.

On a bidge is fa'ing down, fa'ing down, fa'ing down. On a bidge ...

In the hallway, a single stiletto attested to Bibbi's late return home. He nudged it with his toe and found that it was stuck. Crouching down, he discovered that the heel was pressed through the floor. He tugged it out and put his finger in the hole. It was deep. His finger went in, up to his second knuckle, but he felt no wood underneath. They should have waited for woollen carpets. This polyester was rubbish. He wanted to pull it all up. Something was clearly happening underneath. A weird allergic reaction. Something. There had to be some explanation.

There was a knock on the door, a reserved little tap, and Knut found Sonja Flynn outside.

Sonja, good morning, he said in a whisper.

Sorry to disturb you, I'm just calling around ahead of the AGM this evening.

This evening, you're right. I'd forgotten about it. I'll be there – or Une will, at least.

He rested a shoulder against the wall for support, and actually felt more upright, tilted like this. He hoped he didn't seem strange, but he was retired now. He was entitled to be unsteady.

I just wondered whether you've ever had any trouble with your external walls, said Sonja, the one towards the garden in particular. I found bricks missing in mine, you see, and I wondered if it was the same with anyone else.

Bricks missing? No, I'd have noticed that, no. That's terrible.

You haven't noticed any draughts through the wall? Perhaps you haven't thought to check.

She was leaning her head inwards, trying to get a look at the wall in question, but she wouldn't see it from there.

I'm sorry, said Knut, I'd invite you in, only my grandson ...

243

Teddy sounded like he was having a great time, singing, Iron a' steel, bend a' bow, bend a' bow, bend a' bow ...

Oh, sorry, said Sonja, right. Well, see you this evening at the meeting then, but promise me you'll take a close look at that wall in the meantime. There might be draughty spots you've overlooked. I'm sure it can't just be me.

Teddy was hopping from spot to spot in the living room. There was no pattern on the carpet that the child might pretend was lily pads. He was making it all up, in the wide imagination cushioned by those golden curls. Teddy wouldn't stop for a kiss from his grandfather. He kept at his game and, following closely behind him, Knut heard that the floor made a squeaking sound along with the boy's spring.

They had laid the carpet directly onto the parquet flooring – without glue, of course. They didn't want to ruin the wood underneath. The oak parquet had always squeaked in places. What wooden floor didn't? Strange that it now seemed more pronounced. It should be the opposite.

Still overcome by dizziness, Knut lay flat out on the couch. He couldn't help feeling his feet were higher than his head. He turned, exchanging top and toe, and that was better, though he didn't have such a good view of Teddy.

Who was that? said Une.

She walked towards him with legs too wide apart and knees bent for stability.

Sonja wanted to know if there was a draught in here. Don't forget the AGM this evening.

Knut pulled his feet up and Une collapsed on the end of the couch.

I suppose I should go, she said.

Bibbi staggered into the living room.

Do we have any paracetamol? she said.

Teddy was unaffected, though perhaps he simply couldn't articulate what he felt – or enjoyed it. Knut remembered spinning around to make himself dizzy as a child.

I'm too embarrassed to go back to the A&E, said Une. I made an appointment at a private clinic.

We could just have told them we found the marbles in a shoe, said Bibbi. We could say Teddy hid them.

No, said Teddy.

He'll tell on us, said Une, somehow managing to laugh. I don't mind paying, she said, and they can take three of us all at once. That's a great service. Knut, will you wait? We'll be in and out in no time. It's probably the same thing we all have.

But there's nothing wrong with Teddy, said Bibbi. He doesn't need to go.

If we've got some disease, said Knut, I want him tested. Anyway, one of us would have to stay behind to mind him, so he had may as well go along with you.

We'll call you as soon as we know any more, said Une. Get some rest while we're out and keep the windows open. I'm afraid there might be a gas leakage or something.

We don't have gas.

Well, keep them closed then. It has to be something. Until we know what it is, we should take every possible precaution.

They can't have been gone more than five minutes when the doorbell rang. What had they forgotten now?

It was Frida and Fritjof from the opposite block. Knut buzzed them in. He considered going halfway down the stairs to meet them, but he didn't feel up to it, so he let them come up and led them into the living room. The purple chairs were missing. Where had they put them? Frida and Fritjof stumbled onto the couch.

Can I trouble you for a glass of water, said Frida. I hope this isn't PMT again.

Fritjof blushed and elbowed his partner.

Sorry, said Frida, I just think we should speak more openly about some things.

Knut fetched water and coffee, and he pulled over a dining chair for himself, almost tripping on the carpet. Their visit baffled him. They had never called before today.

We got the idea while we were packing away our stuff to get the floors oiled, said Frida. You see, we were talking to Linda just the other day, and she was telling us how nice it was for her to have you and the family close by.

Do you oil your floors often? said Knut.

Do we ... well every few years I suppose, or we should. It's not that long since we moved in.

Knut poured coffee into each cup and sat down before he remembered the milk.

Milk or sugar?

Oh, no thanks, said Fritjof, this is fine. This is lovely. Go on, Frida.

They exchanged one of those glances that could only be understood from inside a relationship.

Well, talking to Linda, and arranging to get all our furniture moved out, said Frida, we had an idea, and it might seem a bit drastic, or sudden, but we just thought we'd see what you and Une think.

I don't entirely follow you.

We'd like to swap apartments.

Swap? Oh! You move in here and we move into yours?

It would be a proper sale, of course, said Fritjof. We can even pay you something extra, since this apartment has a better orientation, with the terrace towards the south-west. We would compensate you for that, of course, maybe 10 per cent or something like that?

They were both looking around them as they sipped their coffee, and Knut was relieved to see that their gazes were drawn more in an upward than a downward direction. They surely wouldn't approve of the carpet.

This is a surprise, he said, and he wondered if he could do it. They were younger than him, but older than Bibbi, and well beyond innocence. They were architects and would probably do a complete rehaul of the whole apartment, so any problem with the floor would be less of a bother to them than to him. It might even be the right thing to do, to leave this troubled home in more capable hands, and they were right: he had to think of Linda.

Take your time to think about it, said Frida. We know it's a big proposal to spring on you.

I'll have to talk it over with Une, but I must say I'm starting to like the idea. It would be a good thing for my mother. I'm sure of it. We tried to buy the apartment under this one, but the old woman there wouldn't sell. We wanted to have my mother in the same stairwell as us, but you could be waiting years for anything to come on the market.

I have to say, Knut, said Frida, we almost didn't come up. It seemed such a madcap idea, but it does make sense, doesn't it? Linda wouldn't have to move herself, which would be a real bonus, I imagine.

You're right there. Une and I were away in Africa when my father fell ill, and we never imagined he would die. You never can tell.

Carpe diem, said Fritjof.

Now, this place isn't perfect, as you can see.

Oh, not to worry, said Fritjof. We wouldn't be able to resist giving it a renovation, putting our own stamp on it. We're both architects, you know.

Yes, it would be in good hands. I was also just thinking that this might not be such bad timing. We only moved in this year, so we're still in the swing of it, if you like. We haven't completely grown into the apartment yet, and we got rid of a lot of stuff when we moved from our old house. Does your apartment have the same layout as this one?

They're practically mirror images, said Frida. We were looking at the plans and there are a few small differences. That window onto the terrace there is on the gable wall in our place, because of the orientation, and the door to the main bedroom is positioned slightly differently. We're not sure why. Mainly the same, just flipped. You should come over. Bring Une when she gets back. The furniture will be cleared away for the sanders, but you'll get a sense of it.

Sanding too. What kind of floors do you have?

All original oak. We spent a good million on renovations, said Fritjof. Of course, it's quite minimalist, compared to here, but when you bring in your own furniture it will feel more like home.

Fritjof was looking at the big wooden chest by the wall as he spoke, and Knut knew he must be wondering how much it weighed.

We might have to get a different moving company this time, said Knut.

We can ask the guys we're using, said Frida. They'll be around any minute now. They're putting all our furniture in storage trailers while we get the floors done. We used them the last time. They're really fast.

Well, there's no harm in asking them, said Knut. Tell them we're interested. I'll give you my number. I mean I'll have to talk to Une about it, and we'll have to call over and have a look, of course, but Une's into design, so I'd say she'll jump at the idea.

You think? said Frida. That would be amazing. It really would.

The best thing for you would be if we could do it before you move all your furniture back in, I suppose.

Well, yes, said Frida. I mean, we won't rush you into anything if you need time to think, but it would spare us the bother of moving everything twice.

The cost too, said Knut. No point paying double.

I really hope Une agrees with you.

She'll be back soon. I sent her a text.

Well, the removal firm will be here shortly, but they should be done in a few hours if you want to call around then — or tomorrow's fine too, if you're busy today. That's no problem.

I'll call you when Une and Bibbi get back.

This is amazing, said Frida.

But what are we doing, sitting here? Have a look around, said Knut.

They seemed almost too pleased with everything. Frida, worryingly, professed to be dizzy with excitement, and Fritjof kept bumping into things. He was sure they were happy with the potential, with what they could do with the apartment, rather than its current state.

We didn't redecorate after my mother moved out, said Knut, because we still wanted her to think of it as her home, but I know Une will relish something more modernized.

You can bring anything you want with you, said Fritjof, any of the fixed furnishings. We'll probably end up getting new stuff anyway. Anything with any sentimental value, just bring it with you. Right, Frida?

By the time they left, Knut's dizziness had metamorphosed into giddiness. He rang Une — no answer. She never had the sound on. He texted her the main details, and then his eyes were drawn to the hole in the carpet left by Bibbi's heel. It was an actual hole.

He went into the cloakroom off the hallway and rooted in the toolbox.

By the combined efforts of a butter knife and the hooked end of the hammer, he prised loose the new glued and tacked-on timber beads along the edge of the floor. He peeled back the carpet a few centimetres and saw a dark spot on the timber underneath. He rolled the new carpet back further, revealing several indentations, actual holes in the wood-work. The biggest was almost a foot wide, a round depression. It was as if the boards had rotted away, in patches, but there was no smell, and the wood didn't feel damp along the edges. Sand. He would fill the holes with sand and roll the carpet back over. He would put out mouse traps and buy a dehumidifier. His family was in danger, and Frida and Fritjof had just thrown him a lifeline. This was their chance.

# Linda

Flink was up to something and unusually vexed. Linda listened to him scampering about the place, growling, grunting and scratching. After her experiences in the past couple days, many of which she couldn't be certain had actually happened, she decided to take everything easy, step by step, so now she lay looking at the ceiling for a moment longer before she rolled over on her side. There were two distinct possibilities: either something extraordinary was going on, something beyond her understanding, or else her family were right and she had started to go demented. Slowly now, she would observe her own thoughts and decide. She looked at the digital display on the alarm clock: 14:07. She couldn't remember the last time she had stayed in bed so long. She heard Flink's feet scrambling out in the hallway and then the sound of something smashing.

Flink! Come here, boy!

He whimpered before obeying her order. He was, more and more, behaving like an unruly child. When he did come into the bedroom, he continued the same rage around the floor. She dragged her legs over the side of the bed, and her feet found her slippers as she reached for her glasses on the bedside table. When she stood up, she was overcome by such a spell of dizziness that she couldn't see well, despite the glasses. The room seemed too dark for this hour of the day. She was careful to support herself as she walked the two steps to the wardrobe, and were it not for her outstretched hand she would certainly have ended up on the floor. At her age, a fall could be one's end. Hips, especially, were delicate as crystal. She held onto the tiny latch on the wardrobe door, stood as still and sure-footed as she could and waited for her breath and her sight to return to normal. Advice from far off, from some other situation, told her not to look down. She was comforted by Flink's licking at her ankle. She flexed it a little to check for a sprain, but it seemed all right.

When she finally did look down, with both thanks and chastisement for Flink on her lips, she saw that the roots of some plant seemed to have broken through the floor. Wooden knees, elbows – they had come right through the floorboards. She attempted to settle her breath, then began to walk across the room, a hand always on a wall or piece of furniture for support, but, even when she turned on the ceiling lamp, she could not make sense of this.

This was not some creeper that had grown at an unnatural speed through her bedroom window. These roots, if that's what they were, were brown and sturdy and gnarled, and they elbowed right through the floor as if it offered no resistance at all. These were the mature roots of some tree or plant, some of them thicker than her arm. She wanted to crouch down and examine them closer. Her eyesight could not be trusted from this distance. She went, instead, into the kitchen, to address the low sugar levels which she was almost certain must be to blame for what she saw. Strange things were happening all around her, and she could not continue presuming nature was to blame, unless it was human nature, the nature of old age. She picked her steps through roots in the hallway, saw more of the same through the open living-room door, and inside the kitchen too.

One root had grown to such a height above the kitchen floor that it hindered the movement of the fridge door. She was just able to stretch in an arm and extract a carton of milk and a jar of jam. She watched her every step, being careful and sensible.

A howl from Flink caused her to spin around. When the ensuing whizz left her vision, she saw that Flink had left one of his few remaining teeth in a large root, over by the window.

She put the milk and jam on the table, plated cracker bread and got out some cutlery and a glass, and she sat down to the slow, familiar process of opening the jam jar with the teacloth, spreading the sweet strawberry paste and pouring herself a glass of milk. When she had eaten her fill, she looked with hope towards the floor. Perhaps it was coffee she needed.

She drank her coffee, ate a banana, and took her tablets with another glass of milk, but nothing changed. Her pulse seemed normal enough. Her temperature was fine. When she inspected Flink's jaw, it was indeed missing the bloody tooth she saw lodged in the root. She wondered if this delirium was due to her decision to be a madwoman following the episode with Teddy and her missing shoes, or if the shoes were also part of her insanity.

It was dark, like a cloudy day, despite the sunshine outside the window. She turned on all the lights.

In the hallway, she put the telephone back on the hook. She was sorry now that she had been so angry at Knut and his family. An indignant old woman: that's what she had become.

Sitting by the phone a while, she hoped it would ring and she could apologize, and so it was no surprise that she started when the doorbell rang. She walked slowly to the door, stepping carefully over the roots, toeing one of them to check again if it was really there. She could feel it, at least, so it was there in that sense.

It was Bibbi outside.

I brought your shoes, Bestemor, she said. I want to apologize.

If Linda let Bibbi inside now, the girl would be able to tell her if this thing with the roots was true. Linda need not even mention the roots, only buzz her in and see if she exclaimed, What happened to the floor? If she let her granddaughter in, she could put her mind at ease, yet her finger hovered, unwilling, over the green button that would admit her. Even if these roots were not really here, Bibbi would notice the strange way Linda crossed the floor, stepping over and around objects that did not exist. She would know Linda was crazy. Together with the shoe episode, senility would be the only possible conclusion. Whether she was mad or her flat was falling apart, there was a problem in revealing either to Bibbi. There were only two bedrooms in Linda's old apartment, though it was a big apartment, with a huge living room and terrace. If she was deemed too senile to live alone, or her living conditions were unsuitable for an old woman, they would insist on her moving back in. This, in turn, would result in Bibbi and Teddy moving out. They would insist on moving down here if it was mad she was, and Bibbi would insist on finding her own place if the floor was the problem. In either case, bringing Bibbi in here would bring her out of her parents' caring gaze, and Linda did not want a lonely, suicidal granddaughter on her conscience. Bibbi's life might be at stake, as well as that little boy's happiness. No, Linda would face her domestic and mental problems alone.

Bestemor, are you all right? Are you still there?

Bibbi's voice was sweetened.

Sorry, said Linda, Flink was kicking up in here. I'm just on my way out with him now. I'll be right there.

Outside, Bibbi agreed to come on a little walk.

Here, she said, I brought your shoes back. You were right. It was Teddy who hid them, of course. He's such a little rascal and Pappa has him spoilt. I'm so sorry about what we said.

Oh, now.

Do you want to bring your shoes inside? I'll hold Flink.

No need. I'll bring them along with me.

When she peered inside the plastic bag, she saw there was a pair of shoes in there that were exactly the same as those she had lost, but these were clearly new. It was not that Bibbi had washed them for her, no, for these shoes had the original round laces on them. Linda could never manage to keep round laces closed, so she always replaced them with flat ones. She wanted to tell Bibbi that she was up to her tricks, so that Bibbi would know she was of sound mind, but she could not bring herself to disappoint the girl. She was a kind child, and, after all, she had her own problems.

Linda treated Bibbi to a cappuccino and a raisin bun at the bakery, telling her she simply had nothing nice to serve with coffee at home. She thought that this might be her opportunity to draw Bibbi out, but it was difficult to find the right words, words that would not cause Bibbi to pick up her things and hurry off. They talked instead about Knut and Une, and they talked a great deal about Teddy, of course.

We've been trying to phone you, said Bibbi.

Oh, I'm so sorry. I only noticed now this morning that I had left the phone off the hook.

Bibbi scraped the foam off the edge of her cup with a teaspoon.

I was feeling a bit sick, said Linda, so I rang the doctor's office, and I was put on hold. It's a funny story, really. The voice told me I was number six in the queue, so, of course, I got tired of waiting. I went away to pour a cup of coffee for myself and came back, and I was still number six in the queue. I watered the flowers and came back, and it was still not my turn, and, well, I eventually forgot all about it.

Are you feeling better now?

Better? Oh, yes, it was nothing, nothing serious, just a headache. Gone now.

Why don't you use the mobile phone I gave you?

The battery ran out, and anyway there's no need. I'm right next door.

I called to the door too, said Bibbi. Did you not hear the doorbell?

I must have had the radio on. My hearing's not what it used to be. Well, we'd better be heading home again, I suppose. Teddy will be wondering where you are.

They walked home, mainly in silence, and Linda wondered how she had ended up talking about herself when all she had wanted was to talk about how Bibbi was feeling.

Bibbi, courteous as ever, insisted on walking Linda to her door. She pointed to a bruise that was darkening on Linda's wrist.

That looks nasty.

Oh, said Linda, deciding she should be honest about as much as possible, I gave it an awful knock off the wardrobe earlier. I stumbled over a – over Flink. The way he hovers around my feet all day, I don't know how I put up with him. I won't invite you in, Bibbi. I'm afraid I have a bit of cleaning to do.

If I didn't know better, I'd say you had a lover locked up in there.

They both looked at Linda's wrist. So that was it.

You're not to blame for how anyone treated you. You know that, Bibbi, don't you?

Bibbi didn't answer, but she gave Linda a hug that was the warmest Linda had received in all the years since Leif passed.

She watched Bibbi walk away – that figure! Flink's tail was wagging faster than sight.

You're in good spirits again, she said, but she still had to lift him in.

Back inside, Flink leapt out of her arms and clamped his jaws around the biggest root in the hallway.

Sitting on a stool, a strange, three-legged stool she did not remember owning, she took off her shoes and tried on the new ones. From where she sat, she could reach out a hand and touch a root. Maybe she should call it a branch, since it was above ground, but it lacked twigs. It was neither warm nor cold. She eased herself onto the floor, holding onto the root for support. She bent her knee to match the angle it grew at, and there was a sisterhood in their forms. The only contrast was that her own limb felt less alive.

# Fritjof

Frida stood with her hands on her hips in the middle of the empty living room. She had her back to him, but he could tell she was smiling. He threaded his arms through hers and kissed her on the ear. He could have swung her around, were it not for his lumbago.

The sun shone brightly on the floor and walls like never before, and Fritjof had the feeling of a quest beginning. They were on the move, more or less, with a few caveats: what Une thought about it, the speed of the sale, and the intangible force of the unexpected. The speed and uncertainty contributed to a feeling of buoyancy. This sunlight would be good for the floor. Whatever water seeped down would evaporate into these rays.

All the furniture was packed away in two storage trailers, now rolling to a warehouse, a safe house. They had planned to keep the terrace furniture, which could take the rain, but it was packed away with the rest without either of them noticing, and they didn't ask the movers to dig it out again. Nothing that might slow things down was entertained.

They intended to stash away smaller items in the basement, but the main door wouldn't open. He sent Eva an email about it. He couldn't remember exactly what they stored there: winter clothes, skis and stacks of stuff they never used. He was willing to forfeit it all, if it came to it, but it wouldn't. The Klevelands were soft as butter.

The empty apartment reminded him of when they moved in, almost four years before.

Frida, he said, detangling his arms, watch this. Ready?

He took a roll of packaging tape from his back pocket and threw it in the air. It spun on its own axis, upwards, and slid right through the ceiling. A second later, it came down again, and Fritjof caught it with ease.

They stood back from each other and played a game of pass, via the ceiling, equally thrilled each time, though perhaps less surprised that it disappeared on the way up than that it re-emerged on the way down.

I'll ring Knut, get him and Une to come over now, said Fritjof. It looks fine, doesn't it?

We should drop in to Raj first. I kind of promised, and I've a string of missed calls from him.

We don't really have time, if Une's to see the place before the AGM. If it's as bad as Raj says, it might be hard to get away from them. I want Une to see the apartment like this, all bright and dry. I'm sure she'll go for it.

I hope he called the police, like I told him.

There was a knock on the door.

Maybe that's Knut and Une now, said Fritjof, or Raj. Should we answer?

It must be someone from our stairwell if they got this far without ringing the bell, said Frida, already in the hallway, checking the spyhole, opening the door.

Angelica! How are you? Were you away?

We've been at the cabin all week. Have you had a leak?

No, said Frida, you mean a burst pipe?

The roof. I just got home now to a huge puddle in the middle of the living room, and everything drenched. It's really fine with you? Hi, Fritjof, did you hear?

Yes, that's terrible, Angelica.

The door was open behind her, and he could see the floor glistening. It smelled kind of mossy.

Typical that it happened the one time we were away.

That is bad luck, said Frida. Have you told Eva?

I phoned her. She's passing it on to the insurance company. What a mess. Listen, the others are still at the cabin and I'm going to Stockholm for the weekend. Could I give you a key, in case it rains?

Absolutely, said Frida.

Just put a bucket under it or something, said Angelica.

She hurried back across the landing to her apartment and returned with a key and a carry-on suitcase.

You're leaving already? said Fritjof. Pity you'll miss the AGM.

Hell, I forgot about it.

Do you want us to mention the leak?

Do, yes. Oh, hell, I'm so late. Wait. She ran back into her apartment and reappeared with an empty envelope and pen.

You can vote for me at the meeting, she said. What's it called?

A power of attorney? said Frida.

That's it. Get them to vote to repair the roof if you can. Maybe we can put in those rooflights at the same time.

The rooflights, said Fritjof, I'd almost forgotten.

We will, said Frida, no problem. Sorry this happened to you, Angelica.

Angelica pressed the envelope and pen into Frida's hands. I have to go. What a disaster.

Have a nice trip, said Fritjof. We'll hold the fort here.

They listened to her trundle down the stairs and, before she was even out of earshot, they fell back into the apartment, laughing.

We're not alone, said Frida.

It almost feels good, said Fritjof. Let's go up and check.

Up?

The roof. I just want a quick look, while we can.

In the stairwell, directly outside their door, there was a small skylight that could be opened to access the roof. Fritjof pulled down the wall-mounted ladder.

You're jinxing it, said Frida, and we should really go down to Raj.

We will in a minute.

He heaved the glass hatch upwards. It thumped on the extent of its hinges, and he climbed up higher, leaning his thighs against the edge. He patted the roof membrane.

How is it? said Frida.

I thought it would be worse.

What?

It looks a bit too ordinary, to be honest.

Come down. Let me up.

He prodded the membrane with a finger, but it only seemed to mock him, behaving as normal. In the valuation it said they had changed it a decade ago, so fourteen years ago now, still fairly new. The roof looked like any other flat roof. Overlapping sheets of bitumen sloped towards a few drains. He pressed the surface again, and there was a give to it, but that was to be expected. Under the bitumen membrane, there would be a layer of sloping insulation.

Fritjof, come down now or I'm leaving.

The roof was astonishingly clean. There was no moss growing on it, or lichen. He had been up on roofs like this before, assessing the state of buildings that would later be demolished, replaced by whatever he created. It gave one a sense of power. This kind of roof was always covered in stains from puddles and a patchwork of white marks left behind after bird shit.

Frida was on the ladder, climbing.

This roof looked like it had just been washed, dried and vacuumed. It didn't look new. It was covered in a fine mesh of hairline cracks. It was too clean. No caretaker had done this.

Frida's head was at his waist.

Make room, she said.

He climbed up further, sat on the parapet and brought one leg and then the other over and onto the roof.

Be careful, Fritjof.

He took off his watch and threw it a little way from him onto the roof. It dropped right through. His stomach constricted. What if it got stuck halfway?

Fool, said Frida. It's probably smashed.

Will you go and push the mattress over to this end of the bedroom?

She warned him not to move until she came back, but he couldn't wait. He lowered his body down to the surface, stretched out like he was rescuing someone on thin ice, wriggled towards where his watch disappeared, paused. He pulled his knees in, began to stand.

Frida's head poked out the hole.

It's still a three-metre drop, she said. Are you sure?

He stood. He looked around, the view transformed with only this three-metre difference, and then he fell.

He didn't sink or slip, or feel he was sliding through something. It was simply that the force underneath his shoes, which had kept him in position, suddenly failed, or ceased. The potential moment of darkness as his eyes passed through the slab was too brief to notice, if it happened at all. It was like falling through air. He dropped straight down onto the mattress, landing on his feet with a jolt through his knees and hips, and then tumbled over, laughing.

He ran out to Frida who was already running in to him.

You have to try it, he said.

She chewed on her lip like a guilty child, standing on the bottom rung of the ladder.

Do it. You'll be fine.

She moved at a lethargic pace.

We mustn't forget about Raj, she said.

She sat on the parapet and squealed. Climbing up behind her on the ladder, he wanted to give her a push. Three times, she went to stand up but sat right down again on the parapet.

You don't have to do it if you don't want to. Give me another go.

He hadn't meant it as a goading, but she took it that way and finally had access to sufficient courage to step away from the hatch.

She made a noise of terror as she dropped.

He listened. When he heard her walking towards the stairs again, he swung his own legs over the parapet, and, going to the exact same position as before, he made a two-legged hop and landed right down on the mattress again. It was a good landing, and he didn't even topple over. He ran out to the stairs and Frida was gone. He heard her landing on the mattress and coming back at a run. He hurried up the ladder and jumped out, laughing. He was only just out of her way when Frida landed on her butt on a springy coil. She gasped and made a run ahead of him to the stairs, up the ladder, out the hatch and right through the roof, and they knew now to get out of the way as soon as they landed. They were children, racing around this loop, and he got ahead of Frida one time, got to the ladder before her, and she pulled at his shoe, but he kicked her off and continued up.

He whooped as he descended and landed well. Frida landed badly beside him, with one foot on the hard edge of the mattress, her body swivelling so she fell with a thump on her shoulder.

She wailed.

Are you hurt?

She wailed on, and when she stopped, she took her hands from her ankle.

I think it's broken, she said.

# Gunnar

Gunnar sat opposite Hildegunn on a matching Bibendum chair and emailed the eviction notice from his laptop.

What's all this stuff? said Hildegunn.

Just a minute.

He sent a copy to all the members of the board of residents. He put the apartment up for sale on his company website as well as finn.no, using the photos and information he had previously sent to the letting agent. It was less than a year since he purchased it, so he would avoid sales tax if he sold it now. This required some juggling with regard to his own official residence, but he could make it work. By specifying that the apartment had potential for renovation or as a rental investment, he could not be accused of promising anyone a beautiful home. Really, he should go down to inspect it. He would. The way they described it, he wondered if there wasn't actually some structural fault. Everything can be fixed, and he had insurance, but he had a bad feeling about it, disgust even. He wanted it off his hands. He wanted out.

Hildegunn shuffled to the edge of her seat. Gunnar moved to help her, but she swatted him away.

Leave me alone, can't you?

Right, right.

I'm happy to have you here, Gunnar. We couldn't let you sleep in your garage, and I'm sure your house will be lovely after the redecoration. Lovely.

Well, said Gunnar, it's no harm to have someone around. Anything else you need, Hildegunn, just ask.

She put her weight on her good leg and rose at an awkward angle, still holding onto the chrome armrests of her favourite chair.

Is it worth it? she said.

You're improving, Hildegunn, you are.

Where did you get it, all this stuff?

He looked around him. The place did look cluttered. She must have been taking knick-knacks out of cupboards while he wasn't looking. He couldn't pinpoint exactly what was new, but the carefully choreographed domestic order that had presided the day before was keenly disrupted.

Why did you put those candles there? she said.

There was a trio of scented candles on a garish golden plate, centred badly on her coffee table. He gathered them together and put them away in a drawer, assuring himself that these were a present she'd hidden away and now brought out, in a moment of stylistic indecency. The nurse had assured him that these forgetful episodes were a temporary effect of the medicine.

Did you buy those lovely plants for me, Gunnar?

The orchids? he said. I didn't buy them, no, I ...

He had never seen them before.

Oh, you brought them from home, of course, and a good thing you did. I'm not a fan of orchids myself, but plants need our constant care. They would not survive without you.

Right, he said, I'll give them a drop of water.

If you don't mind, Gunnar, would you open the windows to air out? There's a strange smell.

He did as requested, opening each window a small angle. He wondered if it was their two individual smells which mixed badly. Perhaps their fragrances were incompatible. It smelled like some other home.

Well, Gunnar, I'm glad you got rid of that brass by the fireplace at least.

He'd seen the decorative kitchenware she referred to the day before and had been equally horrified by it, but it wasn't he who'd got rid of it. If she had flung it out the window, he would not complain. There was so much other junk lying around now that he was impressed she could notice the absence of any one thing.

Don't take this the wrong way now, Gunnar, but I really think you should get rid of all this. Just let it go.

If you like, he said, keeping the here-we-go-again tone out of his voice as a courtesy.

Some charity shop would be delighted to take them, I'm sure, said Hildegunn. You are a single man now, Gunnar. You must cultivate your sense of style. Why didn't you let your wife take them?

My ex-wife?

You should give her all this stuff, Gunnar. You got the house, after all. Give her these hideous armchairs, at least.

Hildegunn was supporting herself on an unsightly purple padded armchair, but she quickly transferred her weight to a more stylish chair close by. Gunnar could not make sense of the purple chairs. He felt sure he would have noticed them if they had been here in the past, but he could hardly accuse Hildegunn of pulling them out of storage. Perhaps they had been covered in some nice blankets, though that didn't ring a bell either.

He had seen workmen coming downstairs yesterday, and a carpet installer's van outside. Whoever it was might have asked Hildegunn if they could store some furniture here temporarily. It was the only thing that made sense, though why they had strewn the chairs around the apartment instead of stacking them in one corner was a mystery. Hildegunn must have told them to do so. That seemed equally astounding. They must have forced her. She must have felt threatened … and then forgotten all about it. Something was off. He had not even been out all that long.

Who brought these chairs in, Hildegunn? Did someone ask you to mind them?

Well, I'm presuming it was you, Gunnar, or one of your crew. How would I know? But Gunnar, I mean no disrespect to the taste of your ex-wife, but these chairs are really not worth holding onto. Did she find them at a bazaar?

You're right. I could never stand her taste in furniture.

He tested the weight of one and thought he might manage it if he held it firmly against his body.

I'll get rid of these straight away, he said.

He brought them both out to the landing, with some difficulty – and then he remembered the keys. The dirty moles. They still had the keys to this door. Now this made sense. Revenge he could understand, at least. Just minutes ago, he had been tempted to avoid his tenants, but now he revelled at the chance to tell them of their imminent eviction in person.

He left the purple armchairs on the landing and tripped downstairs. He pounded on the temporary door with the fleshy part of his fist, but there was no answer. He put his key in the padlock – he had supplied the padlock, so why shouldn't he keep one of the keys for himself? – but he couldn't manage to push the door in. They should be at work; the door should be locked from the outside only, but the vermin must have bolted it on the inside too and snuck out the window. Either that or one of them was at home and refusing to answer. He pounded again and thought he heard a murmuring voice. Part of him was relieved no one answered. He dreaded seeing what they had done to his property. Though he was not the type of man who was prone to exaggeration, he almost believed Pradeep when he described ankle-high earth. What if it was true? It couldn't be. If he sold it without witnessing it, he could not be accused of hiding known damage from the sellers. It would be a few weeks before the new door was delivered, and he could tell the repairman there was no hurry with it. There was the difficulty of finding someone to buy it without a viewing: he could try rental companies and foreign investors. He would get seller's insurance. He gave the door one more push and then gave up. As long as he got 10 per cent more than he had paid for it, it would be worth it. The market was hot.

He heard someone coming down the stairs, and voices:

Slow down.

It's heavy.

We shouldn't be doing this.

We'll get the blame again if we don't.

But it's the middle of the day. We'll be caught.

Gunnar concealed himself at the bottom of the stairs, and waited to see who this was, though the breaking voices suggested teenagers and he already suspected the Blix twins who lived in the apartment under Hildegunn. Their father was a nice man, an accountant. He had supported Gunnar when he was buying the maids' quarters. It sounded like these kids were bringing the rotten armchairs out, and he was not about to get in their way.

Hey! Stop right there! he said.

It was one of Hildegunn's Bibendums they were man-handling.

I told you this was a bad idea, said the long-haired one.

You bring that chair right back up to Hildegunn, or I'll call the police.

Hildegunn? Okay. We just found it, like. We didn't take it.

I don't want to hear it. Get it upstairs, and you can take away the junky chairs you gave her.

Now the question of who had done what was rightly muddled in his mind, but it was easier to put the blame for everything on these two at the moment, rather than trying to tease out what exactly they had done. He wanted to photograph them, but they were minors and he wasn't sure it was legal. One crime didn't necessarily cancel out another.

The purple chairs were gone from the landing when they came up.

Where do you want this?

Right back where you found it, in the living room, you nitwit.

They brought it inside, not without bumping it off every conceivable corner and door jamb.

Put that one here and go get the other one, he said. Do you want me to tell your father about this?

Gunnar sat down on the retrieved chair.

Gunnar, what's going on?

Hildegunn was in bed, fortunately.

Stay there, Hildegunn! Stay where you are! The twins are just helping me get rid of some junk.

The purple chairs were gone, at least.

The twins moaned their way in with Hildegunn's designer chair.

It's heavy, the short-haired one said.

Put it there, said Gunnar. Now, listen: I'm willing to keep this to myself, but I want a favour from you two in return.

What do you want?

Do you know the Indian guys that live in the basement?

Krishna and them?

Yes. How well do you know them?

I've just met them going in and out.

Same here. We just say hello, don't really know each other.

Well, said Gunnar, I want you to make friends with them. Get to know them. That's my apartment they're living in, for now, and I want to know what they're doing to it. Get inside the apartment and tell me what you find, all right?

Are they dangerous?

It's either that or I tell your father.

They looked at each other, shrugged.

Tell our father, the long-haired one said, and they walked out.

He went to close the door after them and found another one of the neighbours standing there. At least, she seemed familiar.

Hi, I'm Sonja Flynn from downstairs, she said. You're Hildegunn's nephew, right?

Sonja, yes, hello. Do you know those twins that just went down the stairs?

They live right underneath you.

Have you seen them up to anything strange? Things have been going missing.

No, they seem pretty normal. Teenagers, you know. Anyway, I'm just calling around ahead of the AGM.

That's right. It's this evening, isn't it? We can bring it up then.

He moved to invite her inside, then thought better of it.

Maybe you could mention it at the AGM, Sonja. I don't want to get on bad terms with Blix, you see. Why don't you just say you saw the twins carrying furniture down the stairs.

I'm calling about the external walls, said Sonja, or the one towards the back garden. I wondered if we could check for draughts. There were bricks missing from my wall, you see, and I'm sure it must be the same in the other apartments. Perhaps if I could speak to Hildegunn, she might even have noticed it.

Hildegunn's indisposed, I'm afraid, and you should be careful about spreading rumours of this kind. If word gets out that there are any structural issues, do you realize what that would do to sales prices? Trust me, Sonja, you'll want to move out some day, and you'll be glad you kept any suspicions of this kind to yourself.

It's a serious problem, said Sonja. We can't just ignore it. It could be really dangerous.

Nonsense. Don't worry about draughts, Sonja. Forget about this. It's just a few bricks, like you say. Believe me, I've sold hundreds of apartments. No one ever asks about bricks. Now, are you going to help me and mention that you saw those twins lifting furniture down the stairs?

Is Hildegunn home? she said, stepping forward, too close to Gunnar.

My aunt is indisposed. She had an accident.

Might I speak to her? She knows me.

Who's that? came Hildegunn's voice.

Just a neighbour, Auntie Hildegunn!

Hildegunn! the woman called out, but Gunnar had had enough. He closed the door on her.

# Eva

There was room for six tightly packed neighbours on the picnic bench, and they added chairs, keeping the middle open as if the table were invisibly extended. Linda sat outside the group, hidden behind Knut on a low camping stool. The grass had grown so long the old woman seemed submerged in it.

Come and sit here on the bench, said Eva. You'll be more comfortable.

I'll stay here. I'm only watching.

She had her dog with her, and he whinged and pulled on the leash, but settled down when Eva called order.

It was an unusual collection of neighbours. Some of the stalwarts, Frida and Fritjof, and Hildegunn, of course, were absent. Knut and Une had both come. One of the Indian tenants was standing tentatively outside the gate, craning his neck to see who was there. Eva gestured for him to come in, but Gunnar shooed him away.

He has a right to be here and to speak, said Eva.

Oh, he's just looking for me, said Gunnar. I'll call over to him afterwards. I'm chiefly here to represent Hildegunn.

The man disappeared.

They hopped quickly through the opening protocol: Eva would chair; Une would write the minutes; Nora and Stella would confirm and sign them. The accounts for the past year were accepted without comment. The budget for the coming year was something Eva wanted to discuss.

A number of maintenance issues have been brought to my attention at the last minute, she said.

The garden wall, said Sonja.

The exterior wall that faces the garden in 14A, yes, is one of a number of issues, along with a seeming deterioration of the party walls in places.

There are bricks missing, said Sonja.

That's in the exterior wall, yes, said Eva. That's something we need to look at, of course. There are problems with the windows too.

Our leak, said Nora. Is that on your list? And the creepers. We can't keep up with their growth.

Forget all that, what about the burglaries? said the petulant accountant from 14A, whose name evaded her. She scanned last year's minutes: Ole Blix. His wife was lovely, and he had such pleasant teenagers. She wished one of them had come in his place.

The doors, she said, yes. There seems to be something wrong with the locks. I asked the company to try replacing mine to start with. A locksmith is coming out next week.

Yours? said the soon-to-be-divorced Ibsen, who was dressed entirely in corduroy for the occasion. What about the rest of us? he said.

This what-about-us attitude was ill-fitting for a member of the board. What have you done about it? she wanted to ask him, but there was no point. He was on his way out.

We can't get our windows to close at all now, said Nora.

Same here, said Linda's bodyless voice.

Us too.

Right, so we have —

I want a different assessor to look at my brickwork, said Sonja. The last one was useless. He just took a few worthless photos and didn't uncover anything, but the builders found bricks missing. They left a patch unfilled so someone can inspect it. I can't leave it open like that for long, and this can't just be me. It must be the same in the rest of the wall, if they just checked properly. Can't they scan it, Eva? Are Frida and Fritjof coming?

Eva, said Blix, is there something in the rule book about harassment? My sons have a right to come home without being accosted by aggressive neighbours calling them thieves.

I was not aggressive, said Une. I found them bringing my dining chairs down the stairs. I could have called the police.

They told you they just found them. They were just being helpful.

I didn't like to mention it, Blix, said Gunnar, and I handled it myself without involving the police or anything, but

I actually caught your twins carting out a pair of designer chairs from Hildegunn's apartment.

Eva thought of her own balcony furniture, and that was not all: Pamela, who lived on the top floor of 14A, beside Knut and Une, had called Eva earlier to say she caught the woman who lived below her – not a Blix – selling her chaise longue out on the street. That there were multiple robberies and thieves only complicated things further.

I've received a number of complaints about theft, said Eva, big things like furniture and pets, from both blocks and with all sorts of accusations and suspicions. As I said in my emails, you must report these instances to the police yourselves, and I know some of you have done so, but this is a worrying trend, I absolutely agree. I'm concerned it's something to do with the locks on our new doors.

And who ordered these new doors? said Blix.

As you said yourself, no neighbour deserves baseless accusations to be hurled their way.

Do you have a master key?

There's no master key, said Eva.

Then how is whoever-it-is getting in?

Our silver spoons too! said Knut. Ow!

Une had elbowed him.

One theory, said Eva, who refused to let her train of words be truncated, even if they were interrupted, one theory is that the doors don't lock properly.

There's nothing wrong with the lock, said Blix. It closes fine. Someone's getting in. We've had loads of stuff stolen, totally random stuff. It's like someone's trying to freak us out.

There was a loud crash from 14A. Everyone turned towards it, and half of them rose from their seats. A cloud of brown dust seeped out through Blix's balcony door. He jumped up and ran inside.

In the rush of his departure, everyone spoke together.

The bathroom above ours leaks when they shower.

The neighbours above us are really noisy.

So are they. We can hear everything suddenly.

We don't even play music.

The paint peeled off one of our walls, but I already repainted it.

Which wall? said Eva, a little too eager.

In the bedroom, an internal wall.

Can we get back to the hole in the external wall?

You're giving me a pain in the ...

Or the burglary?

There's an actual hole in my wall, said Sonja. We can all go and look at it together now if you like.

Not while we're in session, Sonja.

We've nothing to report, said Knut, apart from the burglaries. Same with Pamela, beside us. I have a POA from her, Eva. What about Frida and Fritjof? Do they have any maintenance issues? They said they'd be here.

I can't discuss individual complaints, said Eva.

She heard a dull thud from her own building, and heads turned that way, but there was no cloud of dust, and it had not been such a loud noise. It was an ordinary sound that only startled them now because they were on guard. She saw a couple of neighbours texting, but no one ran off to check.

I hear the angelic – the family on the top floor above me are selling, said Linda, and I saw the two architects beside them moving out furniture this morning.

A wave of whispers and murmurs broke out at this. Knut and Une exchanged a glance, conversed with their eyes and even seemed to come to a conclusion.

Fools, said Gunnar. They'll flood the market. I wouldn't advise anyone to sell at the same time as their neighbours. You'll just be competing with one another. Supply should never exceed demand. It's a principle of growth.

So, you'd advise us to wait with selling? said Ibsen.

You too? said Linda.

We're breaking up, said the pianist.

Ibsen's nostrils flared. No one's interested, he said.

What about the doors? said Gunnar. Have we concluded what to do about them? You'll have to take some responsibility, Eva. Did you choose a reputable company?

There was nothing wrong with the reputation of the company I hired. They've supplied doors to government buildings. But something is wrong with those locks. It has to be.

Nothing's wrong with the locks, said Blix, returning to the assembly with equal vehemence. Someone's got their hands on a master key. That's the problem. See this bolt? – he took a sizeable brass bolt from his pocket – This is going on my door this evening. He eyed his neighbours pointedly. So don't even try.

I'm happy to call the police, said Une, and report this on behalf of the whole block. I don't see the point of doing it individually, piecemeal. Whoever's doing this has a copy of all our keys. It's a common problem. Also, I think we should use a new firm if we're changing the locks. I'm not saying you're in any way to blame, Eva, but it must be someone along their chain of supply who has managed to copy our keys.

The problem with using a new company, said Eva, is we'll have to pay for it ourselves.

Whatever it costs will surely be less than what we lose through theft, and we'll be able to sleep at night.

We could get the company we used to pay for replacement locks, if we can convince them there's been an intruder.

Put up surveillance cameras then, said Gunnar. It's worth the cost, and there are vulnerable people living here. We must consider the elderly. Put cameras in the stairwell.

GDPR, said Eva. We'd have to get everyone's consent.

Then get it, said Gunnar. Whoever's against it is guilty. I call a vote. All in favour ...

All hands went up, including Eva's hesitant forefinger, which was raised with a caveat. We'd have to get consent from those not here as well, she said. It might be better to put the cameras inside, facing the door.

Same to me, said Gunnar. All in favour?

It was irritating how he stole the chair like this.

Let's do this properly, said Eva. Une, if you note that the AGM will vote on whether to purchase and install a surveillance camera for each apartment —

Better leave my rental out of it, said Gunnar.

Whether to purchase and install surveillance cameras for all apartments with owner-occupants, to monitor suspected break-ins. All in favour, raise a hand ... Almost unanimous, wonderful.

I've already been looking into it, said Sonja. I can buy them tomorrow. I'm getting two extras to train on my external wall.

Do you think someone's coming in and stealing bricks out of your wall? said Gunnar. I mean, this whole thing would make anyone paranoid, but –

I just want to know what's happening.

Pay for them yourself, then.

I never asked you to pay for them. I just offered to go to the shop and buy them.

We have enough on our hands with real, tangible problems without succumbing to wild speculation.

My walls are a real, physical problem. Just come and see, anyone. We can go there now if you want proof.

Everyone, calm down, said Eva. We're staying here till this meeting is adjourned. We're already over time.

She waited for silence.

Next issue, said Eva. It's time we got a full structural report on the building.

At whose expense? said Gunnar.

We'll get the exterior and party walls checked.

The balconies too.

Who said that, about the balconies? said Eva.

284

I only meant, said the woman who lived beside Blix, I only thought maybe balconies could have structural issues, that's all.

Check the floor slabs and foundations if you're checking anything, said Gunnar.

Have there been complaints about the foundations? said Linda.

Foundations and balconies would be included in any structural report, said Eva. Windows are, of course, not structural, but I suggest we include them. They're getting old and we'll get a better offer if we change them in bulk. So, a full engineer's report. We'll run any damage they discover through the insurance company. We'll need to vote on that too, Une, to sanction the cost.

How much will it be? said the pianist. I'm against it. Wait until our buyers move in. They'll vote in favour.

We don't need a unanimous vote on this, said Eva, only a majority.

I vote for the motion, said Ibsen.

That would nullify your wife's vote, said Eva.

It's happening, he said.

We're selling too, said Nora. She and Stella had been whispering the whole time.

Just raise a hand if you're in favour of the motion, said Eva.

They both placed their hands pointedly on their knees, to make no mistake, and resumed their whispering. Eva wondered how many years it took before couples could whisper silently with only their eyes like Knut and Une were doing.

We have a majority, said Eva. Wonderful – in my opinion. I'll get onto it first thing Monday morning. Right, anything else?

I have a proposal that might help, said Gunnar. It just occurred to me now, with all these maintenance costs coming in. I'm selling my little rental apartment, you see, and I'd be happy to sell it back to you all. The rental income would be a big help in paying for all these repairs, and, to be honest with you, I need to free up some funds for another investment, so I'd be happy to sell it back for almost the same price I paid for it, say 10 per cent extra. We'd avoid the sales levy, since it's been less than a year. I'm just blue-sky thinking now, but consider it and let me know fairly quickly if you think it would be an idea. I'm just glad to have saved it from vacancy. You could vote on it before we round off.

There was a lot of mumbling and some laughing.

We can note your suggestion in the minutes, said Eva, but we wouldn't be able to decide on something like that now when it has not been mentioned in the summons to the AGM.

Well, note my offer in the minutes, said Gunnar, and say anyone who thinks we should reverse the sale can send you an email within a fortnight. I'm making twenty thousand a month on it, I don't mind disclosing. That's a good lot more than what you'd pay for a loan. Honestly, I'm being nice here. You need it more than me.

Fritjof came jogging into the garden.

Sorry I'm late, he said. Frida broke her ankle.

Knut and Une made room for him on the crowded bench, as if he were the injured party.

I wouldn't recommend breaking a bone right now, said Fritjof. Huge line outside the A&E. We ended up going private. Anyway, what have I missed?

We are just rounding off, Fritjof. We've voted in favour of getting a structural report on the building.

What's wrong with the structure?

There are concerns about the external and party walls, amongst other things.

Nothing wrong with the walls up in our place, but fine by me. I've a POA from Angelica on our landing.

He passed her a crumpled envelope.

They have a leak from the roof. Is that included?

Yes, and we've already voted on it, like I said.

Fritjof, is it dangerous? said Sonja. There are bricks missing from the exterior wall to the garden.

Fritjof scanned the wall in question in a comically professional manner.

That's what the draught was? he said.

Yes. Crazy, isn't it? Do you think it could collapse?

He sucked air through his teeth.

The floor slabs probably span the other way, from the party walls to the gables. It's a shorter span.

The party walls, said Eva, what's happening to them? Could they be overburdened?

No, they're fine, said Fritjof, but do the report, by all means.

We've already voted on the report yes, a full structural analysis. High priority.

Brilliant, said Fritjof. Anything else?

You'll get the minutes, said Eva. We also have a problem with break-ins or faulty locks, so we've voted to install temporary surveillance cameras inside each apartment door.

Inside?

GDPR.

Put ours and Angelica's outside the doors in the stairwell. There's no one else up at our level.

We might do the same at our place, said Knut, since we have a child inside.

Ask Pamela first, said Eva.

Fritjof? said Linda.

Knut leaned to the side to bring the diminutive Linda into view.

Are you and Frida moving out? said Linda. I saw the removal vans.

Fritjof looked caught out, and Knut and Une stiffened.

We're oiling the floors, said Fritjof.

Hey!

The bitter divorcé in the apartment beside Sonja's climbed out of his balcony, tramped through the roses and pulled a vacant chair towards the middle of the circle. His shoes were wrapped in plastic bags, knotted at the ankles. He was visibly inebriated and absolutely filthy. Those beside him edged away, but he didn't notice.

You mustn't climb out to the garden that way, said Eva. Couldn't you come around the block like everyone else?

I would if I could, he said. My entrance is one floor down, and it's completely impassable. That's why I came out.

He pointed a swollen finger at Gunnar.

Your filthy tenants are stinking the place out, attracting rats and trampling muck all over the place. I want them out, you hear! Out!

Eva, said Gunnar, I'll let you deal with this.

Are there rats in your apartment? said Eva.

Rats, earth, worms and rabbits. It's those students. They're coming into my place at night, dumping mud all over the floor. It's bullying. That's what it is.

Eva regretted sending the notice about the smell. This man had come across as quite reasonable in his phone calls and emails. She saw now that she had been gullible. He wasn't the only one to complain of the smell, and he was, quite plausibly, its source. He was covered in dirt. A beetle was crawling up his neck.

She managed to allay his fury with her plan of surveillance and moved to adjourn the meeting. Most of the neighbours hurried away.

If it's over, can you come to look at my wall? said Sonja.

Eva looked at the wall in question. This was getting tedious.

It can wait for the structural report.

You don't understand. It's getting worse.

It can't get worse, Sonja. If the bricks have been missing all along, as you say, then we've been fine all these years without them. It might be best to leave them untouched where we can and repair any problem spots.

But when will the report be made?

I'll ask them to prioritize us. Maybe someone can squeeze us in next week.

There will be nothing left by then.

Gunnar, who should have just kept out of it, said, Don't go for the first available firm, Eva. It's best to compare three offers and choose the best. There's no point in rushing it. What's urgent now is getting our locks replaced.

The bricks are disappearing, said Sonja.

I don't want to get involved, said Gunnar, but you're saying some crazy things.

The bricks are falling out, is what I mean. The missing bricks are causing structural problems that are only becoming apparent now. It's extremely serious and urgent.

Well, it looks fine, said Gunnar.

Sonja, who lacked Eva's scruples about the trustworthiness of her neighbour, asked the drunk if he noticed anything odd about his external walls, any inexplicable draughts.

I bet your wall's the same as mine, said Sonja. You just haven't noticed. Let me come and have a look.

He leered at Sonja as if he had just discovered her.

Let's wait for the professional review, said Eva. We'll need a report anyway, if the insurance is to cover it.

That's your wall there? said Sonja.

It is. Is there something wrong with it? It wouldn't surprise me at this stage.

Sonja folded her chair flat, and Eva hoped this was capitulation at last. Sonja passed through the thorny bushes like someone who couldn't feel pain. She swung her metal chair against her neighbour's section of wall. He roared at her from this side of the bushes. She did it again, at a new spot, and, at the third blow, the chair smashed right through the plaster, all the way through the wall.

I'm calling the police! shouted the drunk. I'm calling your ex too, you vandal. I know who you are.

Realizing he didn't have his phone on him, the man climbed back into his apartment through his balcony. The remaining neighbours stood transfixed, and then they turned to look towards their own apartments and hurried away. Eva waited a while and convinced Sonja to go on home.

Sonja had proved, at least, that this was indeed a structural issue. She had managed to puncture an external wall with a foldable chair. That shouldn't be possible. In a patch more than half a metre wide, there seemed to be no bricks at all. This was highly irregular. The wall could conceivably be built of vaults, or columns and beams, and what Fritjof said about the span was reassuring, but there should be some insulation, something, in the cavity, not just two thin layers of plaster like a double tent. Eva looked up to her own apartment, relieved at least that her part of the façade was in fair-faced brick, its structure reassuringly visible.

Eva crossed her darkened bedroom to close the French windows before she turned on the lights, knocking her shin off the end of the bed as she went. Multiple raised voices echoed across the garden. The windows wouldn't close, but she pulled the blinds down so no one could see in. She bumped her other shin on the way back, and she turned on the lights.

The party wall was bulging inwards.

It was doing so to a small extent, but enough that she noticed straight away. She put aside the unhelpful thought that she might just be light-headed. This load-bearing partition was curving into her bedroom as if it were part of a very large balloon. Her bed was positioned at the middle of the wall, and she could clearly see that the surface curved behind the headboard. The headboard was a tangent to the dividing wall. The legs of the bed were perhaps fifteen centimetres from the skirting board, with the top of the headboard touching the plaster, and she could only conclude that the ballooning structure had pushed her bed away. It was a heavy double bed with built-in storage.

She called the insurance company, thinking they must have some sort of emergency helpline, and was put on hold by an automatic answering machine.

In the kitchen, she found that something similar had happened to the party wall there. The movement, though slight, had been sufficient to loosen the attachment of the overhead cupboards. Glasses and plates had fallen out and lay in pieces on the worktop and floor. She put her phone on speaker and set it aside as she brushed up the shards and carefully removed the remaining contents of the overhead cupboards, placing them on the kitchen table.

When she was finished, she was still on hold. She brought her phone out onto the balcony. It was possible to breathe better out there, and it was the furthest she could go from the two bulging walls. She thought of what Fritjof had said about the slabs spanning between the party walls. What had seemed reassuring then was cause for serious alarm now.

She should be screaming, running. The parents in the block had come together and placed a trampoline in the garden, to the consternation of the gardening committee. If she needed to, if she flung herself outwards, she would land there. This was insanity.

She heard them before she saw them: two dogs and a cat in the back garden, but they could eat each other up for all she cared.

A foldable sun chair hung from a nail on the wall, the only piece of furniture that was left out there, which was another mystery, though not critical enough to compete with her more pressing concerns. She sat in the sun chair, covered by a woollen blanket, and waited to get through to the insurance company. It was absolutely infuriating. They had the audacity to call this an emergency hotline. One option was to hang up and call the caretaker instead, or the fire brigade, but she had now waited so long that she might get through soon, and she didn't want to lose her place. If only they would tell her which position she held in the queue, how many callers were before her. She might have an hour to wait, or only minutes. She pulled the blanket up to her chin.

# Saturday

*Darkness is an underground comfort. Packed in, padded; we have rooms of our own, which stretch our lengths; we sneak out under sinks and in the backs of kitchen cupboards. We are washed on the inside by a steady stream of water, warm or cold. When it flows, we are noisy, though you can't hear us through your shower songs. We are so long-lasting that you forget we are here, but our walls are getting thinner from the slow rub of years. We are heavy metal, but even we have our weak points. Soldered, hammered, bent: I challenge you to find another metal who could take such treatment and remain intact. Find anyone else who would not leak a little after all these years, who would not pling and gush if they got the chance.*

# Sonja

Sonja shivered but kept her eyes closed. She heard footsteps outside, and a beep followed by the double clunk
of a car unlocking. As she listened, a car boot opened: a
recognizably upward click and hiss. Then the thump and
push of a suitcase, perhaps, on the felt card that covered
a spare wheel. She was imagining this, but the sounds
matched her thoughts. The sounds were real, even if
the details were her own. The boot clasped shut. There
were more footsteps and the noise of a car door opening,
a pause, then its closing smack. She heard the back and
forth of an engine starting, the sound of reversing, its
wheely jolting as well as the panicked beeping inside the
car. She could smell the exhaust. She heard tyres turning on tarmac and the gentle scrape of pulling out, and
she listened to the lessening noise of the car driving off,
until it was lost in the haze of the city's vague vehicular
soundscape.

She rose from the kitchen floor, tipped the mattress
upwards and rested it against the kitchen cupboards to make

space. The streets were empty, and there was one empty parking spot along the kerb.

Motivated more by convenience than thirst, she held a glass under the tap, but no water flowed out, not even a gurgle or a hiss. Same with the hot water.

She had been sticking to this side of the apartment: the kitchen, bathroom and hallway, because it was safer. It was possible to sleep here.

The burglar they spoke of at the AGM must be one of the other neighbours, she was certain, because when she came home from the meeting she found a stash of someone else's furniture in her apartment, including two of those expensive Michelin Man chairs. Someone was trying to frame her, and she remembered the self-righteous man from upstairs, whose sons had been caught red-handed, and how he had run inside at one stage during the meeting.

Moving quietly from the kitchen, she stumbled across the hallway. She had dumped all of the incriminating furniture out on the landing, but the floor was still strewn with other objects, small, worthless things that no one could be accused of stealing.

Someone started banging on the door, and she crept towards the noise. There was, unfortunately, a small window in place of a peephole, so the neighbour would see if she opened the metal cover to check who was there. It was probably the same filthy neighbour. He should be grateful she had alerted him to the structural damage in his external wall, but he had pounded at her door the night before, shouting about the police.

She hadn't answered then, and she wasn't about to do so now, though if it was anyone else she would bring them in, a witness. A neighbour who knocked, or even banged on the door, was less of a threat than the neighbour who let himself in, to place false evidence of theft. And all neighbours were petty when compared to disintegrating walls. She couldn't reconcile the reverse burglary – crazy in itself – to the theft of bricks. Nobody takes bricks out of a wall.

The apartment was a sweaty kind of cold.

She opened her bedroom door and froze. Her only movement was a shiver.

All the bricks were gone.

Of the whole wall towards the garden, all that was left was the outer plaster, the thinnest of skins. Her feet brought her close, but she didn't dare to touch it. She could see the impression of the vanished bricks on the plaster.

She looked up to the ceiling, surprised not to find it sagging, but remembered how Fritjof claimed this wall was probably not load-bearing. She knocked on the party wall. It seemed fine, but she was not reassured. Even if immediate structural collapse was not an issue, the fact remained that the external wall was disappearing.

The pace of the change had increased in her mild absence, six steps away in the kitchen. She should have slept here. She should not have let her guard down.

In the living room, the inner plaster was still intact, but it was warped and bulging, hanging like a sail, and she was certain there were no bricks underneath.

She knocked and pawed all over the external wall in the kitchen and the party walls. They seemed completely normal, but how could she be sure?

In the relative safety of her kitchen, she sat on the counter and looked up flights, unsure whether to head to her father up north or her mother abroad. She could take a train or a bus to her father's place – but her mother's home tempted her with its safe distance. Her web search reminded her that the following day was the 17th of May, Constitution Day, and there were no flights until Monday. Booking the first one available brought her credit card precariously close to its limit. An airport hotel was not possible, but she could sleep in the terminal the night before if it came to that.

She filled her three suitcases, along with a large hiking rucksack. Unsatisfied, she replaced packed clothes with books. She brought out her portfolios and took down her framed pictures. Unpacking and re-packing several times, she was forced to admit there would not be enough room for everything. She feared for anything she might leave behind. It was not that she was a worldly person, needy about her things, but her sketchbooks, her etchings. She should have hired a van, or a car with a trailer. An attempt to cancel the non-refundable flight online failed, so she rang the airline's support services and waited. She texted a friend to ask if she could leave some things at her place, and when that didn't work she texted friend after friend. They were all either away or it was a bad time or it was a disaster zone in their apartment. Before an hour had passed, she realized she had no one, not a single friend to help her in the entire city.

She wanted to run outside and scream for help, but her vehemence had worked against her at the AGM. She had gone too far with the chair, but at least she had proved the walls were faulty. Eva had seen it. Eva was her closest ally. She had suggested the structural assessment. She was on Sonja's side, even if she didn't fully appreciate the urgency. Sonja fingered the phone in her pocket. It was early to ring on a Saturday, but such norms could surely not still apply. She had to try.

There was no answer. She tried again. She left a message.

She gathered her best illustrations together on her desk by the living-room window, stacked them by category: birds, insects, plants, people. The categorization didn't help. She wanted to bring them all.

A fly landed on an illustration of a human hand; a ladybird alighted on a pencilled leaf; a spherical bumblebee came to rest on a watercoloured flower. She sifted through the sketches until she found their counterparts: drawings and paintings of flies, ladybirds and bees. When these real creatures flew back out the window, she wouldn't consider them lost, yet she was unable to abandon their representations.

She watched the ladybird as it pattered a jagged path over the page, its wings threatening to open, cracking the semi-sphere of its back. It changed with each movement. Her representation noted only a fraction of what this creature was. The creature did stand still at times, when at rest, when in fear. The remainder, the majority of its essence, went undocumented. She wondered if she should have taken up film instead of illustration. It didn't seem enough.

The bumblebee circled her head and flew out the window.

The tendril of a rose plant blew – grew – in through the window and nudged her browsing fingers. The glass in that windowpane, she realized, was gone.

Along the line of window frame where the glass should have been, which should be sharp with shards of glass and crumbled putty at least, on this edge a skylark landed.

Her hand found paper and pencil. The colours were already mixing in her mind. This most human impulse, to create, she told herself that this also had a value, that this was part of nature too.

# Linda

Flink was growling and snapping, and Linda could feel in the ticking of her internal clock that it was early. She lay in her bed, facing away from the open French windows.

She had been looking at the wardrobe doors for a while now, wondering if they were crooked or if it was just the angle she was viewing them from, without her glasses, that made them seem so. She was well aware that this was a cowardly meditation, that her concern for the wardrobe doors was a way of avoiding her concern for the floor. She still harboured a hope that the roots she had seen and felt were part of yesterday's madness, and today's madness would, at least, be of a different nature. Perhaps today would be the day she forgot how old she was or put on socks that didn't match: some old-womanly madness that held less terror than roots.

Flink jumped up on the bed with something bloody hanging off him. She reached out for him, thinking he was injured, but he dropped the bloody something from his jaws and came closer. In a moment completely devoid of common sense, she wondered if the bloody thing was part of herself, and she looked under the sheets to see if anything was missing.

She was intact, and the bloody thing, when viewed through spectacles retrieved from the wobbly bedside table, was a hairy thing with lengthy ears.

Is that a rabbit, Flink? she said aloud, because talking to pets was a kind of madness that was known and acceptable. Even talking to houseplants was considered fairly sane.

Why did you bring that creature in here, Flink?

His motivation was not her only concern. The practicalities were also an issue. She should be able to believe anything now, looking, as she did, to the floor, where roots protruded further than they had done the day before. They reached up along the walls in thick tangles. What she was most baffled by was Flink's sudden ability to jump in from the garden. Whether he had come in via the balcony or the French windows, it was a metre's jump to the bottom of the balustrade and another metre to the top. It was not impossible. She patted Flink.

I didn't think you had it in you, she said.

Perhaps he just needed the eagerness which having something to fetch brought on. It was strange that he had found a rabbit at all in their urban garden. The animal looked shabby enough to be wild, but it was pretty torn apart. It might be someone's pet.

Oh dear, she said.

Blood was seeping into the sheets and surely ruining the mattress. She picked the creature up by the ears, which seemed made for this purpose, and dropped it onto the floor. She patted Flink again, still proud of his athletic feat, despite the nastiness of his pet murder. The red mark on the sheet was moist and glistening, and she was certain it was already too late to save the mattress, but, if she hurried, she might soak up the worst of it with a cold, wet cloth before it coagulated.

She rotated so her legs hung over the side of the bed. The rabbit on the floor looked like a stuffed toy that had landed in meat. It didn't look like it had ever been alive and certainly didn't look like it had ever been capable of a hop, but that was the way of dead things.

Fresh blood had no smell at all. She was angry with herself for not producing the degree of shock the situation demanded, but it smelled lovely inside her flat right now, just like a meadow, and she could not get the image of a picnic basket out of her head.

A massive tangle of roots had established itself at her bedroom door. It was metres high, impassable to someone her age. The roots were not alone, however. Tangled up in them, and heaped on top, she saw a multitude of things – shoes and coats and one of those kick bikes. In her bedroom too, there were piles of books and bedside lamps and an extra chest of drawers that didn't belong to her. She wondered if the ground had regurgitated these items along with the branches. Other people's possessions felt more of an imposition than the plants, and she even felt affronted on behalf on the roots. She flung alien slippers and dressing gowns out the French windows, pulled out drawers and tipped other people's clothes into the bushes. The safety balustrade was gone. She looked around her bedroom, satisfied, pleased to give her roots space to breathe and stretch. Flink scrambled down the mountain of branches and possessions at the bedroom door, scampered across the floor, and crashed onto the bushes.

She held onto the jamb of the window and watched as the rascal ran off with a few other dogs around the back garden, looping and panting, and maybe he deserved his fun. He came back to his position at the opposite side of the bushes regularly and gave her a little whine before taking off again. One of the dogs was a fawn-coloured pom-pom; another was a mid-sized dog with a slight limp who resembled a brown sheep. The big dog who had been on her balcony the other day was with them too.

Linda felt the weight on her bones more this morning than ever before, but she would have to go after him, and there was only one way out of this room.

If she were in her right mind, she would be worried that the railing at the French windows was gone, but right now it was to her advantage. Getting down on her knees, she lowered a chair into the flower bed below her window. The legs of the chair sunk into the earth as she climbed out, but she managed to get down without falling. No one else was up this early.

She didn't have Flink's leash or any treats to tempt him back to her, and she found herself trailing the dogs as they circled the fountain. She tried to make out how long had passed since the last thing she could remember, which was when Flink had lost a tooth on a big stick, or was it a root? She remembered the meeting out here the evening before too, or at least she thought that was a memory. They always had their meetings inside, and it had the taste of a dream. Her dreams of late were full of the woods, the undergrowth, in some sort of Little Red Riding Hood fable she could not clearly recall now. Her dreams and her waking hours were becoming muddled, so she could hardly tell which was which anymore, except that most of what she remembered seemed likely to belong to the dream world.

Flink and the other dogs were drinking from the fountain, and she felt so thirsty she was almost tempted to join them.

She saw that the garden gate was gone, which must be how all these dogs had come in here. They took off through the missing gate now and continued in a dribble of paws down the street.

It hurt her knees and ankles to keep up with them, but she followed them to the small park across from her old block. She looked up to her old apartment, and the steep tilt this required of her head resulted in a bit of a dizzy spell. She should never have moved out, but it was too late now. Flink was running in and out of the bushes with the other dogs. Linda blamed the glossy dog that belonged to the architects, since he was the biggest and seemed to be leading them in whatever game or hunt they were about. Flink was surely the oldest. It was unusual for a dog to reach his age at all. She had been lucky there.

She called to Flink, told him to come here, told him he was a good boy. The big dog had already continued down the street, and the brown sheepdog took off after him.

Flink and the fluffy mop remained. The little furball ran up to her and yapped, before she took off after the others.

Flink, that's a good boy, come here, she said.

He tottered towards her but stopped when she mirrored his movement. She stepped back again, and Flink inched towards her.

She heard the deep crack of a bark from down the street, and Flink's head turned. The other dogs were waiting for him.

Flink scuttled after them, stopped and turned to Linda. He ran back to her, half the distance between them, then tilted his head and whined at her before scampering off again. He repeated this several times, and Linda found she was following him.

They were good dogs, in a way. They waited for her at every corner.

# Eva

Eva awoke to the noise of something wooden rumbling, or shaking.

It was her mobile, vibrating, and the name Sonja Flynn was on the screen. The phone lay where it had dropped from her limp, outstretched hand, on wooden terrace boards. The boards were really a jigsaw puzzle of small squares, which some people used to make their balconies feel cosy underfoot.

Eva stopped the noise. She didn't know where she was, and almost immediately she knew exactly where she was. This was the ground floor of her own building, a balcony that looked straight out over the garden, a balcony that stuck out, just over the level of the rose bushes, a balcony directly under her own, two floors down.

She looked up to the underside of Nora and Stella's balcony, but that, of course, did not help. She had no idea how she had got down here. This was Linda Kleveland's balcony.

She got up off the recliner with difficulty. Her hips hurt and her back too. She saw, to her increased amazement, that it was her own sun chair she had been sitting on. The thick woollen blanket that had covered her was also her own, yet she had no recollection of bringing them down here, nor of coming here at all. There was quite a collection of terrace furniture on the balcony. It was jammed full of all sorts of seats and potted plants. She saw her own small terrace table and the matching bench. Linda had been busy.

Eva folded the sun recliner in three to make it a more portable size, but it wouldn't fold flat. The hinges were bent and the tubular metal legs slightly contorted. She slid her woollen blanket between the folds of the chair. The balcony door was already ajar, and it didn't creak when she opened it wide.

She heard dogs in the garden and saw that Rhodesian ridgeback running after Linda's dog and two others – with Linda trailing them around the fountain. The fountain had not come on yet. It was too early. She wanted to call out to Linda, but she would wake everyone if she did, and what would she say then? She had no way of explaining how she had ended up down here. She breathed into her hand and found no whiff of alcohol. She might have been drugged, kidnapped. She was completely blank. The last thing she remembered was folding out a sun chair on her own balcony and sitting down with a woollen blanket over her against the cold. She was on the phone. She was on hold. She must have fallen asleep.

There were clothes in the bushes.

Eva pulled into the shady living room, out of sight. She brought the sun recliner with her, tripping repeatedly across the messy floor in the darkness. She couldn't see much, but she could tell the floor was filthy, strewn with who knows what, crammed with furniture, and Linda had let her dog bring in big sticks, which were flung around the floor, big branches lodged under the furniture. She would have to speak to Knut about this. The old woman needed looking after, and Eva was done with being a night-watchwoman – if that's what this was. She stumbled, almost falling over. There was a hole in the floor, and for an instant she thought she saw a pair of eyes in the dark cavity. She didn't wait to check.

Linda's hallway was even worse, with piles of coats and shoes, and furniture stacked to precarious heights in a nightmarish, overgrown mound that blocked the passage to the bedroom entirely, and she heard worrying creaking and cracking noises.

She sent a text to Knut and Une: *Linda in garden. Needs you straight away. Look in apartment.*

On Linda's hall table, atop a messy pile of all sorts of letters, gloves, hats and even shoes, there was a large number of keys in a plastic zipper bag. Eva had ordered and distributed the new keys for the fireproof stairwell doors, so she recognized them immediately. The apartment codes were noted on each key in her own handwriting. This was her collection of spare keys, in her bag, but its presence here made no sense. Her own key was obviously not in there. Rooting in the pile on top of the hall table, she found her own set of keys resting on the heel of a slipper.

The barking and pattering of paws from the back garden had ceased. Eva pulled her own small, three-legged stool from the pile. There might be more, but this was as much as she could carry in one go. She was certain that was her own missing table and bench she had seen on Linda's balcony just now, and the keys ... Linda was their thief, the old devil, and no one to suspect her, sweet and ancient as she was. It was almost impressive how she had managed to lift her loot down the stairs – if she didn't have an accomplice. Knut and Une's daughter had the slight look of a drug addict about her. Eva wondered if this was why Une had been so eager to be the one to contact the police.

She leaned against the wall. Her back was aching. Her eyes had still not adjusted to the darkness, after sleeping so long on the balcony, but she didn't feel safe turning on the light. She had to put these burglaries into context, alongside the greater mystery of her presence on Linda's balcony.

If Linda – or her granddaughter – found Eva's door open one day, then they could take what they wanted. Once they found the bag of spare keys, they had access to the whole building. This did not look like the work of professional thieves. Most of the furniture was badly damaged, unsellable.

There was a loud creak and Eva escaped from the apartment and flew up the stairs. The steps felt oddly shallow.

It was a strange relief to get in home again, considering the worry her walls had been giving her recently. She brought the sun chair through to the balcony and almost stepped right out, hindered only by an uncharacteristic direction in the wind, a gust of air that swept up over her from below.

Her balcony was gone.

Gone.

The slab, railings and everything else were simply gone, not there. She could see straight down to Nora and Stella's balcony below hers. She was surprised that they had no plants in their flower boxes, or any plants at all on their balcony. Perhaps the work with the gardening committee was too much for them. People have their limits.

Her balcony was gone.

Holding onto the door jamb, she looked up and saw that the architects' balcony was gone too. She became suddenly uncertain as to whether they had a balcony in that position, though she would have said she knew this building inside out. Perhaps they didn't have a balcony because they had a terrace. She could see no scar where their balcony had been ripped off, though, looking down again, the same was true of her own. There was a stripe of concrete in the brickwork, where the balcony must have been attached, but it did not look newly sawed off or cracked. If anything, the concrete looked old and weathered.

There was no pile of rubble on the balcony below hers, nor in the garden below. It was as if it had never been there.

# Knut

Bibbi's voice came from her bedroom, Ready or not, here I come!

Where is everything? said Knut, though no one was listening. He was alone in the living room, where half the furniture was missing.

Then he remembered.

We've been robbed!

It must have happened during the night, while they slept. He would have to buy a bolt.

I'm coming to find you, Teddy!

Bibbi's mother-voice was younger than her normal tone.

During the night, Knut had snuck outside and stolen buckets of sand from the playschool down the street. He had rolled back the carpet and filled up the holes as best he could. He would tell Fritjof and Frida they had put down floor covering because of the condition of the wood. He could mention the bad quality without specifying holes. As soon as humanly possible, they must move out.

Keep your place or you'll be caught! called Bibbi, who didn't seem to have noticed that they had been robbed, or worse. She probably thought they stored the furniture somewhere while they were putting down the carpets. She had come home late again last night. She was innocent. He was almost certain.

It was difficult to stand on a floor so damaged without staring at it. He forced his gaze upwards, to the ceiling, the lamps, out the windows to the treetops and the neighbouring building. He went and leaned against the windowsill and looked at the apartment directly opposite, which would soon be theirs. He wondered if he would often stand over there, looking over here, and how it would make him feel. No matter how he felt, he would be standing on a better floor, and any amount of disorientation would be worth it. Fritjof and Frida would never have ordered a polyester carpet. They would understand how to repair floors. They could figure it out.

Is Teddy in here? said Bibbi, creaking open the wardrobe in the hallway. No! Is he in here?

He turned from his perfect neighbours, feeling like the dark side of a theatrical mask, and leaned his backside against the windowsill. The apartment was airy and uncluttered with most of the furniture gone – stolen – and even their various knick-knacks taken. He should be angry, but he felt unencumbered, like he was walking naked in the wilderness. They had each other, and they could get new furniture for the new apartment. Maybe their insurance would cover it.

Bibbi continued. Where could Teddy be? Hmm, not here, not here ...

Between the doors to the dining room and the hallway, his Amundsen chest took on a new prominence, for lack of companions. It had always been there, and he was worried about moving it. It was a piece of furniture he normally overlooked, unless he needed to pull out a rug, but it was significant in itself. Roald Amundsen, Knut's great-great-grandfather on his mother's side, had supposedly taken the chest with him on his polar expedition, or one of his other voyages: they weren't sure. It was covered in engravings and carvings. The carpet fitters had almost broken their backs shifting it. For a chest that had purportedly travelled the world, it was unflinchingly static. It would outlast them all, the whole human race.

Une came in with her palms raised, a gesture Teddy had inherited, a problem he inherited too.

What happened? she said, in a whisper.

We've been robbed, said Knut. The two armchairs are gone and that sideboard that was in the dining room, all the plants and cushions, the record cupboard, the dining chairs ... You didn't put them in the basement?

Everything was moved around for the carpets, she said, but ... where's Teddy?

They're playing. They're all right. They don't realize what's happened.

Une went to join in the chase, though she did not resemble a person playing. Knut went out onto the terrace, but there wasn't much searching he could do there. He wondered what had happened to the potted plants, if Linda took them with her. Linda: he must call down to her and tell her

315

the news. His phone was missing. He had tried checking the usual places – on top of the hall table, on his bedside locker – but the places themselves were gone. They should call the police. Une had lodged an online report of theft for the whole building last night, when they got back from the AGM. He looked across at Fritjof and Frida's apartment again. Was it far enough?

Inside, the chase was still on.

Teddy! Teddy, give us a clue, said Bibbi. Say peek-a-boo, wherever you are.

He heard a distant, muffled peep-peep.

Knut joined in. He opened the wardrobe in the main bedroom and checked behind the clothes. That's where he always hid as a boy, evading his own parents so many times. He checked under the bed and under the pillows. The chest of drawers, with all its contents, had been taken. What if Teddy had been hiding in there when it was stolen? No, it must have been stolen in the night, and he wasn't hiding then. Knut went out to the hallway.

When did you see him last? he said.

Just now, said Une, from the living room, where she had heaved open the trunk and was pulling rugs out onto the floor.

Be careful, said Knut, there might be woodlice.

They both looked at the old chest. It wasn't right to keep this national heirloom at home. It could be stored in better conditions in a museum.

They heard another faint peep-peep.

Teddy?

They heard a tiny voice say, I'm in here!

There wasn't much more checking they could do in the empty living room. In the kitchen, Knut and Une opened all the cupboard doors, checked behind the pots and in the deep pantry.

Bibbi came in and opened the fridge, the oven.

Knut went back to his bedroom and looked in the wardrobe again, checking all the shelves this time, checking tiny pockets Teddy could surely not fit in, but children were flexible. They could roll up small.

In the little cloakroom off the hallway, Une was standing on a chair and searching the hat shelf. He heard Bibbi pulling out drawers in her bedroom. He went in to her and found her opening her suitcase.

They both ran out to the terrace, looked over the railing. They did the same on the empty balcony they hardly ever used.

Teddy! Teddy!

I'm in here! came the little voice.

I hear it best in the dining room, or maybe the living room, said Knut. Check the trunk again.

He did it himself. Bibbi was pulling the couch away from the wall, pulling off the upholstery. She was crying, but forced her voice to stay cheerful: Teddy, sweetheart, come out!

He could hear Une opening the bathroom cabinet. He heard the toilet lid slam.

Did you find him? he called.

No!

Teddy!

I am here.

# Gunnar

Gunnar, is that you?

He had only come back for a change of clothes. The radio was on but, through it, he could hear voices upstairs: Where are you? Teddy, come out! Peep-peep!

Gunnar?

Just a minute, Auntie Hildegunn.

He told himself to be cruel now, if he had to. He couldn't understand his fear of this woman, or the ease at which he obeyed her orders. It was pity, that's what it was. He was too soft. He went straight to his room to change.

Gunnar, come here, can't you?

There was a tone of chastisement in her words, which he by no means deserved. He had just spent the best part of the day bringing a mound of old furniture to a second-hand shop. It was inconceivable, downright creepy, that more of her own furniture had been stolen, and that it had happened while they slept. It was equally appalling that it had been replaced by other junk. Did the thieves really think they wouldn't be able to tell the difference? Rational thought simply didn't match these events.

Gunnar, come here this instant!

She could get away with saying anything, now that she was both injured and in an unstable mental state, but Gunnar had his integrity to protect. His solicitor had told him to guard his self-respect in the first year after divorce. Pride can be a good thing.

He tucked his shirt in neatly before going to Hildegunn's assistance. Her voice was only marginally louder than the calls from the noisy neighbours above. He found her in the dining room. He almost walked right over her.

Hildegunn! What on earth are you doing under there?

She was lying on her back on the ground, underneath a heavy mahogany sideboard, with only her head and one arm sticking out. The sideboard was badly damaged, its legs skewed and splintered.

How did you get in there? he said.

There was only just enough room for her thin body underneath, and those carved wooden legs didn't look like they would hold its weight off her much longer.

Get me out, Gunnar.

He lifted up one end, doing his best to bend his knees and keep his back straight. An image of carrying Hildegunn down the stairs in his arms kept popping into his mind, but the situation didn't require such heroics.

Can you roll out?

His mid-back and his arms strained, and his feet slipped on a rubber mat that was under the sideboard. With ample moaning, Hildegunn began to shuffle out. She moved a centimetre at a time, pushing off with her good leg and leveraging with her elbows. When she was finally free, he let the sideboard down with a thud. Something inside it made an oddly human squeak, but he could hardly be blamed for breakages, given the circumstances. The neighbours' voices grew louder: The game is over, Teddy! You win! Come out now!

It was almost as if their voices rose in response to the gravity in Hildegunn's situation, though she was out now at least.

He got a hold of her under the arms and lifted her up. He didn't trust the armless dining chairs to support her sufficiently. Her body was soft and floppy in his hands, though her bones were hard and resistant, and he was sure he was going to break her. He felt nauseous and retched as he laid her into the wheelchair. He kept a hold of her shoulder until he was certain she would not fall right out again.

Are you injured?

Hildegunn fingered her ribs and her knees, and just looked at her hips.

I can hardly feel anything.

What possessed you, Hildegunn?

She looked at him for a long while before she responded, so he could not trust whatever calculated response she gave.

It came from above, she said.

She was speaking unusually slowly.

I was only doing my exercises, she said, on my mat. I was doing heel slides, like they said I should. There was so much junk lying around, and this was the only free spot. Then that monstrosity came down upon me.

Someone put it on top of you?

He shouldn't have asked. It wasn't wise to play along with her delusions.

No, it appeared from above, Gunnar.

Right, well ...

It did, and I know what you're thinking.

Yes, well, let's not argue.

Gunnar was almost impressed. She had managed to manoeuvre her exercise mat under two legs of the sideboard. He had struggled with its weight himself, though she would not have needed to lift it as high as he had done. She might have tilted the sideboard and slid the mat under, one leg at a time. Of course, there was no logical reason why she should have done so, why she would want to lie underneath a piece of furniture, so he gave up on teasing logic out of her.

I'm glad you're all right, he said. You gave me an awful fright.

It's not safe here, she said.

He wheeled her out to the living room and put her chair in the parked position in a free spot between the doors to the dining room and the hallway. Despite the efforts of a whole morning, the living room was still an unseemly mixture of cluttered and barren.

Contents make all the difference, he said.

They were still shouting above him: Teddy! I'm in here! Please, please, Teddy!

He could hardly think.

It's those dreaded Klevelands, however they're doing it, said Hildegunn. This is their junk. They're trying to scare me away, but I won't abandon my ship.

Can I get you a glass of water?

I won't be pushed aside by anyone. That Linda tried before, you know. She tried to push me out of my own bed, and I'll tell you, I'm not going to let her son do the same. You can go up there right now, Gunnar, and tell them to take all this back.

Was Knut Kleveland in here? I thought it was the Blix twins, but I'd believe anything at this stage.

He didn't want to rule out that something more sinister might be going on. Perhaps Hildegunn had been trying to hide, in a particularly batty manner. He had heard of old women being abused, senile old women who lived at home and who would not be able to report and convincingly explain what had happened.

Tell him to take his horrible furniture back. Tell him we know what he's doing, but I won't be forced out. They've even enlisted the child to harangue me, Gunnar. They have no limits.

The carpenters or carpet installers he met in the stairwell the other day, they must have been going to the Klevelands upstairs. It had to be them. He began to wonder if there might not be a logical explanation there. He thought of the ugly furniture he had just got rid of. The second-hand shop would not have sold it yet, if Knut wanted it back.

Did you let him leave his furniture here, Hildegunn?

I did no such thing. He dumped it on me. Why would I want their hideous furniture in my home? That sideboard is polished mahogany veneer, for heaven's sake.

He was on Hildegunn's side, of course, but he still found it hard to imagine those very normal-seeming neighbours forcing an old woman to store furniture against her will – and stealing from her. The daughter though ... Who had said she was some sort of addict?

What's the name of Knut's daughter?

Bibbi, they call her. She's a drug addict, and an unmarried mother, not that I'd hold the latter against a person, but she's one of them.

Gunnar wondered if it was worth his bother trying to make sense of this. She had obviously forgotten she'd let Knut or Bibbi in, though it was uncharacteristic of her to do her sworn enemies a favour. Her sense of persecution was certainly strong. Whether it was based on actual coercion, he couldn't really say. A bruise was beginning to form on Hildegunn's cheekbone.

He wanted to call the public health nurse, but ... that bruise would cause suspicion. He didn't want to be accused of anything.

I'm going to ring the police, he said.

Hildegunn let him rest a hand on her shoulder as he listened to the tone.

What a nightmare this well-spun, mutually beneficial plan had turned into. He could go back home and live in the garage while they did up his house. It might even be worth the expense of renting somewhere for a month or so.

Hildegunn was groaning.

The voices above had risen beyond what might be considered remotely tolerable. Teddy! Teddy! they called out repeatedly, and a young child's voice called back, I'm in here!

This is going too far, said Gunnar. You're completely right, Hildegunn. Do they think they have the block to themselves?

Teddy, come out and I'll give you chocolate, said a man's voice from overhead. Chocolate, Teddy, chocolate!

Why do they have to roar? said Hildegunn.

There was a noise from the dining room, the creak of a door followed directly by a thump, and Gunnar was certain the neighbours' ugly sideboard had collapsed.

Serves them right, he said.

He went to see.

A young boy, a toddler, was standing between the guest sideboard and dining table, like something from a horror film. His hair was stuck to his head with sweat, his eyes were red, and he was shaking.

The voices overhead continued to call, Teddy! Teddy!

Gunnar must have stood there staring for a long while. All the noise in the building continued, but there was a separate noise, a pressure, in his ears.

What is it? called Hildegunn.

How did you get down here? said Gunnar.

He hadn't meant to whisper. His words must have sounded threatening, because the boy was trembling.

Gunnar pointed at the ceiling, and the child nodded.

This way, said Gunnar, and he led the boy out to the hallway so Hildegunn wouldn't see him, though she called after him with a string of requests.

In the stairwell, the boy knew where to go. Gunnar considered letting him go up alone, but he might not know to knock on the door. At what age did one learn that?

He needn't have worried about blame. When the door opened, Knut and his family tumbled over their child, smothering him in kisses and hugs.

Knut eventually stood to face him.

Gunnar opened and closed his mouth. What could he say?

Your furniture is in Hildegunn's apartment, he said. I think someone switched them, somehow, your carpet fitters or ...

There's nothing here, said Knut. Look for yourself.

They went and stood in the middle of the empty living room together, breathing in time. Gunnar could see through open doors to other empty rooms, and he heard the women feeding and coddling the infant in the kitchen.

Gunnar! Gunnar!

Now it was Hildegunn's voice which passed through the floor.

I'd better ...

# Fritjof

Linda will be delighted when we tell her, said Une.

She was hoarse and had a glazed look in her eyes, significantly degraded from how she had appeared at the AGM yesterday. Knut too. Fritjof hoped they weren't contagious. All the windows were open.

They had been through all the details but lingered in the hallway. Fritjof wondered if he should edge past them and open the door. Any minute now, a flock of geese could fly overhead and foil their plan.

Thank you so much for accommodating our schedule, said Frida. You're right: it will be so much easier just to move everything straight into your place.

They said the paperwork should go through next week, said Fritjof.

We'll be all packed up by then, said Knut.

Oh, it this yours? said Fritjof. He picked a pen off the floor. And these ...

Oh, silly me, said Une. I must have spilled my peppermint drops on the way in. They're all over the place.

Fritjof helped her gather the sweets. Her lips were moving, as though counting, and he hoped she wasn't going demented. That might be grounds for reversing the sale, though she was only just retired, and Knut seemed fine.

The washing machine began to screech the spin programme, a fortuitous prompt that turned the poor old dupes towards the door.

Fritjof pressed pause on the machine. In a strange silence, they listened to Knut and Une descending the stairwell, knocking on Linda's door, calling her name. Then the street door rattled closed behind them. Frida groaned.

My ankle, she said, heading for the mattress in the bedroom, the only remaining piece of furniture now that the clothes horse with its thirty-odd cloths had mysteriously disappeared from the terrace.

They had packed away everything absorbent, all their books and all but their most essential clothes.

There was no shade in this apartment anymore. It was so bright he put on his sunglasses.

Frida was lying on the mattress with both her legs resting vertically against the wall, reading a book. It seemed a bit precarious to lie right there in the spot where she had fallen through the roof. What if the caretaker came and landed on her? They should have moved the mattress to the other side of the room.

What's the book? he said.

She held it up for him to see: *The Woman in the Dunes.*

It's about a village that will be swallowed up by sand if they don't keep shovelling it back every day, she said. I can't imagine how it's going to end – but I wasn't reading. Look at this.

She pulled a folded sheet of paper from the book and passed it up to him. I called Mirek, she said. He can do it next week, but ...

Frida had sketched a system of wooden planks to hold a sheet of plastic in place under the ceiling.

We'll catch anything that comes through the roof, she said, and we could even put a weep hole in the middle with a bucket underneath. Then we chuck the lot before the Kleve-lands take over.

Genius, said Fritjof. Let's build it ourselves. We can't wait.

See the back of the sheet? There's a list of materials. You had better head out straight away before the suppliers close. What's that?

There was a flash, like sun reflected off glass, for just an instant, and afterwards the room was so dark he had to remove his sunglasses. There was a deafening rumbling and then another flash.

Frida sat up in bed.

I thought I felt a drop, she said.

There was another flash and a shattering rumble of thunder almost straight afterwards. The light came from above, but the sound came, amplified, from the void over the back garden, thundering between the two blocks, back and forth like a beating. The rain started up at full force, hammering the floor.

He started mopping in the dining room, because that's where he found the bucket. He thought he heard Frida call, but her voice box was no match for the thrumming rain and the thunder. Running in to the bedroom, he saw she was hopping around on one leg, covering the mattress with plastic – they had bought huge rolls of it – but the floor was so drenched the mattress would soak it up from below.

He pulled the load of hot cloths and towels from the dryer, and Frida almost toppled when he flung them at her. His mop bucket needed to be emptied already.

The forecast for next week was good. He hoped this was the last thunderstorm before the weather broke.

Frida brushed waves of water out to the terrace over the low door saddle. He started to do the same at the balcony door, until he realized that this door now led to nowhere. The balcony was gone. He tried to remember if balconies were among Eva's list for the structural report, but he didn't have time to think. He moved away from the balcony door. It might be structurally unstable.

A huge pond had accumulated in the hallway. He opened the door to the stairwell and brushed the water out with his mop. Not the best implement for this job. Angelica and her family were gone, so there was no one to spy on him, and the accursed surveillance cameras had not been installed yet. The rainwater made the comforting sound of a waterfall as it descended the stairs. Frida was calling him inside, but he continued to brush out the water until he heard a latch open downstairs. He slammed shut his own door and didn't answer when he heard Eva shouting and pounding.

Rain poured over his face, so his eyelids became sore from blinking and squinting. The sun was breaking through, without any respite from the rain, and Fritjof was doubly blinded when lightning struck again.

# Raj

Raj broke into a clattering run when he reached their street. It was late. The windows of the apartment were wide open, but it was too dark inside, and he could not make anything out. The bushes were half-submerged in mud. He heard a noise from Krishna's room, a movement, and he climbed in.

Krishna? Are you there? Did they come?

At first, he thought the room was smaller, the ceiling lower. Then he realized: the earth was really deep. His feet sank into it but didn't reach the floor beneath.

Raj, is that you? What did they say? Did you find a place?

Nothing. Can I turn on the lights?

They don't work, and my phone is dead. Here.

He handed Raj a torch, and Raj lit up the room in narrow circles. The earth was level with the mattress on Krishna's bed, so he seemed to be sleeping on the floor. Raj whacked his head off the metal ceiling lamp. Krishna closed his eyes when Raj shone the torch in his face.

Krishna, you are filthy.

I tried to clean it. I threw it out the window. I worked all day long.

I'm sorry I left you.

What did the postdocs say?

After unsuccessfully attempting to force a meeting with the bank and a tenants' advocacy group, Raj had gone to a symposium. He needed someone, anyone, to witness what was happening here.

Krishna, he said, they were discussing the interface between data analysis and social media coverage of climate change, and then I asked if any of them had time to come and witness the degradation in my apartment. They just looked at me. It was as if they didn't understand the question.

Pradeep is gone.

We can't wait until he gets back. I'm calling the police again.

I told him to go. I told him to save himself. He is going back to his home. He will be married.

Married? To whom?

A woman of his parents' choosing.

No … When did he go?

I believe he has left already.

Raj deleted the number of the emergency services and rang Pradeep instead. He was cut off straight away.

There's no answer.

He would answer if he could, said Krishna. It was not safe for him here.

It's not safe for any of us. Do you think he's on a plane?

He took his stuff. He gave me this.

Krishna brought an envelope from under his pillow and handed it to Raj. It contained a stack of bank notes, a mixture of euros, British pounds, Swedish krone and one Norwegian fifty-krone note. The latter would not buy them much.

It was all he had, said Krishna.

Raj counted the money and made a calculation with rough exchange rates.

We'll take it to a bank on Monday, he said. We'll exchange it for krone and get a bus to some town where the hotels are not full. Tonight ... and tomorrow ... I don't know. We can sleep in the showers downstairs at work, or just go to the station. We both need a wash.

He looked at the money.

This will last us a few days, he said. We can wash and rest, and call the authorities, the embassy. We should not come back here again by ourselves.

I can't move, said Krishna.

I'll carry you.

He rang the emergency number now, and the tone went on and on, repeating.

They do not care, said Krishna.

Raj turned up the volume and put the phone on speaker in his breast pocket. He left Krishna, taking his torch. He climbed in through the window of his own bedroom. It was the same there, maybe deeper.

He broke open the wardrobe door, pulled his suitcases from the top shelf and packed everything he could reach, thanking providence that his most valuable and treasured belongings were stored high up.

He left his suitcases on the pavement and climbed into Krishna's room again. The dial tone continued in his pocket. He packed up Krishna's most important things: documents, electronics, clothes.

Where is your passport, Krishna?

Leave it.

Where is it?

My bedside table.

The low bedside table was completely submerged. Raj used a book to dig away the earth.

Leave it, said Krishna. I will go to the embassy.

Raj continued to shovel and scrape, until he had laid bare the top of the little cupboard. He tugged on the wood, thinking he might be able to tear the top off at least, but it was too well lodged. He sat on Krishna's bed to catch his breath. He took out his phone, unable to believe he could be on hold so long. He hung up and rang a taxi, but then his screen went black. Their electrical sockets were under the ground.

Listen, said Raj. I am going to bring our luggage to the train station now. It is open all night and there are big lockers there. Then I'll be back for you, if the police do not get here first. I will run back, I promise. I will go into a police station.

My mother's teapot, said Krishna.

Is it in the kitchen?

Krishna nodded, and Raj knew he should be annoyed at this, that he should refuse to go searching for a teapot when there was so much at stake and such a hurry, and a plan already formed in his mind, but he knew the story of the teapot. Krishna's mother had saved it from her home during a flood. It was all she could save, and she would not have chosen it, given the choice. She would have chosen photographs, paintings or letters, or her children's birth certificates and examination results, but all she had been able to save was this small, green teapot.

It is not of any monetary value, said Krishna.

Krishna, pray, said Raj. Let me hear you.

The bedroom door was sufficiently ajar for Raj to press through. It was dark in the corridor, and the earth was banked higher up. With Krishna's voice as an anchor behind him, he used the torchlight to guide him towards the kitchen. The ground got higher and higher the further in he went. He was climbing a slope. While he could touch the ceiling in the hallway, he had to bend his head in the kitchen. The earth was up to the level of the worktop. His feet sank into it with each step. He reached to open the overhead cupboard where the teapot was stowed. He had it in his hand when he turned and saw the glassy eyes.

Stumbling backwards, he fell over on the earthy mound, the hill. His scream came out a whisper.

He still had a grasp of the teapot handle, but the lid had fallen off. He felt around him for it, with his teapot hand, keeping the ray of the torch on the badger, who stood completely still, at home. Above the salty congestion of his own breathing, he could hear Krishna's far-off voice.

# Sunday

*Two-legs-no-wings make nests with bottoms like water surface, but solid, no dip through. We found exception, but it floats, nothing under, no spill. They make side-of-nests like cliff but flat-flat on the up-down like nothing else, like water-top turned to the up-down, but no surge to curve like waterfall. They must feel pull from side like we feel pull below, to do to hard what elsewhere does to wet.*

*It was he who first noticed his shit slid through. It was a magical place, he said, the father of our cracked future. We flew down to where the shit landed. Was this how to choose a good nesting branch? It was sturdy, but flat like water-top, thin slivers of tree attached to cliff too flat for real. I laid my eggs on his loose pile of twigs, and he put more in roll-stop along the edge. It was cliff itself that failed. We had been there two suns when I saw with one eye and then the other that my wing stretched through. Look! I shrieked, and he was delight, flew through cliff and back again, twittering like madbird.*

*For a moment it seemed our nest hovered. My wings, his wings, spread. We swooped upwards, away from shell cracked open from outside, our future's death glistening white far below. My mate is gone too. His fright ascended at a different angle. I keep soaring. Tilting down, the landing places all seem ... later.*

# Sonja

The song came first, a rapidly shaken whitty-whitty-whew-whew-whew.

Sonja's eyes blinked towards the clear and speedy, whitit-it-whitit-it-whitit-hew. It was a call she recognized, one which had raised her forehead from her work many times that spring. Her hunch was confirmed by the red and black markings on the bird's head and the shock of yellow on his wings. This was a goldfinch, and he was clinging with astounding lightness to the stem of a cornflower, dipping the sharp cone of his beak into the mess of lilac petals. He flitted down to the soil and nipped up tiny dry twigs, collecting a bundle of nesting material in his bright yellow beak.

Sonja had planted cornflower seeds in the balcony boxes, her only contribution to the flowering of the back garden. She was fascinated by the speed at which they grew, and she was particularly enamoured when they bloomed twice from the same bud. The most wonderful thing about cornflowers, however, was that they were so attractive to goldfinches. One afternoon, a whole family had flocked here to feed.

This cornflower was growing directly from the ground, just a couple of metres away.

Sonja sneezed and sat up, all in one swaying motion. A sheet of sketch paper was crumpled in her hand and – where? She had been sleeping on top of her desk. First she let her feet dangle, then she shifted her weight and climbed down to a floor of earth and weeds.

She turned, stumbled, looked up at the sky.

It was over – the bricks, the walls. The building was gone.

She tripped over a drying rack. Her knees sank into the soil. Between the plants and roots, there were potted plants too, upended. The corner of a flat-screen TV stuck out of the ground: a futuristic crop.

Her shoulder hurt.

All around her she saw piles of sofas, dining tables, coffee tables, chairs of all descriptions, books and pictures and ornaments scattered all around and sticking out of the soil like they had been dumped there.

She moved further, to where multiple wardrobes were toppled over, drawers extended and clothing tipping onto the ground. Three double beds were tilted on top of her own. Looking through watery eyes, she saw branches, or roots sticking out of the pile of mattresses and bedclothes. The roots moved, the – her fingers rubbed dirt into her eyes. These were arms and legs, not branches.

She knocked over the stack, and people crawled out or stayed put, moaning or quiet. Those that could walk staggered away, calling to each other. Someone asked her if she had a phone. It was her neighbour, someone she knew, but she could not remember his name.

Around the toppled beds she moved, past a mound of porcelain, coats and hatstands, to a messy pile of armchairs, side tables, toys, paintings, to her own fridge magnets. Kitchen: even this good room, this safe place, was gone.

Circling, and there were her own drawings again, on her desk, but mostly on the ground. She gathered them up, brushed off soil, smudging, destroying.

On her knees, by the edge, where the wall once was, her fingers dug into the soil and uprooted invasive plants. Others were digging too, so it seemed to make sense. A young man was digging frantically nearby, another neighbour, though they had never spoken. The tenant: he lived downstairs. He used to.

She dug through anything soft and scanned for hard, red clay. She didn't find a single brick, though she dug elbow deep all along the line where they should be.

Somewhere, far off, a marching band was playing.

## Gunnar

Earthquake, he whispered.

He tried to remember if acts of God like this were covered by insurance. He should know. He was glad Hildegunn had turned down his offer to buy. Poor Hildegunn, no insurance could cover the loss of her meticulously specified interior. He crawled around on the ground, looking for his phone, but it was all a muddle and he couldn't find it.

Hildegunn!

He should get up. No one seemed to be coming to help. He couldn't stay crouched here much longer. He was bruised somewhere, but he couldn't locate the spot. It was hard to get his bearings at all, he was so dizzy. He wondered if he'd got a knock to the head.

Has someone called the ... whoever deals with this sort of thing? he said.

There were people there, but no one took any notice of him.

The emergency services, he said. Call an ambulance, someone.

He stood up and leaned against a bunk bed. Looking around from there, he had a somewhat better view, and he realized that he had been wrong. He was not at home at all. He was in some sort of dump, some wasteland or unused lot, and it was creeping with tramps. Some of them were still sleeping. It must be early. Some of them were wandering around in a state of half-nakedness, talking to themselves or screaming. He had wandered into some sort of hippy colony, a band of loony vagrants.

Excuse me, he said to a disturbed-looking young woman. He had seen her somewhere before, he was sure, presumably before she fell from grace. She didn't acknowledge him. Perhaps she wasn't capable.

Can you tell me where I am? he said.

She continued rooting through the rubbish. Her hands were covered in dirt.

Excuse me, he said, I'm sorry, but I wonder if you could help me.

I told you, she said. I told you all, but would you listen?

Right, said Gunnar, I'm sorry. Can you tell me where we are?

Could it be? It was the troubled young woman from the AGM. She wandered away from him. Gunnar made to follow her, but he had to wait for his breath to gather sufficiently in his chest. What was he doing here – with her?

He had to get away from this place. Not a moment longer. The faster he got away, the faster he could receive help. He had to get to safety. If he knew where he was, he would at least know which direction to take. He had an extensive knowledge of the city, though he was not acquainted with its seedier corners.

Eyeing the buildings around the lot, he was struck by how well they looked. Judging by the building typology, this might be Hildegunn's area or somewhere similarly respectable. He didn't want to be noticed by someone he knew, but he would have to take the plunge. There was no alternative.

He walked past a pile of kitchen cabinets that were just like Hildegunn's, and he felt angry at whoever had thrown them out, someone who did not value originality in furnishings. There was a dining table the image of Hildegunn's, with a crack right down the middle. She kept serviettes and candles in a little drawer at the side. He had to force the drawer open, but he found precisely the contents he expected. The napkin he unrolled was even embroidered with the initials HLL.

There was a heavy pine table on top of this delicate piece, and Gunnar shoved it off. He cleared this dining table, which was surely Hildegunn's, knocking off various lamps and candelabras, plates and vases. He left a swirly Alvar Aalto vase in place because, though it was cracked, it belonged to Hildegunn. He recognized the coloured plates of an Arne Jacobsen pendant lamp. He had knocked his head on it at one of Hildegunn's dinner parties, years ago, while reaching for a bottle of Bordeaux.

A theory began to form in Gunnar's mind. The only thing that made sense was that Hildegunn's furniture had been stolen. The band of thieves that had been looting the building lately must have crept in during the night and swiped everything, including him. He presumed his inclusion had been an accident, and perhaps he was the reason they dumped the lot here. This was a heist gone wrong. When they realized they had robbed a man along with the furniture, the thieves must have panicked and dumped the loot here before fleeing.

He spied a mature-looking couple who seemed less crazy than the others, apart from the way they were clinging to one another. He put aside an impulsive hatred for these people —they resembled Hildegunn's upstairs enemies – could it be them? He asked if they had seen who dumped the last load of furniture here.

You didn't notice the registration plate, did you? he said.

How did this happen? said the man.

Do you know? said the woman.

Gunnar moved away. They might be his neighbours, unrecognizably bruised and dirty, but then they must have been kidnapped too. They were in a worse mental state than he was.

He had to get away. He thought of bringing what he could with him – the lamp, for instance – but it would seem too strange, walking along with it, and he must concentrate on getting himself to a hospital. Something was not right, he knew it, and he needed to get checked out.

He did worry about what state Hildegunn's apartment must be in and how she was coping. She had probably called the police. He would ring as soon as he could. As soon as he met a normal person, he would ask for help and borrow á phone. He continued through the dump, still looking for furnishings he might recognize. He wondered if the apartment door was smashed in anew.

He regretted not getting Hildegunn's apartment valued before this happened. The sum of the sales price and the insurance money for the stolen furniture would not be as much as an intact ensemble would fetch. It was sad, unfair in the extreme that this had happened to Hildegunn of all people. There was no one in the entire world of property who was quite so house-proud as his aunt.

He saw a pair of legs, legs with a hip-cast he recognized: her legs.

The rest of her, and he was in no doubt but that it was her, the rest of her was hidden, surely crushed, underneath a massive, carved wooden chest, a great log of a thing from some other time.

He grabbed the carved heads of a snake and a lion on the side of the chest and heaved.

Help! he called out. It's my aunt. She's stuck! Help, everyone, help!

Knut and Une – it *was* them – were beside him, heaving too, and together they lifted one end of the chest. He knew it was Hildegunn underneath, though she was unrecognizable. She was destroyed, crushed like a piece of meat, a flattened set of blood-filled nightclothes and her head – a slice. A pressed butterfly. It was Hildegunn, it was, but she was too flat even for a corpse. He wished the earth would swallow her fully, cover over this harm.

There were feet all around, at the edges of Hildegunn, and they set the chest down beside her, what remained. Gunnar looked away. He looked, instead, at the trunk, and knew there would never be any fairness. Hildegunn, who had furnished her world with choreographed lightness ... to be crushed by such a gaudy, heavy block of wood.

My blocks they are all hives today.
Today, they make rectangles proud,
between the edges, stripes to curl.
The little builders put lengths where

they eat which make the noise of horn,
and sticks bang on the stretched skin of
non-pets. Now big and small are wrapped
in shades of traffic lights, night sky.

They come out of my blocks, tap-tap
down my step-downs, they screech down my
slide close, and down, surprise! They mill
along my lines, where rolling is

outlawed. There is a whistle of
wild celebration o'er my tops,
but I feel flattened anthill here,
so overgrown, spread out too far,

with low-dense tunnels under street.
I should have piled up more, and built
myself up to a greater height.
What I lack most is boundary.

I have the water-edge, though it
is no periphery through time,
fade out with pitter-patter blocks
as I give way to woods. But this

it is the day of wider land,
not mine. I insufficient am.
The builders only know my name.
They hold it true that I belong

to them because they built me up.
I am communal figment and
they say they feel a sense of we
because of me. They use the word

of love, the symbol love they draw
for me. Their leader-blocks my core.
But if I discontinue all,
they will be more downcast than me.

A trace of me will linger on
and I can't say if I'll prefer
that trace to this ne'er-finished patch.

# Fritjof

There was nothing left of either building, no rubble or ruins, not even a structural skeleton. He and Frida stood before the tallest remaining element. It was composed of creepers, rose vines.

A chimney stack? he said.

With a glance between them, they decided. They pulled the creepers apart to see what they were clinging to – but this was the wrong question. The creepers were climbing up one another, without any support structure underneath. They were doing this by themselves.

They left the roses and followed apparent trails between the mounds of furniture and possessions.

These paths are where the walls were, he said.

Walls, said Frida. There is no such thing anymore.

It was still possible to make out which rooms had been where. He could tell by the contents, piled high in categorical heaps: dining, sleeping, cooking, relaxing. It was like a primitive map. It had an accusing quality too, like the piles of separated rubbish at the recycling plant. Without walls or floors to separate them in space, all these possessions became junk.

There was an awful stench of piss.

Help me lift, said Frida.

They each grabbed a corner of a bookcase, took hold of it along the side, because it was no longer one stable element. A naked woman crawled out from underneath and stood at a safe distance, staring at her trap.

Are you hurt? said Frida.

They let the bookcase crash down again.

The woman stood smiling at the splintered wood and splayed books, so Fritjof wondered if she had gone mad. It would only be reasonable.

Smash away, the woman said, and she seemed to be addressing the bookcase rather than them. She lifted the bloodied fingers of her right hand and held them before her eyes, and her smile was gone.

Of all the sorry ends, she said. Could a grand piano not have landed on me, at the very least? His stupid shelves. He won, with his stupid books.

She wandered over to another pile, where she retrieved a trousers and blouse from a toppled-open wardrobe, and put them on with her good hand, devoid of shame. Clothed, Fritjof recognized her. It was the pianist from downstairs.

There used to be a downstairs, he said.

He heard a sudden gurgling of water – a leak? The pianist heard it too and seemed to be led away by the sound.

Look, said Frida.

She was pulling their own stepladder out from behind a smashed piano. She opened it out, and held it steady, though there was no stable flooring anymore, not even any definite horizontal. Fritjof climbed up.

It's the fountain, he said. It's still intact. The garden too, it's still there. Frida, I think I see our geraniums.

Fritjof, said Frida.

I see Sonja, he said. She's okay.

Sonja was running around the block, what was their block. She ran up the one-sided street, turned left at the corner.

Sonja! he called out, and she looked at him but didn't stop.

He watched as she did lap after lap, tracing the edge of their world with her body. There were cars parked along the kerb. The small park across the street was as before. The other buildings that surrounded this lot were entirely unchanged. They looked just the same as he remembered them. Frida kept saying his name, but she didn't let go of the ladder. Eventually, Sonja stopped in front of what was once her own entrance. She pushed through the bushes and disappeared among the furniture.

People started to come out onto the balconies of the surrounding blocks: women in bunad dresses, men in suits, children waving red, white and blue flags. Some of the children had horns and drums, and, in the distance, Fritjof heard the cacophony of multiple marching bands. The people on the balconies were holding glasses of champagne and cups of coffee; they carried top-heavy open sandwiches on paper plates. Some of the children were already eating ice creams. Some of the people still seemed happy. They were particularly clean, and their chins tipped upwards with pride. It was the 17th of May. It was Constitution Day.

How? Had had these people not noticed until now? Their entrances were on the opposite side, facing other streets. They had no reason to walk past here. It was not on the way to anything. They came, as invited, to a 17th of May breakfast; they arrived at a normal front door, climbed stairs, took off their shoes and came inside apartments, pressing cheek to cheek, accepting refreshments, and they did not know — until now. Now they knew.

The neighbours and their visiting friends and families dropped strawberries and smoked-salmon sandwiches and pastries onto their balconies, and they fell quiet.

Fritjof's hand went up. Frida's voice whispered something like, *help*. Parents pulled their flag-wielding children away from the edges of balconies. Fritjof did not break his stare. He had a hold of them with his eyes.

There was a loud bang somewhere nearby, the noise of something heavy falling, or it could have been the single pound of a drum. The balconies emptied. After a pause, the streets filled with rapid footsteps. They fled, all their unharmed neighbours, all who had seen them like this, they fled downhill towards the sea. The sound of their feet was almost musical.

Fritjof and Frida emerged through thorny rose bushes into the garden. The overgrown grass of the lawn was soft underneath their feet. A crowd of neighbours from their two blocks had already gathered there, in the centre of the garden, beside the gurgling fountain, and they looked from one rectangle of smashed furnishings on one side of the garden to another similar rectangle of ruin directly opposite.

Is everyone accounted for? said Frida. Eva, do you have a list?

Oh yes, said Eva, I sleep with it in my pocket. You can count on me.

Fritjof heard a roar, holding words he could not understand.

Raj, said Frida.

She pulled Fritjof with her. They couldn't see him but followed Raj's voice around piles of dining tables and sideboards, bookshelves and a pool table. They found him on his knees, with dirt flying up behind him and landing on Hildegunn's nephew and the Klevelands. They were just standing there, staring, not helping.

Fritjof saw the hand.

It's Krishna, said Raj. You must help.

Raj's face stretched towards them, pleading with the whites of his eyes.

They knelt around Krishna's fist, three points of a triangle, and they dug with their hands, pulled the earth towards themselves and kicked it away behind them. They dug deeper into a compact subsoil, clay. They dug up his whole arm to his shoulder, and Fritjof felt Krishna's hair in his fingers. Frida blinked and whined. Tears made gullies down Raj's muddied cheeks. They scooped and threw off clods of heavy soil as large as they could grasp, and Raj's palms cleaned the earth off his friend's reposed face.

*The musical children blew and banged at the fore. The noisy children gathered in rows behind them, and, wave by wave, increasing in age, they moved forward. Their pace was a slow march. The waves disassembled and were reformed at intervals throughout the morning. A static wall of adults built up on either side of their route through the city, a watchful edge that cheered and waved flags. This was not victory. This was a parade of youth, of peace. It was loud, exhausting. There was a plan. Each wave passed the palace, then flowed out towards the sea, stopping just in time at a designated location, their individuals collected before the slow force of the march submerged them in the fjord. They turned towards home. They paused to chat, then turned towards home. They stopped for ice cream, hot dogs and takeaway coffee, then turned towards home.*

# Knut

In the dream, the young man kept digging and saying, Krishna, Krishna, but Krishna was not helping. A hand was visible, but it was a grown man's hand, too big to be Teddy's.

Come, said Une, and they began to walk back towards the part of the plot over which Bibbi and Teddy had slept.

Une's arm had fallen out of its sling. It was going in the wrong direction.

Wait, he said, and tied the rag around her, tightly. It might make it worse, forcing her bone to stay in the wrong position, but it would keep her arm on, at least, attached.

Une screamed with pain, and then the scream changed into a call for Bibbi and Teddy. Like him, she longed for pain alone, any amount of pain, but not loss.

He tried all the movie techniques, pinching himself and counting his fingers, but he couldn't wake up.

A woman and then a man – Blix – crawled around a mound of sinks and toilets. They were on all fours, patting the ground as they went.

Have you seen Bibbi and Teddy? said Knut.

They looked at him but didn't seem to know that they should reply. They continued in silence, not saying anything, though their mouths were open, ready to reason this all out whenever they should become able to do so.

Hurry, said Une.

He found he could hop along on one leg, holding onto bits of furniture he passed.

Look! said Une, pointing.

Knut saw Teddy's bedspread not far away.

Une took his arm in her good one, and they clambered over the debris where they could not find a way around it.

Bibbi! Teddy!

Their voices clung together in the air. Une picked up the blanket, and they sunk their noses into it and smelled Teddy.

He's here, said Knut.

Where? said Une. Help me push.

Une used her good shoulder and hip to push aside a wardrobe. It had fallen against a mound of beds. The mound toppled. These beds were miniature singles, with Bibbi and Teddy's bunk bed among them, empty. His soft toys were beside it. They checked all the beds, under all the mattresses.

Bibbi! Teddy!

Might they have gone over to Linda? said Une.

They looked in the direction of Linda's block and, only now, realized that it was gone too. The rest of the neighbourhood, all around, seemed intact: no tilting or subsiding, no cracks in the walls. The buildings all around them looked normal. They should have sent Linda one block further.

Bibbi! Teddy!

Where are they?

Dream-Bibbi came running towards them, down the
street and into the wreckage. She was a purplish grey colour,
and when she latched onto him she smelled of vodka and
puke and something else.

What happened? she said. Where's Teddy?

We can't find him, said Une.

Is he not with you? said Knut.

What Bibbi did then could not be called a gasp. She
sucked in and swallowed an amount of air too large for her
lungs and kept it in with both hands clasped to her mouth.

You were supposed to be minding him! she said.

He was in his bed, said Une, here. We found his bed.

Where is he? said Bibbi. Did you bring him over to
Linda? What did you do with him? Where did you send
him, tell me.

Knut turned to face the garden.

Linda! he called out.

We haven't seen her, said Une. We just came to. They
might be together.

Knut took a step towards Linda's block and fell. His
pyjama bottoms were covered in blood. He couldn't feel his
leg at all.

There, it's that woman from downstairs, said Bibbi.

She hurried to the neighbour, and Knut and Une struggled after her.

Have you seen my son, Teddy?

Why did no one believe me?

Teddy, my son. Have you seen him?

I haven't seen any children. Where are they all gone?

Maybe they're together, said Bibbi. Maybe they were scared and ran off together.

Where would they go? said Une. Is there somewhere they would hide if they were afraid?

Bibbi looked at her.

They would run to their mothers, she said. Teddy! Teddy, where are you?

It took them, said the neighbour. First the bricks, then ...

Bibbi and Une were back beside Teddy's bed, and they had started digging there.

Wake up! called Knut, struggling back to them. We have to warn everyone. We must get Teddy out, and Bibbi.

I'm here, Dad.

You're not. None of us are here.

*Before we came to this current, slow-passing state, the transformation that would bring us hence was named: we would rot, degrade, corrode, crumble, sink, pulverize, combine to form new compounds, blow away. We are mineral again, and micro-organic, and more, but we have reached the end of naming.*

# Eva

She was not the only person who felt this pull towards the centre of their former world. A man was drinking from the fountain.

Don't, she said. It's stagnant.

Around her, a crowd of neighbours had gathered – but not enough. She had to look at each of them a moment too long before she recognized them. There was a veil of horror over each identity. Several of them were gaping at her. They stared as if they had just asked her a question.

Well, don't look at me, she said.

What is this, Eva? said Nora. What happened?

Is it over? said Stella.

It's not my fault, said Eva. There's nothing I could have done.

The neighbours continued to gape. They turned slowly on the spot, like clockwork toys whose facial features were painted on in an over-dramatic style: too pale-skinned, their eyes too wide.

You!

The accountant – Blix – who was completely naked, prodded Eva on the shoulder.

Eva looked down over her own body. It was dressed in yesterday's clothes, and she felt a certain dignity, a certain superiority. But it did not fit comfortably.

Don't just stand there, said Blix. Call for help.

She felt her own palm on her chest. It should be moving. It did.

Do you think I can fix everything? she said.

The other blocks all around were still whole. It was only the buildings under Eva's care that had disappeared. This had all the hallmarks of a psychosis. She recognized the world around her to a certain degree. She had a friend who used to live in number 16, and she had chaired meetings about rubbish collection with the boards of numbers 10 and 12. The streets seemed half-familiar, like this was someone else's sketch of her world.

Frida and Fritjof joined the group from the wrong side.

Krishna is dead, said Fritjof.

Who else is missing? said Frida.

If anyone was to understand this, said Eva, it should have been you two.

The roof over us, said Fritjof. We could see it, but it hasn't been working, it hasn't really been there all week.

You didn't report it.

There is no report for something like this. The rules ... structural principles ... load bearing ... barriers ... solidity ... All the words I would use in a report, they have no meaning now. It's just a memory, a design.

We must do a head count, said Eva.

She clapped her hands to get everyone's attention and missed the expected echo from the vanished buildings.

There are forty-six residents, she said, twelve here. Ibsen's gone to alert the police. Sorry, I can't remember your name, I know you are a pianist.

The woman did not look up from where she was slumped in the grass. She smelled of urine.

People are in shock. Who can go and find blankets?

A hand was raised.

Go. The rest of us will divide in two.

She couldn't remember all their names, so she walked a line between them, to divide them into two groups. She made a gesture like an air hostess signalling exits.

Bring anyone who can be moved back here.

On the ground that was once 14A, she found Sonja Flynn digging with hands in the shape of claws.

Do you believe me now? she said. Do you?

You were right, said Eva. We should have listened to you. What you said about the bricks: you knew. I just thought ... It happened so fast.

She touched Sonja's arm. Her skin was moist, warm.

Is this how it ends, Sonja? What happens now?

It didn't crumble, said Sonja. It disappeared. It's gone. Even under the soil, I can't find a single brick.

Eva retched.